"You're a hard lady to keep track of,"

Flynn said. "If I didn't know better, I'd think you were avoiding me."

"But you know better?" Tate asked with amusement.

"Of course," he said. "I'm a likable guy, and you know I wouldn't harm a hair on your head. So I'll pick you up at seven, okay? We'll grab something to eat, then we'll go someplace where you can give me that dance you owe me."

Tate was shocked to feel herself tempted to give in without a whimper of protest. Had she lost her mind? she wondered wildly. Flynn spoke of an innocent evening of fun, but she wasn't fooled for a second into thinking he was innocent. He was a flirt, too smooth to be believed, and any woman foolish enough to fall for that charming, boyish manner of his was asking for trouble....

Dear Reader,

Hot weather, hot books. What could be better? This month, Intimate Moments starts off with an American Hero to remember in Kathleen Korbel's *Simple Gifts*. This award-winning author has—as usual!—created a book that you won't be able to put down. You also might have noticed that the cover of this particular book looks a little bit different from our usual. We'll be doing some different things with some of our covers from time to time, and I hope you'll keep your eye out for that. Whenever you see one of our out-of-the-ordinary covers, you can bet the book will be out of the ordinary, too.

The month keeps going in fine form, with *Flynn*, the next installment of Linda Turner's tremendously popular miniseries, "The Wild West." Then check out *Knight's Corner*, by Sibylle Garrett, and *Jake's Touch*, by Mary Anne Wilson, two authors whose appearances in the line are always greeted with acclaim. Finally, look for two authors new to the line. Suzanne Brockmann offers *Hero Under Cover*, while Kate Stevenson gives you *A Piece of Tomorrow*.

I'd also like to take this chance to thank those of you who've written to me, sharing your opinions of the line. Your letters are one of my best resources as I plan for the future, so please feel free to keep letting me know what you think about the line and what you'd like to see more of in the months to come.

As always—enjoy!

Leslie Wainger
Senior Editor and Editorial Coordinator

Please address questions and book requests to:
Reader Service
U.S.: P.O. Box 1325, Buffalo, NY 14269
Canadian: P.O. Box 1050, Niagara Falls, Ont. L2E 7G7

FLYNN

Linda Turner

Silhouette® INTIMATE MOMENTS®

Published by Silhouette Books

America's Publisher of Contemporary Romance

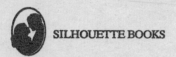

SILHOUETTE BOOKS

ISBN 0-373-07572-3

FLYNN

Printed in U.S.A.

Books by Linda Turner

Silhouette Intimate Moments

†The Wild West

Silhouette Desire

Silhouette Special Edition

LINDA TURNER

began reading romances in high school and began
writing them one night when she had nothing else to
read. She's been writing ever since. Single and living
in Texas, she travels every chance she gets, scouting
locales for her books.

Special thanks to Barbara Catlin, for pointing out
the obvious. You saved me days. Thanks.

Chapter 1

As usual, the rodeo dance was crawling with cowboys looking for easy women and a good time after a couple of days of tough competition. Tate Baxter followed the crowd inside, but even before the door closed behind her, she wanted to cut and run. There was usually a dance after the bigger rodeos, but it had been years since she'd attended one, and she could see in a glance that nothing had changed. The lights were dim, the air smoky, the laughter raucous. A temporary bar had been set up against one wall, and at the far end of the room, a band was belting out a popular country hit about loving and losing. It brought back memories Tate wanted nothing to do with.

At her side, her best friend, Kelly Saxon, suddenly clutched her arm excitedly. "There he is! God, isn't he the most gorgeous thing you've ever seen in your life?"

Tate didn't have to ask who *he* was. Painfully shy, Kelly had worshiped Mitchell Dunn from a distance for weeks now, following him around the circuit, barrel racing in every rodeo he rode bulls in, just for the chance to catch a glimpse of him. When she'd learned he was going to be at the dance tonight, she'd begged Tate to come with her, claiming she'd never have the nerve to go alone.

Following Kelly's gaze across the darkened dance floor to the tall and lean bull rider who lounged against the bar with some of his friends, Tate had to admit that Mitchell was, indeed, one handsome devil. He looked as if he'd just stepped out of a *Bull Durham* ad, but Tate's heart didn't so much as tremble at the sight of him. She'd learned a long time ago to cut a wide path around good-looking cowboys.

"Okay, he's gorgeous," Tate agreed, unable to hold back a smile at the younger girl's enthusiasm. "So what are you doing way over here? Go talk to him."

Kelly gave her a look of pure horror. "Oh, I couldn't! I wouldn't even know what to say."

"Then ask him to dance," she suggested. "Look—his foot's tapping. I'll bet he's just dying to get out on the dance floor. Go ask him and see what he says."

Tempted, Kelly gazed longingly at the man of her dreams, her heart in her eyes, before she finally, regrettably, shook her head. "Maybe later, after I work up my nerve."

It was, Tate decided, going to be a long evening. Lord, had she ever been that young and unsure of herself? "Then I'm going to get something to drink," she said. "It's hot in here."

"I'll get it," Kelly volunteered quickly. "You find us a table."

She was gone before Tate could even open her purse to give her the money, heading straight for the bar...and Mitchell. Grinning, Tate could only stare after her in amusement.

"Well, bless my soul," a familiar gravelly male voice drawled behind her. "I can't believe my eyes! Tate Baxter standing right in front of me waiting for me to ask her to dance."

"The hell she is," a second rough voice retorted. "She wouldn't dance with you if you were the only thing in Levi's between here and Mexico. Can't you see she's waiting for *me?* Tell this overstuffed bozo they're playing our song, darlin'."

Laughing, Tate turned to face Cade Delancy and Wyatt Hogan. One tall and bald, the other short and graying, they'd worked the pro rodeo circuit for years, first as contestants themselves, then as judges when they got too old to climb on the back of angry bulls that wanted nothing more than to stomp them into the dirt. True daredevils, they were both old enough to be Tate's father... and, thank God, perfectly harmless.

Her blue eyes sparkling, she gave the two of them chiding looks. "You guys must have slipped your leashes again. What would Myrtle and Rachel say if they could hear the two of you?"

"Hell, honey, who do you think sent us over here the minute you stepped through the door?" Cade retorted, grinning. "They claim we've already waltzed their feet off, and you're the only sweet young thing around here they trust us with. So who you going to dance with first?"

Wyatt reached into his pocket for a coin and tossed it to his friend. "Here. We'll toss a coin." But as Cade caught it and deftly threw it into the air, Wyatt winked at Tate and pulled her into his arms. "While you're doing that, Tate and I'll catch a fast one. Hang on to that coin. We'll be right back."

"Hey!" Cade protested, suddenly realizing he'd been had. But it was too late. Chuckling, Wyatt danced away with a laughing Tate.

Across the room, Flynn Rawlings watched the cute little blonde laugh as she was swept from one gray-bearded partner to the next and twirled around the dance floor. Like the belle of the ball, she hardly had time to catch her breath in between songs before she was pulled out onto the floor again, this time by a definitely married rodeo clown.

And she was a damn good dancer, Flynn decided, his eyes lingering in appreciation on the graceful sway of her slender, jean-clad hips. Small-boned and delicate, with a waist a man could easily span with his hands, she moved like a dream. He didn't have to hold her to imagine her slow dancing in his arms. Just thinking about it heated his blood.

George Klein, one of the other bareback bronc riders, noted the direction of his gaze with mischief dancing in his eyes. "She's a cute little thing, isn't she? Do you know her?"

Unable to drag his gaze from the woman on the dance floor, Flynn shook his head. "Nope, but I'd like to. Is she on the circuit?"

Biting back a smile, George nodded. "Yeah. Her name's Tate Baxter. She's a barrel racer, and a damn good one at that. If you think she can dance, you ought to see her on a horse. Talk about smooth!" He shook his head at the memory. "The world title is hers for the picking anytime she decides to compete the full season instead of part of it, but she's not interested in stuff like that. She just wants to ride to earn money for college. I think she wants to be a doctor, so she must be pretty damn smart. 'Course, the whole world's smarter than I am," he admitted with a self-effacing grin. "Why don't you ask her to dance?"

Flynn had been thinking of doing just that, but something in the other man's voice had alarm bells clanging in his ears. He'd only been riding the rodeo circuit for two months now, but the first day, he'd learned that rodeo cowboys enjoyed practical jokes every bit as much as the ranch hands on his family's ranch back in New Mexico. There was no such thing as being too cautious when a rodeo cowboy was being helpful. And right now, George was being so helpful, he looked like an angel trying to earn his wings.

His blue eyes narrowed suspiciously. Flynn gave his friend a hard look that warned George he was nobody's fool. "Why? What's wrong with her?"

"Nothing," the younger man assured him with wide-eyed innocence. "I swear it. Ask anyone here," he urged, gesturing to the grinning cowboys gathering at Flynn's back. "They'll tell you the same thing. Tate Baxter's the cutest thing to come down the pike in years. And when she lets herself, she can be a hell of a lot of fun. I'm sure she'd be tickled pink to dance with you."

"Yeah, right," Flynn retorted, unconvinced. "If she's so special, how come the rest of you aren't tripping over each other trying to get to her? She's married, isn't she? Or maybe separated? I swear to God, George, if she's got a jealous husband hiding in the shadows, waiting to jump out and strangle the first man that holds her a little too tight, I'm going to hunt you down and string you up by your thumbs."

His eyes dancing, George raised callused hands like a victim being held at gunpoint. "No husbands, now or at any time in the past or future as far as I know. I swear it. She's as free as a bird and just your size. Quit hemming and hawing and go show the rest of these stiff-legged cowpokes how to two-step with a lady who knows how to dance. You know you're dying to.''

He was; he couldn't deny it. His gaze locked on the delicate blonde, Flynn had a gut feeling he was about to make a mistake—a big one. But it had been a hell of a long time since he'd waltzed across a dance floor with a woman who knew what she was doing. And Tate Baxter certainly knew how to move. Smiling up at her partner— who was old enough to be her grandfather—she was light as a feather in his arms and so damn graceful, she left Flynn's mouth dry.

If he hadn't been so taken with her, Flynn would have heeded the voice of caution whispering in his ear . . . and seen the other cowboys starting to nudge each other behind his back. But he had eyes only for Tate Baxter. "All right," he agreed. "But if this is a setup, you'd better enjoy it. Next time'll be my turn and it won't be a pretty sight."

Unperturbed, George only laughed. "I'm shaking in my boots, Rawlings. Quit being so damn paranoid and go dance while you've got the chance. Tate doesn't socialize very often and when she does, she always leaves early."

Flynn didn't wait to hear more. The minute he started across the dance floor, the betting started.

Her cheeks flushed and her eyes sparkling, Tate was breathless when Cade finally managed to cut in and claim a dance. Muttering about cunning best friends who were old coots, he held her at a proper distance and pushed her around the dance floor like a tugboat trying to maneuver a canoe through rapids without capsizing it.

Unable to hold back the laughter that bubbled up inside her, Tate clung to him as the music came to an end, chuckling. "Enough!" she cried. "Uncle! I've had enough."

Not the least perturbed, Cade only shook his head at her affectionately. "You can't be tuckered out so soon. The band's just now warming up. You probably just need a shot of something to recharge your batteries. Stay right here and I'll get you a beer."

She would have rather had a Coke, but he was already pushing his way through the crowd, leaving her in a shadowy corner where Wyatt wouldn't be able to find her. Grinning, Tate watched him make his way through the crowd, his eyes constantly searching for his wily friend, and she had to laugh. She could just imagine him and Wyatt in their heyday, when they were young and single and the two hottest riders on the circuit. They probably had to beat the women off with a stick.

"I know this sounds corny, darlin', but I think they're playing our song. How 'bout a dance?"

Caught up in her thoughts, it was a long moment before Tate realized that the invitation, issued in an unfamiliar teasing drawl, was directed at *her.* Surprised, she turned and found herself alone in the shadows with a cowboy with roguish blue eyes and a flirty grin that just dared her to try and resist him.

Trouble, she thought, biting back a curse as her heart jerked into an erratic rhythm that irritated her no end. She knew trouble when she saw it, and the engaging cowboy standing before her was the kind that a woman with any sense of self-preservation would go a hundred miles out of the way to avoid. He was tall, just under six foot, lean and tanned, with a square jaw and a face that would have been rugged if not for the laughter that skimmed his features, giving him the look of an overgrown boy bent on mischief.

There'd been a time in the not-too-distant past when she would have taken one look at those wickedly amused eyes of his and thrown caution to the wind. A man who laughed at himself and the rest of the world had once been able to call to her heart with nothing more than a grin. But not anymore.

Drawing herself up stiffly, she resisted the urge to wrap her arms around herself protectively and instead gave him a cool look that said all too clearly she wasn't the least impressed with what she saw. "Sorry. I don't dance."

At first, Flynn was sure she was joking. "Don't dance?" he echoed in laughing disbelief. "C'mon, lady, who're you trying to kid? I've been watching you. You could give Ginger Rogers lessons in two-stepping. So whaddaya say? Are we going to catch this song or not?"

"Not," she retorted without apology or explanation. "Now, if you'll excuse me, I have to go. Good night."

She was gone before he could so much as sputter a protest, stepping past him and walking away without a backward glance. Stunned, Flynn stood flat-footed on the edge of the dance floor, ignoring the couples that cast him curious looks, and scowled after her. He wasn't such an egomaniac he couldn't handle a little rejection once in a while, he thought irritably. But dammit, if the woman didn't want to dance with him, why hadn't she just said so? She didn't have to lie. Shooting her a hard glare, he turned away and headed for his friends across the room.

Grinning as he walked up, George gave Flynn a sympathetic slap on the shoulder. "Struck out, huh? It happens that way sometimes."

"What are you talking about...*sometimes?*" Randy Jordan grumbled, shoving a wadded-up ten-dollar bill in George's hand. "It happens that way *all* the time with Tate Baxter and you know it. Why I let you talk me into betting on Flynn I'll never know. Just because he can charm the fangs off a rattler doesn't mean a damn thing to Tate. She likes charming cowboys about as much as I like getting stomped on by an angry bull.''

Just then noting the exchange of money going on between the other men who had stood on the sidelines and watched his ignominious defeat, Flynn's eyes narrowed on George, who only grinned and shrugged unrepentantly. Exasperated, he growled, ''All right, you've had your fun—and obviously made a dollar or two, too, at my expense. Now suppose you tell me what the hell's going on here. What's Tate Baxter got against cowboys?''

''Everything,'' George replied. ''Some low-down skunk of a bull rider got her pregnant when she was seventeen and ran for cover the second he found out he was going to be a daddy.''

''He dumped her?''

''Faster than a hot potato,'' Randy chimed in. ''As far as anyone knows, she hasn't seen hide nor hair of him since . . . which ain't necessarily a bad thing. As far as I'm concerned, the sleazeball is lower than dirt and she's better off without him.''

''Maybe so,'' George agreed, ''but she hasn't had an easy time of it. God only knows how she manages to support her little girl by herself. She drives a beat-up old pickup and camper that's older than she is, and the only money she's got is what she earns barrel racing in the spring and summer. And that goes for her schooling. I don't know how the hell she does it.''

From the looks on the faces of the men who surrounded him, it was obvious that the little barrel racer was well thought of . . . even if she wouldn't give any of them the time of day. His gaze drawn like a magnet to Tate, Flynn watched her hug the two old geezers who had danced with her earlier, then turn to a pretty redhead who was shyly talking to Mitchell Dunn. Seconds later, she was heading for the door. Alone.

The lady didn't look his way once as she slipped outside, but Flynn had the distinct impression that she was cutting short her evening because of him... because he'd dared to approach her and had unwittingly made her uncomfortable. And that bothered him more than he cared to admit.

Some of his best friends were women. He adored them—their softness, their wit, the damned intriguing way their minds worked and their curves seduced. He couldn't remember ever meeting one he didn't like, and he'd never, ever, consciously hurt one. True, he was a flirt; he didn't deny it. But a woman always knew right up front with him that he wasn't looking for anything serious. And dammit, all he'd wanted from Tate Baxter was a dance!

"Well, she doesn't have to worry about me bothering her again," he said, dragging his gaze from the doorway where she'd disappeared. "I know how to take a hint, and there are plenty of other women around to dance with. Where'd the rodeo queen go?"

Leaving behind the exhibit hall where the dance was being held, Tate struck out on foot across the fairgrounds and headed for the campground that had been set up for contestants on the far side of the arena. For the past couple of days, the campground had been full to overflowing, but now that the Red Rock County Rodeo was over, many of the cowboys had already left for various other rodeos down the road and there were only a handful of campers nestled under the oaks of the RV park. Of those that remained, her pickup and camper was the only one with a light still burning.

Not surprised, Tate smiled ruefully. She didn't fool herself into thinking that the light had been left on to guide her home. Not that Ellie Saxon, Kelly's seventeen-year-old sister and Haily's favorite baby-sitter, would intentionally leave her in the dark. Ellie was much too conscientious to do that. But she was also a Stephen King fan who loved to scare herself silly with his books. She'd brought his latest novel with her tonight, and Tate didn't doubt for a minute that the blazing lights were for Ellie's benefit, not hers.

The crunch of her feet on the gravel path the only noise as she crossed to the camper, Tate slipped her key into the lock and pulled open the door in one smooth motion... and nearly sent Ellie jumping out of skin. Startled, her eyes big as saucers, the younger girl slammed her book shut and shot up off the couch in alarm. At the sight of Tate standing in the doorway, she practically wilted, her muffled laugh emerging as a nervous giggle. "Thank God, it's you! You scared me to death!"

"And here I thought it was the book." Tate chuckled. Glancing past her to the bunk over the cab, where she could just see the tousled buttercup curls of her daughter, her eyes softened. "I see the squirt went to bed on time. Did she give you a hard time?"

"She wanted to watch 'Star Trek,' but she could hardly keep her eyes open during the news. I convinced her to lie down and close her eyes until it came on, and I haven't heard a peep out of her since. How was the dance? Did you have fun? Who was there?"

Tate had to smile at the younger girl's enthusiasm. "Oh, the usual crowd. Pete Saunders, Joe Jackson, Mitchell Dunn."

At the mention of her sister's heartthrob and two other good-looking cowboys on the circuit, Ellie sighed dreamily. "Oh, wow! I bet Kelly was on Cloud Nine, huh? They probably had to beat the women off with a stick. Did you dance with any of them?"

Tate wouldn't have even if she'd gotten the chance, but she only laughed and shook her head. "They didn't even know I was alive, but right before I left, Kelly told me Matt had asked her out—"

"That's great!"

"So the evening wasn't a total washout," she continued with twinkling eyes. "Cade Delancy and Wyatt Hogan were there, too, and they made sure I wasn't a wallflower. I had a good time."

"But they're old! And *married!*" Ellie replied, horrified.

And safe, Tate silently added as she chuckled. "So? What's a wedding ring got to do with anything? And age is just a state of mind. Cade and Wyatt might have a few years on me, but they're still a lot of fun."

"I know. I like them, too. But..." She hesitated, struggling for words, but diplomacy evaded her and she finally blurted out, "But you can't hang around your married friends all the time and expect to find a man. You've got to circulate, get the word out that you're available and wait for the single guys to ask you to dance instead of two-stepping with the married ones."

Touched by the girl's earnestness, the genuine worry in her eyes, Tate couldn't take offense. Ellie reminded her too much of herself at seventeen—young and naive and a die-hard romantic, so anxious for love that she'd ached for it. And vulnerable. God, she'd been so damn vulnerable, so itchy to live life and taste all that it had to offer, that she'd been a sitting duck for the first man who came along with a twinkle in his eye. He'd shown her a little bit of attention and she hadn't stood a chance.

She might as well have handed him her heart—and her pride—on a platter, she thought in disgust. But no more. She could never, ever, regret having her daughter, but they had both paid the price for the mistakes she had made with Rich Travis. Haily was growing up without a father, and she was a mother, but she'd never been a wife. She'd never known the joy of having a lover in her bed every night or the comfort of having a husband beside her during the tough times to share the responsibilities of raising a child. And that wasn't likely to change. Because she'd never again make the mistake of letting a man get close enough to hurt her or her daughter.

"I'm not looking for a husband," she told Ellie gently. "I found out a long time ago that I don't need a man to make me happy."

Ellie looked at her in growing dismay, unable to believe she'd heard her correctly. "But you're so pretty! And all the guys are crazy about you. I've seen them watching you. You could have any of them you wanted. Even Mitchell Dunn and Pete Saunders!"

Tate struggled with a smile, her blue eyes twinkling. From Ellie's tone, Dunn and Saunders ranked right up there with Mel Gibson and Tom Cruise. If either of the men deigned to so much as smile at Ellie, she'd think she'd died and gone to heaven. She'd never understand that her ideal of heaven and Tate's ideal were two different things.

"Thanks, but I'll pass," Tate replied with a smile as she dug in her purse for the money she owed Ellie for babysitting. "I'm just not interested." She handed her a ten-dollar bill, then stepped outside with her so she could see that Ellie made it safely to her family's motor home parked on the other side of the campground. "Thanks for staying with Haily, sweetie. I really appreciate it."

The girl mumbled a good-night as she started across the campground. Watching her walk away, Tate didn't have to read her mind to know what she was thinking. At seventeen and in love with love, Ellie couldn't understand why anyone *wouldn't* want to fall in love. Tate only hoped she never found out.

He'd drawn Hornet, one of the trickiest broncs on the entire circuit. Cursing the Fates, Flynn made his way through the crowd behind the chutes at the outdoor arena in Garden City, Kansas. It was a hot day, and all around him cowboys were cursing the sun that blazed down unrelentingly, but Flynn hardly noticed. He might as well hang up his spurs right now, he thought in disgust, and save himself a fall. Only a handful of riders all year had managed to stay on Hornet till the buzzer, and it would take a miracle to add his name to the list. Damn!

Lost in thought, he didn't see the woman whose path converged with his until he plowed into her and almost knocked her out of her boots. Spitting out an oath, Flynn grabbed her, catching her only seconds before she could end up flat on her backside. It was only when she looked up, her blue eyes wide with surprise, that he realized it was Tate Baxter he held between his hands.

It had been a week since she'd all but told him to get lost, and during that time, Flynn would have sworn he'd put her completely out of his mind. He wasn't a man to brood over rejection, and it wasn't as if she were the only female on the circuit to dream about. There were rodeo queens at every stop, not to mention groupies whose slow smiles and come-hither looks boldly advertised that they were available. If he'd wanted a woman, there were plenty available.

The only problem was, in the days since she'd snubbed him, he hadn't wanted a single woman . . . to flirt with, to dance with or to do anything else with. It wasn't until now that he knew why. Nobody else had seemed damn near as interesting as Tate Baxter.

His upcoming ride on Hornet pushed aside for the moment, he stared down at her in delight, a slow smile stretching across his face. "Well, if it isn't the lady who doesn't dance."

With her shoulders caught in the grip of his strong hands and his body so close that she could smell the enticing spice of his after-shave, Tate's heart started to pound. If this was what dancing with Flynn Rawlings was like, she thought, her throat dry, then she didn't want to ever try it.

Struggling to appear unruffled, she stepped back, forcing him to release her. "Obviously you're not used to rejection, Mr. Rawlings," she said coolly.

"Oh, it's not the rejection," he retorted, unperturbed. "I've got a thick hide. But I do have a problem with little white lies. And you lied, sweetheart. Just like a rug. You want to tell me why?"

Heat threatening to climb into her cheeks, Tate tried to bluff her way through. "I didn't—"

But she'd hardly begun when Flynn leaned down abruptly, his nose a heartbeat away from hers, and looked her right in the eye. "Look me in the eye when you lie, honey. It's much more effective."

"I—I—" Blushing, she glared at him in exasperation. "All right, Mr. Rawlings, you win. I lied, and I apologize. Is that what you wanted to hear?"

Satisfied, he grinned and straightened, prepared to enjoy himself. "Actually, I'd like to know how you know my name. You asked around about me, didn't you?"

Impossibly, the hot color stinging her cheeks deepened. Did the man have no shame? His horse was already loaded into the chute; his ride would begin any second. If he wasn't on the bronc's back when it came time to open the gate, the horse would be turned out without him and Rawlings would be fined. Yet he was as relaxed and carefree as if he had all the time in the world.

Though, once she thought about it, she didn't know why she was so surprised. Yes, she'd asked around about him. Just because she hadn't recognized him, she assured herself, not because she was interested in him. And what she'd learned about him, she hadn't liked.

Flynn Rawlings was the charming, youngest son of a wealthy New Mexico family and was obviously on the circuit just for the fun of it. She didn't begrudge him his money, only his attitude. She and a lot of the others on the circuit were busting their butts just to win enough prize money to put food on the table and still have enough cash left over for entry fees and gas money to get to the next rodeo, yet Flynn didn't care if he won or not.

Glancing over at the chutes, where men were scrambling to help the cowboy who was riding right before Flynn, she turned back to Flynn with an arch look. "Shouldn't you be getting ready for your ride, cowboy?"

His eyes followed hers and narrowed on the activity around the chutes. Swearing under his breath, he took a step away from her, then another. "You owe me a dance," he told her hurriedly. "So when do I get to collect? How 'bout tonight?"

He was running out of time and they both knew it. Smiling sweetly, Tate said, "How about one night during the summer of 2010? That'll work for me. How 'bout you?"

"Aw, come on, don't be that way. I'm a nice guy," he assured her with a grin. "Ask anyone. They'll tell you I'm as harmless as a flea."

Unimpressed, she merely arched one brow at him. "That's not much of an argument in your favor. Fleas carry the bubonic plague."

Flynn snorted on a laugh. Damn, why couldn't he have run into her fifteen minutes earlier? Then he would have had time to talk her around. Frustrated, he glanced over his shoulder to see Dutch Larkon burst out of the chute on Buttercup and his friends yelling at him to hurry. Muttering a curse, he ran for the chute, calling back to Tate over his shoulder, "We're not through discussing this. Wait for me."

Scrambling up on the metal rails of the chute, there was no time to think of anything but the ride. Positioning himself over the horse, he pulled his rigging up tight and carefully eased himself down on Hornet. Beneath him, he could feel the seething anticipation of the horse as she patiently waited for the gate to open. She was docile... for now. But Flynn knew from having watched her at other rodeos that the minute she exploded into the arena, she was as unpredictable as a mad hornet.

"Dammit, Flynn, we thought we were going to have to turn her out without you. You set?"

"The arena's clear, cowboy. We're ready when you are."

"Slide and ride, Flynn. Go for it."

The comments flew at him, but Flynn hardly heard them. Tugging his black cowboy hat low on his ears, he made sure his left hand had a good grip in the handhold of his rigging. Moving into position, his knees grasping the mare's neck and his spurs not yet touching the animal, he took a deep breath and let it out. His heart pounding, a rush of adrenaline streaking through him, he nodded his head, giving the signal to open the gate.

Time seemed to stop, and then all hell broke loose. The latch opened with the now-familiar clang, the gate man jerked open the gate and Hornet broke free of the chute and rocketed into action. Planting her feet, she shot up into the air, twisting and turning and blowing steam in an effort to loosen the flank strap that had tightened around her belly.

Feeling like a puppet being jerked around on a string, Flynn hung on for dear life and concentrated on the mechanics of the ride and staying on the angry animal's back. From the moment Hornet had jumped into the arena, he'd raked her with his spurs in the neck to start the ride, which was one of the requirements of bareback riding, then tried to set a smooth motion that would earn him a good score with the judges. But Hornet didn't make it easy for him.

If Flynn hadn't known better, he would have sworn the animal knew exactly what he was trying to do and was determined to thwart him at every step. She started a smooth jump-kick motion that made it much easier for him to stay on her back, but just when he caught the rhythm, she whirled without warning, and it was all he could do to hang on and wait for the buzzer signaling the end of the ride. Then, a split second before it sounded, Hornet suddenly whirled back in the opposite direction, into a spin. Unprepared for the change in direction, Flynn went flying just as the buzzer blared.

He hit the dirt hard, but thankfully well away from Hornet's flying hooves. Grunting at the bone-jarring landing, he picked himself up and dusted himself off, scowling at the mare, who was as docile as a lamb now that she had got Flynn's spurs out of her neck and him off her back. Her tail lifted high in triumph, she trotted out of the arena with what Flynn would have sworn was a grin.

Over the public-address system, the announcer chuckled and told the crowd, "Let's have a nice round of applause for Flynn Rawlings, ladies and gentlemen. That's the eighth rider in a row Hornet's bucked off and she's one of the favorites to win the title of bucking horse of the year. But Flynn gave her a run for her money. Better luck next time, cowboy."

Grinning ruefully, Flynn waved at the clapping crowd, snatched up his hat out of the dirt and made his way out of the arena. Half expecting to find Tate watching his ignominious defeat from the sidelines, he hurried around behind the chutes, only to stop in consternation when she was nowhere in sight.

"Well, hell," he muttered under his breath.

What was it with the lady? he wondered irritably. From the way she stiffened up like a poker every time she caught sight of him, anyone would think he really did have the plague. And he didn't like it one little bit. All right, so some jerk had hurt her badly in the past. He sympathized with her and could understand why she'd be leery of getting involved with anyone again. But *he* hadn't done anything to her, and she had nothing to fear from him. He wasn't looking for a relationship—far from it! He was just interested in a little harmless flirting. If she'd have stuck around long enough to finish their conversation, she'd have found that out for herself.

Wanting to shake her, he circled around behind the chutes toward the entrance to the stands, intending to watch the rest of the competition. Since he hadn't made it to the buzzer, he was out of the competition for the grand prize, but if his ride tomorrow turned out better than today's, he could win one of the daily jackpots. And it never hurt to scout out the competition and learn a few things.

But he never made it to the stands. There, standing by one of the concession stands and drinking a Coke, was Tate. His eyes hard with purpose, Flynn headed right for her.

"You're a hard lady to keep track of," he said easily. "If I didn't know better, I'd think you were avoiding me."

Startled, Tate whirled to find him just behind her, that maddening grin of his telling her he knew exactly what she was up to and he wasn't letting her get away with it. In spite of her best efforts to remain coolly aloof, she found it nearly impossible to hold back the smile that twitched at her lips. Looking him up and down, she drawled, "But you know better?"

"Of course," he chuckled baldly, his blue eyes twinkling. "I'm a likable guy and you know I wouldn't hurt a hair on your head. So I'll pick you up at seven, okay? We'll grab something to eat and then we'll go someplace where you can give me that dance you owe me."

Staring up into his mischievous eyes, Tate was shocked to feel herself tempted to give in without a whimper of protest. Had she lost her mind? she wondered wildly as her pulse started to throb. Flynn spoke of an innocent evening of fun, but she wasn't fooled for a second into thinking he was innocent. He was a flirt, too smooth to be believed, and any woman foolish enough to fall for that charming, boyish manner of his was asking for trouble. And she was too smart for that.

"I don't think so," she said stiffly. "I don't date. Ever."

Far from being put off, Flynn only studied her in amusement. "You don't dance and you don't date. Or at least you didn't until now. Honey, we're just going to have to do something about your social life. I'll pick you up at seven.''

"No!"

"Okay, seven-thirty," he said agreeably. "Now go get ready for the barrel racing so you can win. We'll celebrate tonight."

"Damn it, Flynn, I'm not going out with you!" she began. But it was too late. With a cocky grin, he ran a finger down her cheek, then turned and walked away.

Chapter 2

Tate tried to convince herself that if she stood Flynn up that night, it was because he'd forced her to. She'd told him no when he'd asked her out; he'd just refused to accept it. The nerve of the man! He might flash those dimples of his at other women and hear only what he wanted to hear, but he'd soon find out that those little tricks wouldn't work with her, because she wasn't interested in the dratted man. She couldn't be! And if she had to stand him up to get that point across to him, then by God, she would.

Still, she couldn't help but feel guilty when she made sure she and Haily were far away from the camper when he showed up at seven-thirty. They had dinner with Kelly Saxon and some of the other barrel racers, then played gin rummy until ten. By the time Kelly dropped them off at the campground, it was dark and quiet and there was no sign of Flynn.

Relieved, Tate urged a sleepy Haily toward the back door of the camper, only to stop at the sight of the bouquet of wildflowers that had been left on the overturned milk case she used as a step. At her side, Haily stopped, too, her green eyes widening in surprise. "Hey, Mom, look...flowers. Who're they from?"

Tate stared at the bouquet as if it were a rattler waiting to strike. She didn't see a note, but she didn't need one. Only one man would dare to leave flowers on her doorstep as if he were courting her, making a mockery of her efforts to ignore him. *Flynn Rawlings.*

Swallowing a curse at the curiosity suddenly dancing in her eight-year-old daughter's green eyes, she quickly snatched up the unwanted gift and unlocked the door to the camper. "Someone probably left them here by mistake," she said casually as she swept open the door. "They're probably for Cindy Johnson. Her camper's a lot like ours and she's always getting candy and flowers and stuff like that."

"But maybe you've got a secret admirer," Haily said hopefully, clearly intrigued with the idea. "Gee, Mom, wouldn't that be fun? Who do you think it is?"

Tate forced a laugh that didn't come as easily as she'd have liked. "Nobody, sweetheart. Now enough about secret admirers. It's time for bed. It's getting late."

That started the usual grumbling, just as Tate had hoped, and the subject of the flowers was dropped. But long after Haily was asleep and Tate crawled into her own bed, the sweet fragrance of the wildflowers she'd reluctantly put in water on the kitchen cabinet teased her senses. And with no effort at all on her part, she found herself unwittingly thinking of Flynn Rawlings. Damn the man. What was she going to do with him?

Like a thorn pricking her side, the memory of his wickedly boyish smile worried her all through the night and into the next morning, refusing to be ignored. When Haily reminded her there were junior rodeo activities at the arena for the kids at noon, she decided some extra practice with the barrels before that afternoon's competition was just what she needed to push the infuriating man from her mind.

But when she walked over to the Garden City fairgrounds with Haily, it didn't take her long to discover she'd made a mistake. Everywhere she looked, she was reminded of Flynn and her encounter with him behind the chutes. She couldn't concentrate worth a bean, and she knew if she didn't get her wits about her before the competition later that afternoon, there was a good chance she wouldn't even place in the money.

Thoroughly disgusted with herself, she left Haily at the arena with the other kids and returned to the campground, determined to keep her mind and hands busy cleaning the camper. But Flynn had already beat her to the punch. Armed with a bucket of sudsy water, he was busily cleaning her pickup and camper.

Stunned, Tate could only stare at him. "What do you think you're doing?"

Not the least surprised to see her, he glanced over his shoulder and grinned. "Washing your rig for you. I had some time on my hands this morning, so I thought I'd do it for you. Haily at the junior rodeo?"

She nodded, refusing to let him distract her. Her hands on her hips, she glared at him in exasperation. "Damn it, Flynn, I can't let you do this!"

Unperturbed by her tone, he turned back to his task. "Do what? Clean the truck? Sure you can. I'm already doing it. Want to help?"

"No!" Lord, she'd never met a more infuriating man. What did it take to get through to him that she wasn't interested? "If this is another little trick, like the flowers, to charm me into going out with you, you're wasting your time," she warned bluntly. "I'm not looking for a man—*any* man."

"Good." He chuckled. "Because I'm not just any man. Not that I expect you to know what you're trying to pass up here," he amended with dancing eyes. "You won't give yourself a chance to get to know me yet. Once you do, you'll wonder what you were so scared of. I'm harmless."

She snorted at that, not believing it for a second. Harmless? Flynn Rawlings? Maybe on the day he was born, but even then, she doubted it. The man was a charmer who obviously wasn't used to being turned down, and pursuing her was just a game to him. What did she have to do to make him realize that she wasn't a woman who played games?

"I don't care if you're as harmless as the Easter Bunny," she retorted, stepping around him to unlock the back door of the camper. "Just stay away from me and what's mine and we'll get along fine."

She stepped inside without another word and slammed the door behind her with so much force, the windows rattled. Wincing, Flynn stared up at the camper and watched as she yanked the curtains shut one by one. Amused, his mouth sloped into a wicked grin. For someone who wasn't interested, she certainly went out of her way to make sure she couldn't catch sight of him. He whistled softly to himself and went back to washing her truck. He was, he reminded himself, a patient man.

* * *

Knowing better than to push his luck, Flynn steered clear of Tate the rest of the day, but he was in the stands when she won the barrel racing competition that afternoon. Not surprised that she'd grabbed the top prize for herself—she was a darn good athlete and she and that midnight-black mare of hers were quick as lightning when they ran the barrels—it took all his self-control to stay where he was when what he really wanted to do was go down behind the chutes and congratulate her. But he'd had all afternoon to think over his strategy, and he'd decided it was time to give the lady a taste of her own medicine.

Avoiding her, however, was proving to be more difficult than he'd expected. Deciding to skip the rodeo dance that night, he left early for the next rodeo he'd preentered, a four-day event in Wichita Falls, Texas. But he'd hardly settled in at the campground nearest the rodeo grounds the following day when he saw Tate's familiar green pickup and camper pull up before the campground office.

A slow, mocking grin tilted up one corner of his mouth. Fate was a crazy thing, he thought ruefully. Just when he'd decided to back off from the lady for a while, she practically dropped on his doorstep. Obviously, she was once again entered in the same rodeo he was, though he hadn't realized that until just now. Not that he'd have changed his plans if he'd known, he acknowledged with a chuckle. When a man found destiny in his corner, who was he to argue?

He knew the exact moment she realized that once again their paths had inexplicably crossed. She came out of the campground office with a receipt in her hand, only to stop short as her gaze fell on his truck. Recognizing it immediately, her brows snapped together in a scowl. It took only a shift of her eyes to find him relaxing in a lawn chair, whittling. For pure devilment, Flynn grinned and waved. If looks could kill, he'd have dropped dead on the spot. Unable to stop himself, he laughed. God, he loved a woman with spirit!

Tate, however, was not amused. From fifty yards away, he saw her hesitate, her indecision clearly giving away her thoughts. She was tempted to get back her money and find another campground. But the nearest one was over fifteen miles away and was hardly convenient to the rodeo grounds. He knew because he'd checked it out himself.

Tate obviously had, too, and seemed to decide that even his annoying presence could be tolerated for the sake of convenience. Dragging her gaze away from his, she stuffed the receipt into her pocket and climbed into her pickup. Since the campground director let campers pick their own sites rather than assign them, Flynn wasn't surprised when Tate turned toward the opposite end of the campground, away from him. Her message was loud and clear. In case he'd forgotten, she wanted nothing to do with him.

Amused, Flynn returned his attention to his whittling, a boyhood hobby he'd picked up again when he'd joined the rodeo circuit. Stuck in towns where he didn't know a soul, with more time to kill than he knew what to do with, whittling not only gave him something to do with his hands, it provided a creative outlet for a talent he hadn't even realized he had. Without quite realizing how it had happened, he'd found himself carving bucking broncs and bull riders and the rodeo clowns who threw themselves in front of two-thousand-pound bulls to save a cowboy's life.

At first, of course, his pieces had been rough and crude, but he'd stuck with it, enjoying the feel of the knife slicing through the wood. Then, sometime during the next three months he'd been on the circuit, the wood had come alive under his knife. In his carvings, he found a way to capture the grace and beauty and sheer guts of rodeoing and, in the process, surprised himself. Now his pieces were in hot demand by other cowboys and rodeo fans alike, and a source of income he'd never expected to find on the circuit.

Shaking his head over the ironies of fate, he carefully worked on the face of an ornery bull that didn't want to be ridden. Every line, every angle of its twisted horns and powerful body spoke of the animal's rage.

With all his concentration focused on the carving he held in his hands, Flynn didn't realize he had a visitor until a shadow fell across him. Surprised, he glanced up and almost dropped his knife at the sight of Haily Baxter standing in front of him in a green-and-white playsuit, her gamine face bright with curiosity.

"Hi," she said with the quick, open smile of a child who'd never met a stranger. "Watcha doin'?"

"Whittling," Flynn responded, captivated as he handed over the carving. "Here. Take a look."

She took it with a reverence that surprised him, her small fingers slowly moving over the bull as if she were committing every inch of it to memory. Fascinated, Flynn studied her just as intently.

He'd seen her around, of course. There were a number of kids who traveled with their parents during the summer, but he'd have known Haily was Tate's even if he hadn't known her name. A pint-size version of her mother, with yellow-gold curls that would no doubt darken with age, she had a smile that was a mirror of Tate's. And her eyes. Lord, those big, expressive eyes of hers would be the downfall of some unsuspecting fool years from now when she left childhood far behind. One look into those midnight-blue depths and any man with blood in his veins would find himself tumbling head over heels.

Not that *he* was in any danger of losing his head over her mother, he assured himself quickly. He was made of sterner stuff than that. Before his wayward thoughts could skip farther down that unwanted path, he turned his attention back to the child in front of him. "Well, what do you think?"

"It looks just like Bullwinkle," she announced, unwittingly paying him the highest compliment by naming the very bull he'd modeled the carving after. "Have you heard of him?"

"Oh, yeah," Flynn said, smiling. "He's the meanest son of a...gun on the circuit. Nobody's ever ridden him."

Expecting her to chatter on about all she knew of the famous bull, he was surprised when, instead, her blue eyes narrowed suspiciously. "Are you a bull rider?"

"Nope. Why? You got something against them?"

"My mom says they're all accidents waiting to happen."

Flynn laughed and recognized a kindred spirit in the mischief sparkling in her eyes. "I've done some crazy things, sunshine, but even I'm not crazy enough to get on the back of a bull. Some things just aren't meant to be ridden. I'm a bronc rider." Solemnly holding his hand out to her, he introduced himself. "I'm Flynn Rawlings. And you must be Haily Baxter. I've seen you around with your mom."

Delighted at being treated like an adult, her dimples winked as she gave his hand a businesslike shake. "I'm not supposed to talk to strangers," she confided, "but now that I know your name, you're not a stranger."

Pleased with that deduction, she changed the subject lightning quick and held up the smoothly chiseled bull. "How'd you learn to do this? Can you teach me?"

Flynn hesitated, his glance moving past her shoulder to Tate's camper parked under the trees on the other side of the campground. "I don't know about that, sunshine. This knife's awfully sharp and your mom might not approve."

"Oh, but I'll be careful," she pleaded. "*Pleease?* And you'll be right here to watch me to make sure I don't do anything wrong. Please, please, please?"

The little minx was hard to resist and she knew it. Shaking his head at her antics, Flynn grinned and picked up a small branch that had fallen from the trees that surrounded the campground. "All right," he said reluctantly, "but we're going to take this slow and easy. You cut yourself and your mom'll have my head."

She giggled, and just that easily, Flynn found himself becoming friends with Tate's daughter. He hadn't planned it, wouldn't have even thought it was possible. He liked kids well enough, but he hadn't ever been around any except Mandy, his brother, Gable's, little girl, and she was only nine months old. But an eight-year-old with the gamine face of her mother and a line of conversation that kept him thoroughly entertained was not a baby.

Lord, that child could talk! Bright, funny, open, she showed up at his campsite for the next two mornings as soon as breakfast was over, anxious for her whittling lesson and chattering to beat the band. With a trust that he found incredibly touching, she told him all about how she and her mother lived with her grandfather during the school year, how they hit the rodeo circuit in the summer and got to camp all over the country, how neat it was going to be when her mom became a doctor.

He should have stopped it. Deep down in his gut, Flynn knew Tate would resent him inviting her daughter's confidences. Not that he was encouraging her, he assured himself righteously. He just wasn't doing anything to *discourage* her. Especially when Haily guilelessly told him the next five rodeos they were going to and how Tate had let her map their route so she could practice her geography.

"So can you come?"

Lost in thought, Flynn glanced down at her and frowned. "Come where?"

"To supper," she said with adultlike patience. "Mom already said you could come and we're not having anything fancy—just hot dogs and chili—so can you come?"

Flynn only stared at her, unable to believe he'd heard correctly. "Let me get this straight. Your mom said it was all right for you to invite me, Flynn Rawlings, to supper?"

For the first time since he'd met her, Haily's gaze didn't quite meet his. Fiddling with a stray string that hung down from her shorts, she hedged, "Well, not exactly. I didn't mention names or even that I knew you because Mom's got this thing about cowboys. But she's always telling me I can invite friends to supper anytime I like and tonight seemed like a good time. Okay?"

Flynn almost choked on a laugh at that. *Okay?* Not if he valued his life! Playfully pursuing Tate Baxter when she'd like nothing more than for him to take a hike was one thing. Getting himself invited to supper by her daughter was quite another. He might find the situation amusing, but not everyone shared his sense of humor. Tate would be livid and no doubt throw him out on his ear, and Haily would never understand.

Already shaking his head, he said quietly, "I don't think that's a very good idea, sunshine. When your mom said you could invite a friend, she meant another squirt like you, not an old cowboy like me."

"But you're not that old!"

Chuckling, Flynn ruffled her hair. "Gee, thanks, sweetheart. It's nice to know I'm not ready for a rocking chair yet. But I am still a cowboy, and you said yourself your mom doesn't like cowboys."

"But she doesn't know you," she pointed out with maddening logic. "So how does she know if she likes you or not? If you come to supper, she'll have a chance to find out."

Unknowingly, she held a carrot of temptation out to him he couldn't resist. After all, what harm could it do? the voice of mischief whispered in his ear. Tate was already avoiding him like he was contagious, and all he'd done was dare to ask her out. What more could she do to him if he showed up on her doorstep for supper? Slam the door in his face? It wouldn't be the first blow she'd given his ego.

"All right," he reluctantly agreed. "I guess I'm game if you are. Just don't blame me if we both end up in the doghouse over this."

The hot dogs were shriveled, the chili a thick glob on the stove and Tate was growing impatient. She'd held supper back almost thirty minutes, and Haily's friend still hadn't shown up. Glancing at her daughter's disappointed face, she said gently, "Sweetheart, I'm sorry, but it's getting late and I don't think your friend's going to make it. Why don't we go ahead and eat?"

"But he'll be here. He promised. Please, Mom, can't we wait just a few more minutes?"

"But, honey, are you even sure he asked his mother if it was okay? He might—"

At the sudden sharp rap at the camper door, Tate turned, expecting to see one of the other campers' little boys standing outside the screen door staring up at her. But there was nothing little about the man patiently waiting for her to open the door, and the only thing boyish about him was his all-too-familiar mischievous grin.

Her heart tripped at the sight of that grin, infuriating her. The man was up to something, she told herself, and she didn't like her sudden suspicions at all. Through the screen, her narrowed gaze locked with his. "What are you doing here?"

He opened his mouth to answer, but Haily never gave him the chance. "Flynn!" Bounding up out of the camper's built-in booth, she squeezed past Tate in the narrow aisle and pushed open the door, her dimples flashing impishly. "Mom was afraid you weren't coming. We were going to eat without you."

His sapphire eyes twinkling down at her, Flynn stepped into the camper and gave one of her pigtails a teasing tug. "I wouldn't have blamed you if you had. I would have been here thirty minutes ago, but George Klein's truck broke down after the rodeo and I had to give him a tow to a garage." Glancing at Tate, he said, "Sorry I'm late, but there was no way to call."

Stunned, she could only stare at him. "*You're* the friend Haily invited to supper?"

His lips twitched, but he knew better than to grin. The lady was hotter than a firecracker with a short fuse and he wasn't about to give her a reason to blow up in his face. All innocence, he lifted a brow at her. "Yeah, didn't she tell you? We met a couple of days ago and I'm teaching her to whittle. If that's okay with you, of course."

"Oh, Mom doesn't care," Haily answered for her. "She likes for me to learn new things. Don't you, Mom?"

Put on the spot, her daughter's bright, innocent eyes turned up to her so trustingly, there was nothing Tate could do but graciously go along with her. But just as soon as the opportunity presented itself, she was going to tell Flynn Rawlings just exactly what she thought of a man who would use a little girl to get to her mother!

"Of course I do, sweetheart," she said easily, ruffling her hair. "You can tell me all about it while we eat. You and Flynn sit down and I'll get the food."

Determined not to let Flynn's presence rattle her, she ignored him and turned back to the stove. But she had forgotten how small the camper was and just what an imposing figure of a man Flynn was. Tall and lean, he seemed to take up all the available space without moving so much as an inch. Then, when he stepped toward the booth to sit down, he had to ease past where she stood at the stove.

Realizing her mistake too late, she started to suggest that he just stay where he was until she got the food on the table and took a seat herself, but he'd already turned sideways to get past her. Crowded up against the stove, she froze, but the aisle was simply too narrow. His chest brushed her back, his hips nudged hers and suddenly there wasn't enough oxygen in the air.

Her fingers curling around the oven handle, Tate held herself perfectly still and told herself not to be fanciful. If her heart was pounding like a jackhammer, it was only because she was still furious with the man for striking up a friendship with Haily to get to her. And if her nerve endings were throbbing in awareness of him, it was simply due to the fact that she resented the way he was not only pushing his way into the camper, but into her life. It had nothing to do with Flynn himself.

"Excuse me." His softly murmured apology whispered in her ear like a lover's caress as he slowly pushed past her, his hands settling on her shoulders for just a second before he stepped away and eased into one side of the dinette booth across from Haily.

Her eyes squeezed closed, Tate carefully released the quick breath she'd sucked in at his first touch. A devil, she thought, shaken. The man was a seductive devil with ways that would tempt a saint. She couldn't let him get to her.

Still, it was a long moment before she was able to turn and face his knowing eyes. Straightening her spine until it was as stiff as a fence post, she scooped up the food to be transferred to the table and plastered on a smile that never reached her eyes. If the infuriating man was going to trick his way into her life, he couldn't expect her to welcome him with open arms.

"So," she said lightly, taking a seat at the table across from him, "how did you and Haily meet?"

If she'd expected to put him on the spot, she was disappointed. With a cheerfulness that set her teeth on edge, he told her how Haily had stumbled across him right there in the campground. Haily excitedly joined in, and the two of them were soon talking and laughing as if they'd known each other for years.

Tate tried to hang on to her resentment at Flynn's pushiness, but the rogue was so damn charming, she couldn't take her eyes off him. He was as relaxed as if he were in his own home. His legs were comfortably stretched out under the small table, and he teased Haily as if she were a favorite niece. And Haily loved it. Joking with him, she chattered like a magpie, thoroughly enjoying herself. Watching the man and child together, Tate felt her annoyance melt away and could do nothing to stop it.

How could she resent a man who made her daughter laugh so easily?

If she let herself, she could like Flynn Rawlings. *More than like him.*

The thought, like a cat burglar on the prowl, slipped up on her, surprising her before she could avoid it, taunting her, mocking her caution. And terrifying her. Her mind, only too eager to remind her of all the reasons why she'd be a fool to let down her guard with him, dredged up images of Rich Travis. But it was Flynn Rawlings her eyes were eagerly taking their fill of, noting the way his shirt molded the strong breadth of his shoulders, the way his black cowboy hat was rakishly pushed back from his brow, the teasing, tormenting flash of his dimples. And her heart . . .

She didn't even want to think about the message her heart was wildly beating out. From the moment she'd turned and found him on the other side of the screen door, it hadn't stopped its thundering.

All too aware of his closeness, the feel of his legs occasionally brushing hers under the table, she steeled herself against the sexual heat he exuded just by breathing and wondered where she'd lost control of the day. She hadn't done well earlier in the barrel racing—she'd finished a dismal fourth—and she had no one to blame but herself for her poor performance. Her mind just hadn't been on the ride. She'd called her father an hour before the rodeo started, and something in his voice had warned her he wasn't feeling well. He'd denied it, of course, but he hadn't fooled her. Tough as an old boot, Allen Baxter was the type to claim he was fit as a fiddle even when he was sick as a dog, and she was worried about him.

The last thing she needed, on top of all that, was Flynn Rawlings and that inviting gleam in his eyes as he sprawled across the table from her as if he belonged there. But she could hardly push him out the door without having a darn good explanation for Haily, and Flynn didn't seem in any hurry to leave. Frustrated, she drew in a calming breath and struggled for patience. It didn't come easily.

It was, however, a full forty minutes before Flynn announced that he had to leave. He'd drawn supper out as long as he could, then entertained Haily with stories about his brothers and sister and life on his family's ranch in New Mexico. Another time, another place, another *man*, and Tate might have allowed herself to enjoy the stories. But she had a feeling Flynn knew just exactly how he was irritating her by staying far longer than she'd expected, and she wanted to throttle him.

The minute he reluctantly came to his feet, she was at his side before he could change his mind. Amused, he lifted a brow at her, but he had no intention of letting her rush him out the door. "Thanks for supper, sunshine," he told Haily, ruffling her bangs. "Next time it'll be my treat at McDonald's."

"Hey, okay!"

Tate wanted to tell him there wasn't going to be a next time, but that was something she intended to say in private. Gritting her teeth in a grimace of a smile, she only shrugged. "We'll have to see." Glancing at her daughter, she said, "Why don't you get started on the dishes, sweetheart? I'll help you just as soon as I show Flynn out."

It was a clear dismissal, one that not even Flynn, whose hide was as thick as an elephant's, could ignore. His mouth twitching ruefully, he stepped outside with her right on his heels.

Twilight had thickened while they ate, and the long shadows of late afternoon had given way to the quiet stillness of early evening. Most of the other campers had gone inside for the night, and at any other time, Flynn would have enjoyed the fact that he finally had Tate alone. But one look at her flashing eyes told him the lady was in no mood for anything but a fight.

Giving her a crooked grin, his gaze met hers in the gathering darkness. "I guess you're mad, huh?"

"Mad?" she echoed sarcastically in a low voice that wouldn't carry to Haily in the camper behind them. "Me? Now why would I be mad? You've only followed me halfway across the country—"

"You don't have to make it sound like I'm stalking you or something," he said with a sudden frown. "It's not my fault that we just happened to be entered in the same rodeos. For all I know, *you* could be following me."

"In your dreams, cowboy," she snorted. Her patience at an end, she glared at him, wanting to shake him. "I've tried to be reasonable about this, but it's like I'm talking to a brick wall or something. What do I have to say to get through to you? I've told you I'm not interested, but you haven't heard a word I've said. You sent me flowers— don't deny it," she said quickly before he could so much as open his mouth to protest. "I know they were from you. You're the only man I know who won't take no for an answer."

Working up to a full head of steam, the frustration that had been building for days exploded and she let him have it with both barrels. "And striking up a friendship with my daughter to get to me is pretty darn low! If you'd spend half as much time working on your rodeo skills as you do thinking up ways to get to me, you might win a few competitions. But you don't have to win, do you? Your family's got money, so you're just looking for a good time. Well, I'm not it. You got that? *I'm not interested!*"

Flynn didn't consider himself thickheaded. Or a masochist. When something didn't work, he knew when to cut his losses. And if he had any sense, he'd walk away from Tate Baxter and make sure he never had the misfortune to run into her again. But damn it, he had something to prove to the lady and she wasn't the only one who had run out of patience.

Throwing caution to the wind, he reached for her, hauling her close before he could ask himself what the hell he was doing. He saw her eyes widen, heard her gasp, and in the next instant his mouth was on hers.

At the first touch of her soft, sensuous lips, he knew he'd made a mistake in reaching for her. At the first taste of her, his heart slammed against his ribs and he knew he was in a mess of trouble. He'd kissed his share of women and had enjoyed every second of it. But it only took the feel of Tate Baxter in his arms, the hot, honeyed taste of her on his tongue, to make him realize that he didn't know a damn thing about kissing.

Heat lightning. There was no other way to describe it. Holding her, kissing her, was like getting hit with a bolt of lightning on a clear, cloudless day. It came out of nowhere and nearly knocked him out of his shoes.

He should have put her from him then and there and not stopped running until there were at least two time zones between them. But her mouth was as sweet as sin, fragile, intoxicating. A man could walk away from sin; he could even learn to avoid intoxication. But combine the two with a subtle vulnerability that made him want to sweep her up and protect her from hurt, and he was lost. With a groan that could have been her name, his arms tightened until every smooth, delicate inch of her was pressed against him from chest to knee.

Tate stood perfectly still and tried to tell herself that she wasn't a woman who invited—or welcomed—a man's passion. It had been nearly nine years since anyone had dared to kiss her, and she wouldn't have complained if it had been decades. She didn't need this—didn't want him. All she had to do was not respond and Flynn would finally get the message and let her go. It was that simple.

Or at least it would have been if she hadn't felt the thundering of his heart pounding in time with hers. And then his tongue slipped into the dark, secret recesses of her mouth, stealing her breath, and she could actually *taste* his longing, his need.

Stunned, she wanted to yell at him for using unfair tactics. What woman could resist a man who let her see exactly what she did to him? But she couldn't manage the strength to push him away, couldn't find the words to tell him what she thought of him. Instead, her knees weakened, her arms slid up around his neck and the cool, unshakable aloofness that no man had been able to get past for years went up in smoke. Before she could stop herself, she was clinging to him, unable to remember why she couldn't let herself want him.

When he finally let her up for air, Tate was sure he was as shaken as she was. But in the blink of an eye, that bold, lazy grin of his was back. "Still want nothing to do with me, sweetheart?" he drawled teasingly, lifting a hand to trace the hot color spilling into her cheeks. "Go ahead, look me in the eye and tell me you're not interested. I dare you."

If she'd thought that she could get away with murder, he would have dropped dead on the spot. Since that was out of the question, she did the only thing that any self-respecting woman would. She looked him dead in the eye and lied through her teeth. "I'm not interested," she said flatly, her blue eyes flashing. "There, I said it—again! Would you like it in writing or will you take my word for it?"

Torn between laughter and fury, Flynn could only glare at her, not sure if he wanted to shake her until her teeth rattled or snatch her up in a laughing hug. Either, he knew, would be a mistake. If he touched her now, he wouldn't let her go anytime soon. Muttering a curse, he turned on his heel and stalked away while he still could.

[faint text from previous page showing through]

Chapter 3

The fourth contestant in the barrel race rounded the third and last of the barrels, leaned low over her horse and raced across the finish line at a full gallop, her pigtails flying out behind her. A roar of appreciation went up from the crowd, nearly drowning out the announcer's congratulations to Becky Donaldson for a record-shattering ride.

Behind the chutes, waiting her turn to compete, Tate wouldn't even have noticed the time she had to beat if Haily hadn't pointed it out to her. Lost in her troubled thoughts, she looked down at her daughter, who had to repeat the time to beat twice before she heard it. Frowning, she said, "Are you sure?"

"Well, yeah," Haily said, bewildered. "They just announced it. Mom, are you okay? You're acting kind of funny."

Tate felt heat climb into her cheeks and could do nothing to stop it. If she was acting strange, it was only because there was a certain cowboy she couldn't get out of her head and it was driving her crazy. Damn Flynn Rawlings! She was going to kill him!

"I'm fine, honey," she quickly assured Haily, forcing a smile that didn't come easily. "I was just thinking about something else." Like a kiss that had haunted her for two straight nights now. "Why don't you go up in the stands and root for me? If I'm going to beat Becky's score, I'm going to need all the help I can get."

She expected Haily to jump at the chance to sit by herself in the stands, but she didn't budge. Her blue eyes dark with concern, she stared up at Tate searchingly. "Maybe I should stay back here with you. You might need me."

Anyone hearing Haily would have thought *she* was the mother and Tate the daughter, instead of the other way around. Chuckling, Tate gave her a quick hug, then sent her toward the stands with a gentle push. "Go on, worrywart. I promise I'm not going to miss my ride, so there's no need for you to hang around here when I know you're dying to be up front. Now scat!"

She went, but not without a last motherly word of advice. "Make sure you walk Sugar around back first. You know how skittish she gets if she doesn't have time to warm up to the crowd and all the noise."

"Yes, Mother," she teased. "Whatever you say."

Grinning impishly, Haily wrinkled her nose at her and skipped away to the stairs that led to the stands. Shaking her head, Tate watched her until she was out of sight, marveling at the wonder that was her daughter. Eight going on forty. What would she do without her? she mused with a wry grin as she returned to where she'd left Sugar in a holding pen.

Talking softly to the mare, she led her through the crowd of cowboys and chute help who crowded the area behind the chutes, helping contestants get ready for their upcoming events. The wait before it was her time to ride was always the most difficult for her to get through. Tate tried to concentrate on what she had to do to beat Becky Donaldson and win the prize money she so desperately needed. But every time she tried to close out her surroundings and focus her thoughts, it wasn't her upcoming ride that came to mind, it was Flynn.

Muttering a curse, Tate turned Sugar back the way they had come. She hadn't been able to get the infuriating man out of her thoughts from the moment he'd surprised her with that kiss the night before last, and it was driving her crazy. It was just a stupid little kiss that should have been forgotten immediately. Dwelling on the dang thing only gave it a significance it didn't deserve.

"You've got a rodeo to win, girl," she muttered sternly to herself. "If you want to worry about something, worry about that. You're coming up next."

Pulling Sugar to a stop near the entrance to the arena floor, she was making last-minute adjustments to the cinch when she absently looked up to find Flynn watching her from thirty feet away. Startled, she sucked in a sharp breath, her heart jerking into an uneven rhythm in her breast.

All around them was the general mayhem that usually took place behind the chutes during a rodeo, but there might have been no one within ten miles for all the attention Tate showed them. She'd avoided him for two days, even going so far as to steer clear of the chutes during the bareback competition just so she wouldn't have to see him, wouldn't have to remember....

And now she knew why. The minute her eyes met his, his touch, his kiss, his taste, came flooding back as if it were only minutes, instead of days, since he'd grabbed her to prove a point. And in spite of all her best efforts to deny it, he'd done what he'd set out to do. Like it or not, she wasn't nearly as indifferent to him as she wanted, *needed*, to be.

And he knew it. You could have driven a truck through the space that stretched between them, but she could see the knowledge written on his face as clearly as if he stood right in front of her. Patience. It was there in his eyes, a hard glint of resolve that promised her it was only a matter of time before he kissed her again.

Her heart slamming against her ribs, it took all her strength of will to drag her gaze from his. Over the loudspeaker, the announcer gave the time of the contestant who had just competed. It was her turn.

Forcing her mind back to the matter at hand, she quickly mounted Sugar, who was already tensed in anticipation of the nudge from Tate that would signal the beginning of the timed run. Tightening her grip on the reins, Tate tried to relax, but the adrenaline pumping through her veins made that nearly impossible. Instead, she had to be content with a quick, steadying breath. The next instant, she leaned forward in the saddle and Sugar went flying into the arena at a full gallop.

Later, she never knew how it happened. She would have sworn that she was totally focused on getting around the three barrels she had to circle without mishap—after all, it wasn't as if she were one of the fresh young things just getting into barrel racing. She'd been on the circuit for years and could circle a barrel with her eyes closed and her hands held behind her back. But not today.

She rounded the first barrel at record speed, hugging it so close that she felt the metal brush her knee as Sugar flew past. Exhilaration streaked through her. They were going to do it. She and Sugar were going to leave Becky

Donaldson and that old spotted mare of hers in their dust! Two more barrels and they'd be home free.

But when she raced toward the third barrel, hoping to shave even more time off the clock, she pushed too close to the envelope of disaster. One minute everything was fine, and the next, Sugar's shoulder bumped the barrel, which immediately started to teeter. A collective gasp went up from the crowd, but all Tate could do was put her head down, spur Sugar to go faster and head for the finish line, praying that the barrel would somehow miraculously right itself.

It didn't. Just as she flew across the finish line and darted behind the chutes, she heard the groan from the crowd that signalled the barrel had lost the tug-of-war with gravity and tipped over like a fallen soldier in the dirt. And for that mistake in judgment and concentration, she would be awarded penalty seconds that would completely take her out of the running for any type of prize money.

To her horror, she felt tears sting her eyes and quickly blinked them back, all the while telling herself that the loss was no big deal. But she knew that it was. Before she hit the circuit late every spring, she mapped out the rodeos she would enter and decided which ones she had to win so she'd have all the money she needed to support Haily and herself during the school year. And this one had been a "must win."

Feeling a sickening lump in her stomach, she hauled back on the reins and brought Sugar to a stop near the holding pens, knowing she had only a few short minutes to conceal her disappointment before Haily rushed out of the stands to find out what had gone wrong. Tate didn't want her daughter taking on adult troubles, especially when there was no need to. There would be other wins down the road where she would make up the difference, and it was still early yet in the summer. There were a lot of rodeos ahead of her, and if she kept her nose to the grindstone, she could win more than her share of them.

If she steered clear of Flynn Rawlings.

In the next second, her innate honesty forced her to admit that he hadn't lost this race for her. No, she'd done that all by herself, she thought as she dismounted. She'd let him distract her, and that was her fault, not his. And it had to stop. Even if she had been willing to risk her heart for a charming flirt again—which she wasn't—she literally couldn't afford to get mixed-up with the man. Now all she had to do was find a way to convince him of that.

As if she'd conjured him with her thoughts, she looked up to see him striding toward her with Haily at his side. Mocking her efforts to remain unmoved, her heart skipped a beat, silently greeting him and irritating her to no end.

"I can't believe you didn't win!" Haily said as she rushed forward the last few steps to give her a quick hug. "You were *so* close. What happened?"

Forcing a rueful smile, Tate returned her hug. "I guess I got a little too close. It happens sometimes."

"Tough break," Flynn said quietly, his eyes meeting hers over Haily's head. "You had everybody else beat by a mile."

The sympathy in his voice was almost her undoing. *Don't be nice to me,* she wanted to cry. *Don't give me another reason to like you.* But she couldn't say that, not without revealing just how his persistence was finally getting to her. "I messed up," she said with a shrug, then turned her attention to her daughter. "You ready to hit the road again, sweetheart? If we hurry, we can be in Oklahoma by nightfall."

So she wasn't staying for the dance, Flynn thought. Not that he was surprised. After the kiss they'd shared the night before last, he'd seen the stunned passion clouding her eyes. And the fear. When he'd gotten up the next morning and climbed out of his tent, he'd fully expected to find her camper gone. He should have realized that she was too professional to let anything interfere with the rodeo competition. Now that it was over, however, she was going to bolt like a scared rabbit before he could get any ideas about touching her again.

His lips twitching, he opened his mouth to warn her it wasn't going to do any good to run—she'd just meet him down the road since he was already entered in six of the next seven rodeos she was signed up for—but he never got the chance.

Before he could open his mouth, Tom Daily, the chute boss, yelled over at her, "Hey, Tate, you've got an emergency call. You can take it in the arena office."

Startled, Tate paled, suddenly remembering her last conversation with her father. "Oh, God!" she whispered. "Dad! Yesterday when I talked to him, he wasn't feeling well—"

She didn't wait to explain further, but ran to the arena office with Haily and Flynn right behind her. The rodeo official who had taken the call took one look at her ashen face and motioned to the phone lying on the desk. Her heart in her throat, Tate swallowed and snatched it up. "H-hello?"

"I'm all right," her father began testily. "I'm in the hospital, but there's nothing for you to worry about. I wouldn't even have called you, but Doc Kramer threatened to if I didn't. And you know what an old woman he is. Worries about everything."

At any other time, Tate would have laughed at his disgusted tone, but she knew her father. He didn't like people fussing over him, worrying over him, and he'd go to his grave swearing he was fine. "He worries because he knows how you are," she retorted, sinking down onto the chair behind the desk. "And he wouldn't put you in the hospital unless he felt it was necessary. What happened?"

"Nothing."

"Don't give me that, Dad," she warned. "You either tell me or I'm calling Doc Kramer as soon as you hang up."

"Oh, all right, all right," he grumbled. "I don't know what all the fuss is about anyway. Nothing drastic happened.... I just had a little dizzy spell. I told Kramer it was just because I forgot to take my blood pressure pills, but the old goat insisted on putting me in the hospital, anyway. Said he wanted to monitor me overnight, just to make sure everything was all right." He snorted, giving his opinion of that idea. "I got stock to feed, a farm to take care of. I don't have time for this."

Encouraged by her murmur of sympathy, he rambled on about all the things he had to do, how the place was going to just fall apart if he wasn't there to see about it. Amused, Tate couldn't hold back a smile. Anyone hearing him would think he had a huge farm to run, when in actuality, all he had was two acres and a couple of pigs and cows.

"I'm sure the neighbors will look out for the animals while you're gone," she assured him when he let her get a word in edgewise. "I'm more concerned about you. Are you sure you're okay? Because I can come home, you know. Haily and I can be there by late tomorrow afternoon if you need us."

He clicked his tongue at that, and she could just picture his fierce frown. "You'll do no such thing," he said gruffly. "I'm fine, you hear? Bored out of my mind, but fine. There's no need for you to come rushing home like I'm on my deathbed or something. You'd just be wasting your gas money and you need that to get to your next rodeo."

He sounded so positive that Tate just let him talk. But when she finally hung up and turned to face Haily and Flynn, she announced flatly to her daughter, "We're going home for a while, honey. Grandpa's having trouble with his blood pressure again and I need to see for myself that he's all right."

In less than an hour, Tate was nearly ready to go. Flynn had helped her hitch up her horse trailer, then loaded Sugar in the back. There was nothing left to do but say goodbye. Haily, with the ease of an affectionate child, gave Flynn a fierce hug, promised to look for him somewhere down the road, then climbed into the cab with a jaunty wave. For Tate, it wasn't quite so easy.

Suddenly as unsure as a teenager on her first date, she turned to him, emotions she hadn't expected squeezing her throat. She tried to tell herself that he had been nothing but a playful irritant and she should be thanking her lucky stars that she now had a legitimate excuse to put some space between them. By the time their paths crossed again, she would have the crazy, mixed-up feelings he stirred in her firmly under control and the kiss they'd shared would be nothing more than a distant memory.

But as she stared up into blue eyes that were, for once, serious, she was shocked to realize that she was going to miss him. Somehow, someway, he had forced himself into her life, and it was hard to picture a day going by without her heart jumping into a gallop at the sight of him.

"Well, I guess we should be going," she said in a voice that was revealingly husky. "Thanks for your help."

"It was nothing," he said with a shrug. "I just hope your Dad's all right. Be careful, okay?"

She nodded, unable to tear her gaze from his. For a wild, tense moment, she was sure he was going to reach for her—she could read the hot intent in his eyes—but then Haily poked her head out the window and asked her where the map was, and the moment was broken. "In the side pocket on the door," she answered, then forced a rueful grin as she turned her attention back to Flynn. "Well, that's my cue that it's time to go," she said with a chuckle that sounded hollow even to her own ears. "See you down the road, cowboy."

Flynn almost grabbed her then and gave her a kiss she wouldn't soon forget, but she'd already slid behind the wheel before he could make up his mind, and all he could do was echo, "Yeah. See you down the road."

As she jammed the key into the ignition, he hooked his thumbs into the front pocket of his jeans and stepped back out of the way. But instead of firing to life when Tate turned the key, the motor refused to turn over and started to grind. Frowning, he made a motion for Tate to stop. "Have you been having trouble with your battery?"

"Not really," she said, her brows snapping together as she glared at the gauges on the dash as if the answer to the problem lay there. "It's been a little slow to start, and I just thought the water in the battery was low. But when I checked it, it was fine."

Already moving to the front of the truck, he said, "Pop the hood. Maybe the connections are just loose."

But once the hood was up and he checked the battery cables, he saw they were tight and clean. Wiping his hands on his handkerchief, he came around to the driver's side. "I'll get my truck and give you a jump," he told her. "I'll be right back."

Within minutes, he had his pickup parked nose to nose with hers and jumper cables linked between the two batteries. Revving his motor, he motioned for Tate to try the ignition. She flicked her wrist, and grinned as the truck started immediately.

Flynn, however, wasn't satisfied. Leaving the two trucks linked by the jumper cables, he walked over to join her. "How old's your battery?"

She shrugged. "I don't know. It was on the truck when I bought it."

"The truck was used?"

If Tate had needed any verification that they came from two different worlds, he gave it to her with that question. The Rawlingses of New Mexico had probably never bought a truck that hadn't been driven new off the showroom floor, while she, on the other hand, didn't have any idea what it felt like to be the first-time owner of a vehicle. Her chance would come, of course, but only after medical school; and that was years down the road.

Smiling, she said, "*Very* used would probably be a better description. But it's been a good truck. I haven't had a bit of trouble with it."

Until now. "I hate to tell you this, sweetheart," he said reluctantly, "but you need a battery."

Tate heard the endearment, but it was the other that she protested. "Oh, no! Surely not. It'll build back up while I'm driving."

"It won't if you've got a dead cell. You turn the motor off for any reason—even to put in gas—and you could be in trouble. And you've got a long way to go," he reminded her. "Do you want to take a chance on getting stuck on the side of the road out in the middle of nowhere with Haily?"

"No, of course not—"

"Then get a battery, honey. Trust me, you need one."

Troubled, her eyes searched his. Why now? she wanted to cry. She didn't need this, couldn't afford it. She was already short on funds, and now she had to make an unscheduled trip home, which would cut even deeper into the money she'd expected to win over the next few months. How could she even think about buying a battery when she was worried about having enough cash to get home and then on to the next rodeo?

"I'll get one somewhere down the road," she hedged, too proud to discuss her finances with a man who probably didn't even know the meaning of the word *budget.* "I don't have time right now."

Biting back a curse, Flynn wanted to ask her if she had the time to sit on the side of the road when the damn truck died, but the stubborn set of her jaw told him he'd only be wasting his breath. Muttering a curse, he stepped back. "Have it your way. Let me disconnect the jumper cables and you can be on your way."

Seconds later, he slammed down the hood on her pickup and watched, grim-faced, as she drove away. She was lying. He knew it as surely as he knew that he and the lady weren't through with each other by a long shot. She was going to try to drive across two and a half states with a battery he wouldn't trust on a go-cart. And there wasn't a damn thing he could do about it.

It wasn't his problem, he decided as he stored the jumper cables in the space behind the cab seat of his pickup. *She* wasn't his problem. But as he climbed behind the wheel and slammed the driver's door, he couldn't ignore the niggling voice that reminded him that she was a woman alone, a single mother with a child who had no man to help her. Even if she'd been a complete stranger, he would have worried about her heading out on a cross-country trip with an iffy battery.

He made no conscious decision to follow Tate. But suddenly without quite knowing how it happened, he found himself putting his truck in gear and turning down the road after her. The rodeo in Price wasn't far from her father's place in Utah, he reasoned. There was nothing that said he couldn't take the same highway she did and, in the process, make sure she got home safely. He'd keep his distance and she'd never know he was behind her—unless she had trouble. She'd also never know that until this minute, he hadn't once considered entering the Price rodeo.

Tate drove all night, stopping only for gas and an occasional rest break. Every time she turned off the motor, she made sure there was always someone close by to give her a jump if she needed one, but her precautions proved to be unnecessary. The truck fired to life every time she turned the key, though not without stubborn reluctance. But it started, and that was all she cared about.

Then, when she was only an hour from home and dawn was still only a promise on the eastern horizon behind her, the truck died without so much as a whimper of protest. One second she was racing along, telling herself she could make the last leg of the trip without falling asleep, and the next she was staring in disbelief at the speedometer that was dropping like a rock. Swearing under her breath, she tightened her grip on the steering wheel and eased the truck over to the shoulder of the road.

The minute she braked to a stop, silence, thick and heavy, pushed in on the truck like the darkness that surrounded them. A darkness, she noticed with a mounting sense of dread, that her dim headlights barely cut a swath through. Her heart thumping, she pushed off the lights to save what little power she had left and glanced over at Haily, who she was still sound asleep and slumped against the locked passenger door. Relieved, Tate reached for the key and gave it a turn.

Nothing. Absolutely nothing happened.

Groaning, she leaned back against the headrest and closed her eyes. How could this happen now? She was so close to home, she could practically smell it, but with a dead battery and no help in sight for as far as the eye could see, she might as well be half a continent away. Great! This was just great!

Her head back and her eyes still closed, Tate didn't see the vehicle that appeared far on the horizon behind her. Then her side mirrors caught the glare of its headlights, reflecting the high beams right in her eyes as the vehicle pulled over to the shoulder behind her.

Startled, Tate straightened, her gaze narrowed against the lights that blinded her. She couldn't see a thing, and suddenly it wasn't the dead battery she was worried about but the stranger who had hopefully stopped to help her. If he had other ideas, she and Haily were in big trouble.

Dear God, why hadn't she listened to Flynn when he'd warned her this could happen? she wondered wildly as her heart started to pound. How could she have been so irresponsible when she had Haily with her?

Fighting panic, she reached for the tire iron she always kept under the seat, then quickly shook her daughter. "Wake up, honey. The truck died and somebody's stopped to help us—"

"Huh?" Always a deadhead whenever she got less than twelve hours' sleep, Haily only mumbled under her breath and curled against the door.

Behind her camper and horse trailer, Tate heard the slam of a door, the crunch of booted feet in the gravel on the side of the road. Her throat dry as dust and her palms damp, she tightened her grip on the tire iron and braced herself for God only knew what kind of danger was walking her way.

In the side mirror, a man's tall, thin silhouette came closer and closer, but the light of his headlights was behind him and his face was in shadows. Sick apprehension spilling into her stomach, she could do nothing but wait.

With her gaze locked on the man in the mirror, she didn't realize he was so close until he suddenly appeared at her window. Startled, Tate jumped and glanced up... only to wilt in relief at the sight of Flynn scowling down at her.

"Oh, thank God!" she breathed, quickly rolling down the window. "You scared me to death! What are you doing here?"

Seeing her wide, frightened eyes as big as saucers in her bloodless face, he swore, glaring at her. "You damn well ought to be scared! Dammit, woman, I warned you this could happen. But did you listen? Hell, no!"

He'd kept his distance all night, only occasionally catching a glimpse of her taillights far down the road, and had just begun to think he was being overprotective when he'd topped a rise and seen her truck pulled over to the shoulder. The fear that had clutched him by the throat had been unexpected and immediate. He'd been at least fifteen minutes behind her. If someone else had stopped—

But no one had, a voice in his head reminded him. She and Haily were obviously both safe.

But that didn't make him any less furious. When he thought of the scumbags who could have stopped to investigate her predicament, it was all he could do not to jerk her out of her truck and paddle her backside good.

Glancing past her to where Haily slept curled against the passenger door, he brought his scowling gaze back to hers. "If I hadn't been on my way to Price, you could be in real trouble right now," he said harshly, lowering his voice to a low roar so as not to wake Haily. "And it would be no more than you deserved, taking off cross-country with a battery that hasn't got enough juice to light a light bulb. It was a damn fool thing to do. Are you okay?"

Just that quickly, he went from chewing her out to worrying about her. Blinking at the lightning quick change of subject, Tate found herself struggling to hold back the sudden smile that threatened to slide across her face. He wanted to be furious with her, but he couldn't quite hide his concern. "I'm fine," she assured him quietly. "But I'd be better if I'd had a breakdown in my father's front yard instead of out here in the middle of nowhere."

"Give the key a turn," he said. "It probably won't do any good, but I want to hear what it sounds like."

She did as instructed, and just as before, nothing happened. There was no sound at all but the click of the key in the ignition. A quick glance at Flynn's grim face told her that she'd run out of luck. This time it was going to take more than a jump to get her going.

"You've reached the end of the line," he told her flatly. "We'll have to unload Sugar, then unhitch the trailer from your truck and swing it around to mine. Once we get to St. George, we can drop Sugar at your dad's place. Then I'll take you to the hospital to see him."

"What about my truck? We can't just leave it here."

"Sure we can," he assured her. "It'll be perfectly safe. It's not going anywhere fast the way it is, and after you see your father, I'll bring you back with a new battery."

"Oh, no, I couldn't let you do that," she protested. "You have to get to Price, and I've held you up enough."

"Don't be ridiculous," he chided. "It's not going to take that long to get a battery and bring you back. Anyway, I've got some time to kill before the rodeo starts, so there's no hurry. So you're not inconveniencing me, okay? Any more objections?"

She could think of a whole slew of them. He was getting too involved in her life, riding to her rescue, showing up just when she needed him the most. He was acting like a hero; the only problem was that she knew for a fact that there was no such thing as heroes anymore. A woman who let herself need a man in today's world could expect nothing but heartache. And she'd had enough of that to last her a lifetime.

She could, *would,* stand on her own two feet no matter what, she told herself fiercely. But she had to get to the hospital and assure herself that her father really was all right. *Before* he somehow talked his doctor into releasing him before he was ready to go home. Reluctantly giving in, she said with a sigh, "I guess not," and pushed open her door.

The three of them packed into Flynn's truck like sardines, and they were soon on their way to the Baxter farm. Haily had awakened when Tate had tried to move her from one truck to the other, and was thrilled that Flynn had rushed to their rescue. Rested and wide-awake, she chatted like a magpie, and Tate was more than content to let her. The adrenaline that had given her the energy to drive through the night was quickly waning now that

Flynn had taken over the responsibility of driving, and fears about her father that she had successfully ignored for hours took advantage of her tiredness to raise their ugly heads.

With all her heart, she wanted to believe that he'd been honest with her about his condition. But she couldn't shake the feeling that Dr. Kramer wouldn't stick him in the hospital unless something was seriously wrong. Worried sick, she stared blindly out the window and prayed she was wrong as dawn slowly crept over the eastern horizon.

An hour later, as soon as they dropped off Sugar at her father's farm and had unhooked the horse trailer, they headed for the hospital. Her heart in her throat, Tate knocked softly at her father's door and pushed it open. Prepared for just about anything, she stopped in her tracks at the sight of him sitting up in bed, eating a breakfast that a lumberjack would have had trouble downing.

"I thought you were sick!"

Not the least surprised to see her, Allen Baxter grinned at her accusing tone and took another bite of pancakes dripping in syrup. A big man with a thick head of white hair and a solid build that came from years of good living and hard work, he looked the picture of health.

"I told you I was fine," he reminded her. "But you didn't believe me, did you? You never do." Shaking his head at her, he opened his arms wide. "Come over here and give your old man a kiss."

"I ought to give you what for," she retorted, smiling in spite of her best efforts not to as she hurried over to the bed to wrap her arms around him. "You scared me to death."

"Aw, you worry too much," he scoffed, tugging at her hair affectionately. "Where's that granddaughter of mine? And who's this?" he asked in surprise, spying Flynn in the doorway.

Heat spilling into her cheeks at her father's suddenly speculative look, Tate wanted to kick herself for not expecting the kind of interest Flynn's presence was sure to generate. The last man her father or anyone else had seen her with was Rich Travis, and that was months before Haily was born.

"Flynn Rawlings," she said quickly, introducing the two men. "Flynn's entered in the Price rodeo and happened to come across Haily and me when we broke down about fifty miles outside of town."

"Broke down—"

"It's nothing serious, sir," Flynn assured him. "She just needs a battery. When we leave here, we're going to stop by an auto parts place and get one."

"Good," the older man grunted. "I told her she was pushing her luck with that old truck, but I might as well have saved my breath. I'm glad to see she's finally met a man she'll listen to."

"Dad!"

Flynn chuckled, liking Allen Baxter immediately. He had a feeling once the older man got talking, he would give him an earful about his independent daughter, and Flynn couldn't wait to hear it. It was about time he found out what made the lady tick.

But Tate made sure that didn't happen. Quickly changing the subject, she said, "Haily wanted to come up, too, but kids aren't allowed past the lobby, so you'll have to wait till you're kicked out of this joint before you can see her. Have you seen Dr. Kramer yet this morning? When's he going to release you?"

It was the wrong thing to say. His grin disappearing, her father grimaced irritably. "Who knows with that old reprobate? He doesn't know himself what he's going to do from one minute to the next."

But Dr. Robert Kramer knew exactly what he wanted to do concerning Allen Baxter. "He needs a keeper," he told Tate bluntly when he caught up with her and Flynn in the hallway outside her father's room. "This isn't the first time he's forgotten his blood-pressure medicine—from the hints he's dropped, he seems to do it on a pretty regular basis—and next time he may not be so lucky."

Whatever Tate had been expecting, it wasn't that... especially after she'd just seen her father put away a breakfast fit for a field hand. She paled. "Are you saying he could have a stroke?"

A close family friend in spite of Allen's grumbling, Robert Kramer hated to scare her, but he couldn't hide the truth from her just because it wasn't what she wanted to hear. Slipping a consoling arm around her, he gave it to her straight. "I know you have to raise money for school, honey, but Allen's not as young as he used to be. He's forgetful, doesn't eat like he should, doesn't take his pills. And yes, that could lead to a stroke—even a heart attack. He shouldn't be living alone."

Stricken, her eyes welled with tears. "But—"

"I know, you can't be there all the time," he said quickly, anticipating her objections. "That's why you need to think about getting someone to stay with the old cuss when you and Haily are on the road. And I know a woman who's just perfect for the job."

Chapter 4

Tate handed the clerk at the auto-parts store the money for the battery she'd just bought. Half her gas money gone in one fell swoop, she thought with a wince, but she didn't have any choice. Without that battery, she'd be stuck at her father's farm the rest of the summer...and out of school in the fall.

She tried not to panic at the thought, but it was too late. Her heart was already sick with anxiety and pounding a mile a minute. She was so close to finishing, so close to finally getting into medical school that she could almost reach out and touch the dream. She'd literally spent years trying to get there, struggling all the while, and she hadn't done it alone. Poor Haily.... She'd dragged her from one rodeo to another, wondering all the while what kind of mother she was to haul her daughter up and down the highway every summer of her young life. Only the knowledge that she'd eventually be able to provide a better life for both of them had kept her going. She couldn't—wouldn't—quit now.

You need to think about getting someone to stay with the old cuss when you and Haily are on the road.

Doc Kramer's words echoed in her ears, haunting her. How was she going to feed another mouth? Take on another responsibility? Every month, her father's small Social Security check came, just like clockwork, but he just barely got by on that. There wasn't enough left over for so much as an occasional dinner out, let alone live-in help.

And even if by some miracle she could somehow scrape up the money herself, how in the world would she talk her father into the arrangement? she wondered in growing despair. He was a proud, independent man who hadn't answered to anyone, especially a woman, since Tate's mother had died when she was a little girl. He wouldn't take kindly to a stranger moving into his home and watching over him as though he didn't have the sense to come in out of the rain. Not only would he resent it, his pride would take a real beating, and she didn't know if she could stand by and be a party to that.

But what other alternative did she have? If she couldn't leave him alone, then she had to be prepared to stay with him herself. Catch-22, she thought grimly as she and Haily followed Flynn out to his truck with the new battery. She was caught in a catch-22 that was nothing but a vicious circle, and from where she was standing, there was no way out.

That did not, however, stop her from worrying about it. Flynn and Haily chatted all the way out to where they had left the camper, but Tate couldn't summon so much as a smile. Antsy, needing to do something—*anything*— she didn't notice Flynn watching her until he suddenly slid his arm along the top of the seat and reached over to squeeze her neck. Startled, she jumped, her eyes flying to his.

"It's going to be okay," he said gruffly. "You heard what the doctor said. As soon as your father takes his medication on a regular basis, he'll be back to his old self. All he needs is someone to look after him."

He made it sound so easy, she thought, and for the Rawlingses of New Mexico, it probably was. When you had money, all you had to do was make a couple of phone calls and write some checks, and you could get whatever you wanted. But when you didn't have two nickels to rub together, you were playing by a whole new set of rules.

She opened her mouth to tell him just that, but then stopped. He hadn't released his grip on the back of her neck as she'd expected. Instead, his fingers began to unconsciously knead the tension he found there, burrowing under the fall of her hair to gently stroke and rub, pressing against her tight muscles, working a magic that stole her breath and sent warmth seeping through her.

Distracted, Tate felt her heart lurch, her throat grow dry, and alarm bells clang to life in her ears. She should do something, lean forward until he was no longer touching her, reach up and pull his hand from her. But pleasure oozed from his fingers, melting her muscles one by one, heating her all the way to her toes. Caught in the trap of his suddenly dark gaze, she swallowed, unable to tear her eyes from his.

What was he doing? Flynn asked himself. He hadn't meant to touch her, but she'd looked so serious sitting there that he hadn't been able to resist. Without even knowing how it had happened, he found himself wanting to comfort her, to bring a smile back to her face, to hold her close and assure her everything was going to be all right.

And that scared him to death. This was supposed to be a game between them, a lighthearted duel of wills in which he found a way to make her admit that she wasn't as indifferent to him as she liked to pretend. Neither of them was supposed to get serious; they weren't getting involved. Why, then, did he find himself getting caught up in her problems? Why did he have this driving urge to do whatever it took to make her world right again?

At the sudden, unexpected blare of a horn, Tate dragged her eyes from his and cried, "Look out!"

Jerking his gaze back to the road, Flynn saw that while he'd been staring at Tate like an infatuated teenager, he'd let his truck drift over the center line…right into the path of an oncoming car that was frantically trying to get out of his way. Muttering a curse, he snatched his hand back from Tate and gave the steering wheel a sharp turn that brought them back into their own lane. Seconds later, the oncoming car whizzed past them, its horn blaring.

Silence, thick and tense, filled the cab, and for what seemed like an eternity no one broke it. Then Haily sat up straighter and breathed out in awe, "Wow, that was close!"

A muscle jumping in his clenched jaw, Flynn looked down at her where she sat between him and her mother and forced a smile. "You ain't kidding, honey," he said tightly, quickly returning his eyes to the road. "I got a little distracted there, but it won't happen again."

Seated on the other side of her daughter, her heart still thumping madly, Tate stared straight ahead and didn't say a word.

Her camper was just where they'd left it on the side of the road, lurching off the shoulder like a drunk who couldn't stand up straight, but unharmed. Relieved, Tate sat in the driver's seat while Flynn, with Haily's chattering assistance, installed the new battery. Only minutes after they'd arrived, he poked his head out from beneath the hood and told Tate, "She's all hooked up. Give it a try and see what she'll do."

Holding her breath, she turned the key. Without a moment's hesitation, the motor roared to life. "Finally!" She laughed in relief. "Something's working the way it's supposed to."

Flynn, however, wasn't so quick to celebrate. Slamming the hood down on her truck, he opened the door for Haily to climb in on the passenger side, then walked around to the driver's side, where Tate still sat behind the wheel enjoying the steady hum of the engine. "How are the gauges?" he asked, looking through the open window at the dash. "Everything running okay?"

Surprised, she looked at the gauges and shrugged. She knew what they were all for, but except for the gas gauge, she very seldom looked at them. Her father did a tune-up on the truck every spring before she left to join the circuit, and she'd never had any problems with it. Until now. "Yeah, I guess. Why wouldn't it be? The battery was the problem, and it's been corrected."

"Maybe," Flynn said. Poking his head farther through the window, he got a good look at the battery gauge and swore under his breath. "It's still discharging."

"What is?" Tate asked in alarm, staring in confusion at the dash.

"The battery is discharging, and since it's brand-new, that can only mean your alternator isn't working right." At her blank look, he explained, "The alternator is like a little generator that builds up the battery when the motor's running. If it's on the blink, there's nothing to recharge the battery and it eventually goes dead."

A sinking feeling of apprehension spilling into her stomach, Tate swallowed thickly. "Don't tell me I need an alternator, too," she warned. "Not after I just bought a battery I might not have needed after all."

"Oh, you needed it," he assured her. "Yours had a dead cell. But you're going to have to get an alternator, too, or you're not going to get very far before you find yourself right back in the situation you found yourself in last night…stuck on the side of the road in the middle of nowhere."

After everything else, it was too much. Tate felt a lump of emotion form in her throat. "How much will it cost to fix it?"

Flynn watched her brace herself for the bad news but there was no way he could sugarcoat it. Wishing he could spare her, he quoted her a ballpark figure she could expect to pay at any decent garage.

It was too much. Pale, she mentally did a quick count of the gas money she had left, but no matter how many times she counted it, she still came up short. And even if she'd had the exact amount right down to the penny, she wouldn't have any left over to buy gas to the next rodeo.

"I see," she said huskily. Forcing a smile, she tried to make a joke of her lack of funds, but the words just wouldn't come. Instead, hot tears spilled into her eyes, horrifying her. Dear God, what was wrong with her? she wondered wildly, blinking rapidly. She wasn't a crybaby; she didn't fall apart just because life threw her a curve once in a while. She was tougher than that. She had to be.

"Mom? What's wrong? Why are you crying?"

At Haily's cry of alarm, she glanced quickly down at where her hands were clenched on the steering wheel, letting her hair fall forward to hide her tear-streaked face.

"I'm n-not," she sniffed, making a pathetic attempt to regain control. "I'm just a little t-tired—"

"Tate?"

She wouldn't look at him, but she didn't have to. In the split second before she'd hidden behind her hair, he'd caught a glimpse of her blue eyes swimming in tears, and the sight had almost wrenched his heart from his chest. Stunned, he fought the need to touch her, knowing this was one battle he was going to lose. And he didn't give a damn.

She always seemed so strong that he'd thought she could handle just about anything without blinking an eye. How could he have known that she would break so easily? Suddenly needing to hold her, he reached for her, but the truck door was between them, and with a muttered curse, he jerked it open. A single step brought him to her side, but still she kept her head stubbornly down. "Honey, look at me," he growled roughly, and took hold of her chin to turn her face to his.

Even then she fought him, refusing to meet his eye... until he slipped an arm around her shoulders and drew her close. Startled, her eyes flew to his, and suddenly they were both remembering a kiss that refused to be forgotten.

Let her go, the voice of reason ordered in his head, but he couldn't. It seemed as if he'd been waiting an eternity to hold her again, and what could it hurt, anyway? Nothing was going to happen. They were on the side of the road, for God's sake, with Haily as a chaperon. He couldn't even kiss her.

But he wanted to.

And she wanted him to. He could see the need deep in the depths of her midnight-blue eyes, a fire that burned like a star in the night. Cupping her cheek in his palm, he rubbed his thumb across the tracks of her tears with slow deliberateness, working his way to her full bottom lip. Heat spilling into his loins, he watched her eyes darken, her lips part ever so slightly and knew he was playing with fire. But considering the circumstances, it was as close to her mouth as he was going to get.

Dazed, a hot ache churning in moist, dark secret places of her body, Tate tried to remember why she didn't want this, didn't want Flynn. But her mind was fuzzy, her heart jumping crazily, her lips where he rubbed them throbbing. She knew she needed to move, but it was a long, breathless moment before she could force herself to pull back from his hand at her cheek and the arm encircling her shoulders.

"Don't pay any attention to me," she said with a forced, shaky laugh as she quickly wiped the last of her tears away. "I always go to pieces over alternators." Especially when she didn't have the money to pay for one.

Studying her through narrowed eyes, Flynn said, "I know you weren't expecting this, especially after just buying a battery. If money's tight—"

He was going to offer her a loan, and something in her cringed at the thought of taking money from him. "Money's always tight," she retorted ruefully. "But I'll manage. I always do. Dad takes his truck to Leon's Automotive Service, and they've always been fair with him. I'll call them when we get back to the farm and see what kind of price they can give me."

She didn't seem too concerned about her ability to come up with the cash, Flynn thought with a frown. In fact, she seemed downright casual. And she was lying through her teeth. A couple of weeks ago, she might have fooled him, but since he'd gotten to know her, he'd learned that there was one thing the lady was never casual about, and that was money.

And there was no way in hell she'd take it from him or any other man. She was too proud, too independent. Which meant he had to pick his way very carefully through the offer he intended to make her. "If you can't come to terms with them, you can always go to an auto-parts store and buy the part yourself. Your dad probably knows how to put on an alternator. 'Course, he's laid up for a while, so you'd have to wait till he was feeling better, but it would save you a ton in labor charges. Or…you could let me do it for you."

"You!"

She sounded so surprised, he had to laugh. "Yeah, why not?"

"But you have to be in Price—"

"Not for a few days, I don't. Anyway, it won't take all that long to fix it after you get the part, and even if it does, there's no hurry. I've got some time to kill, and I'd just as soon do it here as there."

Tate hesitated, fighting the urge to jump at the offer. He was the answer to her prayers, a knight in boots and jeans holding out the perfect solution to her problem. But could she use him that way? her conscience asked, needling her. After she'd done everything she could to discourage his interest in her, could she turn around and take advantage of his generosity?

Already shaking her head, she said, "I appreciate the offer, but you've got better things to do than work on this old truck. And I couldn't pay you what the job deserves," she added, unwittingly admitting the real cause of her dilemma. "But thanks anyway."

Flynn told himself to let it go. She didn't want to be beholden to him, and that was her choice. She wouldn't thank him for butting into her business or trying to take on her problems. Anyway, she'd found a way to handle her troubles before she'd met him, and she'd do so now. If he really wanted to help her, he'd take her at her word and head north just as soon as he made sure she'd gotten back to her father's farm.

But something in his gut twisted at the thought of driving off and leaving her all alone with a sick father, a broken-down truck and a nearly empty pocketbook. Before he could stop himself, he found himself suggesting, "You don't have to pay me. We could barter. Right now, I'd do just about anything for a couple of home-cooked meals and a real bed to sleep in. Eating out all the time and bedding down in a sleeping bag is beginning to get awfully old."

"Does that mean Flynn's going to stay with us for a while, Mom?" Haily chirped excitedly. "Wow! That'll be great! I can show him the pond and my secret place and my cat...."

"Yeah, Mom," Flynn teased, "it'll be great. Whaddaya say? Have we got a deal?"

"Please, Mom? I can practice my whittling and everything. Please?"

Her gaze bouncing between her daughter and Flynn, Tate hesitated. Every ounce of her common sense screamed out in protest that she was crazy to even consider such a suggestion. She was too drawn to the man already; spending more time with him would only make the situation impossible. And she didn't, under any circumstances, want to be in his or any other man's debt.

But who else would work on her truck in exchange for a few simple home-cooked meals? the voice of temptation whispered in her ear. She could have her cake and eat it, too, and how often did she have that kind of luck? The repairs would be made, but she'd still have the money to get to the next rodeo. Why was she even hesitating?

"Just a few meals and a bed? That's all you want?" she asked, studying him through narrowed eyes.

He nodded, his blue eyes glinting with amusement at her suspicious tone. "That's it. Scout's honor."

Far from appeased, she could only stare at him, torn. She'd bet her uncle Clyde's overalls that Flynn hadn't been a scout in this lifetime or the last. But still, every instinct she possessed told her she could trust him. Only God knew why.

"All right," she said reluctantly. "But this is strictly a business transaction, and if the repairs turn out to be more complicated than expected, I'll make up the difference in cash." It would leave her strapped, but she'd find a way to manage. She always did. Holding her hand out to him through the window, she smiled. "Okay?"

He nodded. "Deal."

But when his fingers closed around hers to seal the transaction, that age-old energy that was never far from the surface whenever he was within touching distance sparked to life, leaping between them like a bolt of electricity. Trouble, she thought, as her heart lurched in her breast and took up a pagan beat. As skittish as a virgin, she abruptly tugged her hand free and dropped her gaze, but it was too late. They had both just set themselves up for trouble, and there didn't seem to be a thing they could do to avoid it.

By three o'clock that afternoon, Allen Baxter was back home and napping in his room, Haily had gone over to a friend's house to play and Tate was in the kitchen starting the spaghetti and meatballs she'd planned for supper. Left alone in the garage, Flynn quickly replaced the alternator on Tate's truck, only to find himself with hours to kill before supper. Retreating to the back porch with his pocketknife and a piece of wood, he set down to whittle.

Normally he would have found the routine relaxing, but he could hear Tate in the kitchen, banging pans and humming, and he couldn't concentrate. Her voice was pitched low, an unconsciously sensual murmur that was as distracting as hell. Half tempted to join her, he found himself listening to her instead of watching what he was doing and he almost sliced open a finger.

"Dammit, Rawlings, get a grip," he grumbled softly to himself. "If the lady's that disturbing, then maybe you'd better hit the road while you still can."

But it was already too late for that. The peace and quiet of the farm had wrapped around him the second he'd stepped foot on it, reminding him, on a smaller scale, of the Double R and home. And seeing Tate on her own turf, humming and carefree in a way she never allowed herself to be on the circuit, was too enticing to resist. He didn't want to leave—at least, not just yet.

But he wasn't going to sit on her front porch and moan about the lady, either, he warned himself. He had to find himself something to do.

He didn't have far to look. The farmhouse was at least as old or older than Allen Baxter, and like its owner, was showing signs of age. The faucet in the bathroom had a slow, irritating leak, the closet door in the guest room was warped—and consequently tended to stick—and the up-stairs' porch railing looked as though it were hanging on by a thread. After searching in the garage for the tools he would need, Flynn set to work.

He was in the bathroom, struggling with the faucet, when Tate found him. Standing in the open doorway, her hands on her hips, she took in the disassembled faucet in a single glance and frowned. "What are you doing?"

Not the least abashed at being caught in the act, he looked up and grinned. "Putting a washer in this thing so it'll quit dripping. Hope you don't mind."

Tate only snorted at that, unable to stop her own lips from curling up at the corners. He looked as happy as a pig in a mud puddle and couldn't have cared less if she minded or not. "What about the truck?"

"Finished it hours ago," he said absently, returning his attention to the rubber washers he'd been searching through. "Runs like a top." Swearing under his breath when he couldn't find what he was looking for, he glanced up abruptly. "Has your dad got any more washers around here? None of these look to be the right size."

"In a drawer in the kitchen," she retorted. "Next to the refrigerator. But—where are you going?"

"To get the washers." Grinning, he stopped only inches away from her, waiting patiently for her to step back from where she was blocking the doorway. When she only stubbornly lifted her chin, he cocked an eyebrow at her in amusement. "Are you going to move or what?"

She wasn't amused. "Dammit, Flynn, we had a deal. You were just supposed to fix the truck. Nothing else."

"Did I say that?"

Confused, she shook her head. "No, but I just assumed—"

"There's your first mistake," he cut in, his eyes dancing wickedly as he reached out and drew a greasy finger down her cheek. "Never assume anything. It'll get you in trouble every time."

Obviously pleased with himself, he took another step forward, crowding her until she had no choice but to stand chest to chest with him or give way. Heat flying into her cheeks, she gasped and stepped back, her hand lifted to her face. Beneath her fingers, she could feel the grimy mark he'd left behind...and the fire of his touch. Her heart pounding, she watched him head for the kitchen, whistling, and wondered how he could manage to steal her breath with nothing more than a touch.

"Hey, Tate!"

Still bemused, she glanced up from her thoughts to find him standing at the kitchen doorway, his grin full of mischief as he watched her watch him. Her blush deepening, she tried to shake off his charm, but it was impossible. "What?"

"Wash your face. It's dirty." He chuckled, and disappeared into the kitchen.

Tate didn't plan to throw her shoe at him, but somehow in the next instant, it was hitting the kitchen floor with a satisfying thunk. It didn't hit him, but then again, she wasn't trying to. Infuriating man, she thought, amused. What was she going to do with him?

Over the course of the rest of the day, she asked herself that same question at least a half-dozen more times. After he finished with the faucet in the bathroom, she found him sanding the door in the guest room, then working on the upstairs' balcony railing. She wanted to be miffed with him—at the rate he was going, she would owe him meals for the next six months!—but he made that impossible by being so gracious about the whole thing. Frustrated, she finally told him she never would have agreed to let him stay in the first place if she'd known he was going to turn out to be so nice.

He'd laughed and, hopefully, hadn't realized that she'd been dead serious. A flirting Casanova she could have handled, but a funny, generous, caring man who seemed to be going out of his way to take a load off her shoulders was a whole different kettle of fish. She kept trying to remind herself that even if he tore down the whole house and built it back for her again, he was still nothing but a charming rodeo cowboy who would soon be heading down the road again. That should have been enough to make her heart stop racing every time he smiled at her, but it wasn't. And that scared her to death.

Disturbed, she was quiet all during supper, then afterward escaped to the front porch while Flynn coaxed Haily into doing the dishes with him. She needed to think, but she'd hardly settled herself in the porch swing when she heard the creak of the screen door and her father joined her.

"I thought I saw you sneak out here," he teased, sinking down onto the seat beside her. "With everything that's been going on, we haven't had much time to visit. Everything okay?"

She wanted to tell him . . . about how she'd finished out of the top money in the last couple of rodeos, about how the recent truck repairs had left her so short-funded, she'd need a wing and a prayer just to get to the next competition, about what the doctor had said about leaving him alone now that he was getting forgetful. But most of all, she wanted to tell him about Flynn, how he confused and scared her and made her feel things that were dark and dangerous and tempting, things she'd locked away in a secret corner of her heart when Rick Travis left her alone and pregnant, things she'd sworn never to feel again for any man. But she couldn't say the words. She couldn't unload on him when he'd just gotten out of the hospital, and he would hate the fact that *he* was one of her worries.

"Just fine," she said easily, giving the swing a gentle push as she stared out at the night. "I just thought I'd sit out here and relax for a while. You just can't get this kind of quiet in town, and lately, that's where I seem to spend all my time. If I'm not in school, Haily and I are parked at arena campgrounds, and the quiet there just isn't the same.''

Over the creak of the swing, they could hear the chirp of the crickets and the occasional croak of a frog. But it was the laughter from the kitchen that couldn't be ignored. At the sound of his granddaughter's giggle, Allen Baxter chuckled. "Flynn's a real hit with Haily. I can't remember the last time I heard her laugh so much.''

"Yeah, she's pretty taken with him.''

"How about her mother?'' he teased. "Is she taken with him, too?''

"Dad—''

He grinned at her warning tone and reached over to give her a hug. "I know, I know. The last thing you need is a man, and I need to mind my own business. But you know I can't do that—never could. Besides, you are my business. Haven't you figured that out yet? And I want you to be happy.''

"I am happy.''

"No, you're not *unhappy*,'' he corrected gently, patting her shoulder. "There's a difference, and one of these days, the right man is going to show you that.''

Staring up at him in the darkness, she said quietly, "And you think Flynn might be that man?''

His smile a flash of white in the night, he shrugged. "I don't know. *That's* none of my business. You get to pick the man. I just don't want you to let some jerk from the past blind you to what's right in front of your nose. Even when you're not looking, sweetheart, it doesn't hurt to be aware of all the possibilities.''

Satisfied that he'd got his point across, he ruffled her hair and pushed himself to his feet. "Well, that's enough preaching for one night. Guess I'll turn in. 'Night, honey."

"You're going to bed so soon?"

"Yeah." He chuckled. "That's the trouble with getting old—you find yourself going to bed with the chickens. And getting up with them, too. See you in the morning, sweetheart."

"Sleep in," she called after him. "I'll bring you breakfast in bed."

He nodded agreement, but she knew he wouldn't. He was a farmer; he'd kept farmers' hours all his life. She couldn't expect him to change the habits of a lifetime just because he was getting on in years.

Where had the time gone? she wondered, setting the swing in motion again. Her father had always been there for her, even when she found herself pregnant and jilted at seventeen, and it was difficult for her to accept that he was growing older. She hadn't told him of her talk with the doctor and didn't quite know how to bring it up. In his eyes, he was still as strong and competent as the day she'd been born, and he wasn't going to take kindly to anyone telling him differently. Dear Lord, what was she going to do?

Inside, she heard her father and Haily go upstairs, calling good-night to each other just like John Boy and the Waltons. She was still smiling a few minutes later when Flynn stepped outside and joined her on the porch.

His eyes as sharp as a hawk's, he easily pierced the darkness to find her sitting in the swing in the shadows. "Mind if I join you?" he asked quietly, already moving toward her. "It's been a long time since I sat in a porch swing with a pretty girl."

Tate felt her heart skip a beat and told herself not to read anything into his flirtatious remark. She knew what a charmer he was. And she was no longer a girl willing to be charmed.

Still, it took more of an effort than she liked for her to say easily, "Sure, if you'll settle for a tired mother instead of a pretty girl. What are you doing downstairs still, anyway? After driving all night last night and the day you've put in, you've got to be dead on your feet."

"I don't need a lot of sleep," he assured her, easing down into the swing beside her. "And you drove all night, too. Why aren't you upstairs in bed? Or do tired mothers stay up until they're sure everyone's safely tucked in for the night?"

She smiled. "This one does if she expects to sleep at night."

He stretched out his long legs next to hers, his thigh innocently brushing hers. "So you're a worrier," he concluded. "I figured as much. But then again, I guess most single parents are, especially if they're carrying the load you are. What are you going to do about your dad?"

She hadn't meant to discuss her problems with him. She was used to handling them alone, and in a few days, he would be leaving, going in a different direction from her and Haily, and would probably be out of her life for good. That was the way she wanted it, but for just those reasons and because it was so much easier to confide troubles in the concealing darkness, she found herself talking to him, telling him things she hadn't planned to tell anyone.

"I don't know. I've got to start winning soon or I'm never going to have enough money to get through the fall. But how can I leave Dad? You heard Dr. Kramer. The next time he forgets to take his blood-pressure medicine, he could be in serious trouble."

"What about the woman he suggested you call?" he reminded her. "She sounds like the perfect solution."

"For someone who's got the money to pay her, she is," she retorted ruefully. "I don't."

Since she'd brought the subject up, it was the perfect time to mention the idea that had been bouncing around in his head all afternoon, Flynn decided as he made himself more comfortable in the swing. The problem was, the lady was touchy about accepting help from anyone—especially him—and he had to find a way to do it without stirring up her suspicions.

Half turning to face her, he slipped his arm along the back of the swing. "Speaking of money," he said casually, "I noticed in this morning's paper that there's a couple of one-day rodeos in Cedar City and down in Mesquite this week. You know anything about them?"

She blinked at the change of topic and struggled to switch gears. "I haven't ever entered them myself, but I've heard they're small. And the prize money's not all that much, though it's nothing to sneeze at. Why? You thinking about entering?"

"Maybe. I've still got some time to kill before Price. And the competition probably won't be much—just locals."

"That's true," she agreed. "The prize money is hardly more than the entrance fee and gas money, so the big boys won't bother with them. But since you're already so close, your expenses won't be that much."

"So why don't you go with me and enter the barrel racing?" he asked smoothly. He watched her eyes widen and realized she hadn't even thought about competing herself. "You know you could win," he told her, grinning. "And after all the trouble you've had with your truck, I'm sure you could use the prize money."

"But Dad—"

"Isn't an invalid," he reminded her. "He just needs someone around to remind him to take his medicine. And unless you're planning to give up rodeoing completely so you can be here all the time to do that personally, you need to talk to the woman Dr. Kramer recommended."

"I know," he continued quickly when she opened her mouth to protest. "You think you don't have the money...now. But winning at Cedar City and Mesquite would certainly help. And if you had someone here with Allen while you were on the road, you wouldn't be worried about him all the time and you'd be able to concentrate on winning the bigger purses."

He made a lot of sense and he knew it. Caught between a rock and a hard place that was his logic, Tate had no choice but to agree with him. "All right. I'll interview Mrs. Donovan and see if we can come to some sort of terms."

"And the rodeos? You going to go with me?"

A frown wrinkling her brow, she tried to glare at him, but her mouth kept insisting on smiling. "Do you always have to have your own way?"

"Not every time," he said, chuckling. "Just nine times out of ten. So can I take that as a yes?"

Beaten, she laughed. "Yes, dammit. Yes!"

Chapter 5

Tate didn't deliberately set out to deceive her father, but it just happened to work out that the next morning, when Maggie Donovan came out to the farm to be interviewed, he was in town at the feed store. Her conscious prickling her, Tate tried to convince herself that it was better this way—there was no use upsetting him until she knew for sure that she and Mrs. Donovan could work out a deal. And in order for that to happen, the woman would have to agree to an insultingly small salary, which she probably wouldn't do. Why should she? She could go just about anywhere and make more.

Prepared for rejection, Tate convinced herself that she would find someone else if Maggie Donovan didn't work out. But within five minutes of meeting the older woman, she was racking her brain trying to figure out a way to come up with enough money to hire her on the spot. She was perfect for the job.

A large, rawboned woman without an ounce of pretension in her body, she was a widow with no family of her own and tired of living alone. She said what she thought and expected others to do the same because God only knew how much time anyone had on this earth and there just wasn't time for dillydallying. She was gruff, blunt, no-nonsense. And she took one look at Haily playing in the yard and melted like a marshmallow. Tate couldn't help but like her immediately.

"Kids," she said, shaking her head at Haily's antics, the weathered lines of her face folding into a grin. "Aren't they the darnedest things? I bet she's got a sweet tooth that drives you crazy, doesn't she? I'll have to make her some of my superduper brownies. I haven't met a kid yet that didn't just love them."

So she was already planning on taking the job. Pleased, Tate tried not to let her hopes get too high. They still hadn't discussed salary. "Mrs. Donovan, about the job—"

"Call me Maggie, hon," she cut in. "I'm not one to stand on formality. I never did understand how people living in the same home with their hired help, eating the same food, could call each other by anything but their first names. I don't know about you, but it's just too stuffy for me."

"I agree," Tate said quickly, wondering how she had somehow lost control of the interview. "About the job, Maggie—"

"You have family dishes that you'll want on the menu," the older woman said, incorrectly guessing what she was going to say. "That's fine with me. It seems like I've been cooking for a hundred years, and by now I can make just about anything. Just give me the recipes and we're in business. And if there's anything you don't like, just let me know and you'll never see it on your table."

Tate had to smile—she couldn't help it. As far as Maggie was concerned, they had a done deal and the question of her salary hadn't even come up. "It's not that simple, Maggie. I'm sure you're an excellent cook and we'd be lucky to have you. Dr. Kramer wouldn't have recommended you otherwise. What I'm not so sure of is how I'm going to pay you what you're worth. With my schooling and Haily growing like a weed and needing new shoes practically every other week, money's in short supply—"

"Did I say I wanted money?"

Tate blinked at her bristly tone, confused. "Most people applying for a job expect to get paid."

"But it doesn't have to be in money," the older woman pointed out. "I don't need money. My husband left me more than I can spend in a lifetime, and I've got no one to spend it on. We didn't have any kids, so it's just me, and I'm tired of cooking for myself and rambling around an old house that's too big for just one person. I need to be around people again, and from what Dr. Kramer has told me about your situation with your father, you need me, too. We don't need to cloud that by bringing up money."

"But you should get some sort of compensation," Tate argued. "Cooking and cleaning is hard work—I know— and I'd feel funny not paying you anything."

"Hon, if you'd been alone as long as I have, you'd know that there are a lot of things more important than money...like someone to say good morning to every day, and someone to cook for and pick up after and make you feel useful. Believe me, if you just give me room and board and treat me like a member of the family, I'll be as happy as a clam at high tide.''

Her brown eyes were nearly black with sincerity and shadowed with years of loneliness she couldn't quite hide. Tate felt her heart twist in sympathy and knew she couldn't turn her away. ''I think we're going to be getting the better end of the bargain,'' she said ruefully, ''but if those are your terms, I accept. Welcome to the family, Maggie.''

She chuckled, clearly delighted. ''I'll start today before you have a chance to change your mind.''

''Oh, I'm not going to change mine,'' Tate assured her, grinning. ''But you might when you meet my father. I haven't told him anything about this, and I've got a feeling he's not going to be too thrilled about me hiring you behind his back.''

''You just leave him to me,'' Maggie said confidently. ''Once he gets a taste of my homemade biscuits and apple pie, I'll have him eating out of the palm of my hand.''

As soon as she put her bags in one of the downstairs guest rooms, the older woman started lunch, leaving Tate free to go looking for Flynn. She found him up on a ladder, working on one of the eaves that had started to rot through. Hands propped on her hips, she glared up at him in exasperation. ''Dammit, Flynn, if you don't stop playing handyman, I'm going to have to throw you off the place. You're here for a few home-cooked meals, not work. Remember?''

''A man's got to work up an appetite,'' he retorted with a grin, ''so quit your nagging, woman. Believe me, I'll get my money's worth when I sit down at the table. How'd the interview with Mrs. Donovan go?''

"Maggie," she corrected him. "She's cooking lunch right now."

His smile smug, he leveled dancing eyes on her. "And you were so sure you couldn't afford her."

"A gentleman wouldn't rub it in."

Unperturbed, he arched a brow at her, his dimples flashing rakishly. "Who said I was a gentleman?"

Caught in the trap of his roguish smile, Tate felt her mouth go dry, the wild drumming of her heart loud in her ears. Lord, he was a handsome devil! And dangerous as sin. Any woman with any brains in her head would know that he was a heartbreak waiting to happen, a mistake to be avoided like the plague. But somehow he'd finagled his way into her life, and she didn't quite know how it had happened. And with every passing day, she found it harder and harder to remember why she couldn't let herself be taken in by his charming grin and dancing eyes.

"Tate? Something wrong?"

Suddenly realizing she was staring at him, she jerked back to attention with a start, heat flushing her cheeks. "No. I was just wondering how I was going to tell Dad about Maggie."

"You mean he doesn't know?"

She shook her head. "Not yet. I'm going to tell him just as soon as he comes home."

Picturing the reaction that news was going to get, Flynn grinned. "Oh, boy, the fat's going to hit the fan. Maybe I'll just go to town for a hamburger or something."

But in the end, he couldn't make himself leave. If Allen Baxter was going to blow his stack, Flynn planned on being there to at least offer Tate moral support. Not that she'd need it, he reminded himself. The lady was independent to a fault and, for more years than he cared to count, she had gotten along fine without a man to back her up. Her relationship with her father was none of his business. He knew that, accepted it. But for reasons he wouldn't allow himself to examine too closely, he couldn't leave her to face her old man alone.

At five minutes till twelve, Allen Baxter pulled up in front of the barn, the back of his pickup loaded with feed. Tate, obviously watching for him, hit the back screen door before he'd had time to so much as throw the truck into park. Only seconds behind her, Flynn climbed down the ladder at a leisurely rate and sauntered over to the truck.

"Dad, there's something you should know—" Tate began, only to break off with a frown as Flynn walked up.

"Don't mind me," he said easily, ignoring her frown. "I was just going to help unload the feed. Where do you want this, Allen?"

"Over in the corner," the older man said as he climbed out of the pickup. "Thanks for the help, son. I appreciate it." Motioning to the right side of the barn, he turned his attention back to Tate. "Can this wait, sweetheart? I'd like to get this unloaded before lunch."

She hesitated, oh, so tempted to just swallow the confession and let him find out for himself what she'd done. But that really would tick him off, and she didn't want to risk upsetting him when he'd only just gotten out of the hospital. "Actually, lunch was what I wanted to talk about."

Distracted, his attention on where Flynn was stacking the feed, he didn't see the guilt that flashed in her eyes. "What about it? If it's about whatever we're having, you know I don't care what you cook. Just so it's hot and there's plenty of it. I'm so hungry, I could eat a horse."

Suddenly feeling like a child who didn't have the guts to confess that she'd broken a window, she cast Flynn a helpless look, then wanted to kick herself for the weakness. Since when had she needed someone else's help to talk to her own father? Stiffening, she blurted out, "That's what I'm trying to tell you, Dad. I didn't cook lunch."

Confused, her father glanced from her to the house and back again, his thick salt-and-pepper brows snapping together in a frown. "Honey, I can smell the chicken frying. If you're not cooking it, then who is? Haily's not—"

"No, it's not Haily," she quickly assured him. "I hired a live-in housekeeper this morning."

For a moment he just looked at her as if he couldn't have possibly heard her correctly. "A housekeeper," he repeated, dazed. "You hired a housekeeper? Without discussing it with me? What do you plan to pay her with?"

"We worked out a deal." Explaining the arrangement with him, she pretended not to see the irritation gathering in his eyes. "So you see, no money's involved. It's really the perfect arrangement. I won't have to worry about you being here all alone while I'm on the road, and Maggie has a family to look after again. It's going to be great."

Through narrowed eyes, Allen Baxter studied her without saying a word. "Why do I have the feeling that there's something going on here that I don't know about?" he said finally with an ominous scowl. "Kramer put you up to this, didn't he?"

"He was just concerned about you—"

"Concerned, hell," he snorted. "He just wanted me under the thumb of a baby-sitter, and dammit, I'm not a baby! Get rid of her, Tate. I mean it. You either talk to her or I will."

"She's gone to a lot of trouble to cook lunch," Flynn reminded them both quietly, adding his two cents. "Don't you think you should at least eat it before you throw her off the place?''

Disgusted, the older man grumbled, "All right. But that's it, you hear me? Just as soon as lunch is finished, I want her paid for her trouble and sent on her way.''

Without another word, he stalked off toward the house to wash up for lunch. "Well,'' Tate said, releasing her breath in a huff. "I guess that didn't go too bad, did it?''

Surprised, Flynn laughed. "You tell me. He's your dad. From where I was standing, it sounded like he just chewed you out.''

"Nah, he was just blowing off steam. Stubborn old coot,'' she said, chuckling affectionately. "He wouldn't admit he needed an umbrella in the middle of a thunderstorm.''

"So what are you going to do? Fire Maggie three hours after you hired her?''

"Of course not!'' she retorted indignantly. "I wouldn't do that to her. We made a deal, and I can't go back on my word. Once Dad's had time to cool off, he'll understand.''

"And if he doesn't?''

"Then the fur's going to fly because Maggie's not going anywhere.''

With the matter settled as far as she was concerned, Tate marched into the house for lunch with Flynn at her side, braced for fireworks. Introductions were made, and her father, as Tate had expected, was as gracious as always to a guest in his home. But the look he shot her warned her not to mistake his hospitality for acceptance. Untroubled, Tate took her place at the old oak round table that had been in the center of the kitchen for as long as she could remember. It was loaded down with enough food to feed an army.

Maggie, in her element with so many people to cook for, brought a napkin-covered breadbasket to the table and sat down next to Tate. "There's more biscuits on the stove," she said happily as soon as the grace was said. "And more chicken. So eat up, everybody. There's plenty."

Platters and bowls were passed around, the conversation limited to murmurs of approval as plates were filled. Buttering a hot biscuit that was so light, it made her mouth water, Tate watched her father bite into his own biscuit, only to freeze, his eyes widening in startled disbelief. "Dad? Is something wrong?"

He swallowed. "No, no...I just..." Hesitating, he glanced at Maggie with new respect. "I just haven't tasted anything like this since your mother died. Maggie, if the rest of your cooking is half as good as your biscuits, I'm going to have to call Doc Kramer and thank him for sending you to us. This is great!"

Chuckling, Tate glanced over at Flynn to find him watching her with a wide grin. It was going to be all right.

Still riding high over her father's acceptance of Maggie into the household, Tate was antsy with expectation the following day as she prepared to leave for Cedar City. Her mind on the upcoming rodeo she was sure she was going to win, she was hitching her horse trailer to Flynn's truck when Haily announced that she wanted to stay home and make cookies with Maggie. Since Maggie welcomed the company, Tate gave in, and a few minutes later she and Flynn were racing off with Sugar safely loaded in the trailer behind them. Preoccupied with the competition to come, it wasn't until they were five miles down the highway that Tate realized what she'd done by agreeing to leave Haily behind.

For the first time since she and Flynn had met, they were totally and completely alone.

Her heart thundering in her chest, she lectured herself for miles, silently telling herself there was no reason to act like a teenager on her first date. The fact that Flynn had asked her to ride with him didn't mean a thing. Other rodeo contestants split expenses all the time on everything from gas to hotel rooms because it was a smart business move. And considering the current state of her finances, she'd have been a fool to insist that they each go in their own vehicles.

This was just business, nothing more.

Then why are you aware of every move the man makes? Every breath he takes? a voice in her head taunted with maddening logic. *Come on, Baxter, who do you think you're trying to kid?*

His eyes bouncing from the road to the sudden fierce frown that sat on her brow like a thundercloud, Flynn said, "Something wrong? You're not having second thoughts about leaving Haily behind, are you?"

"What?" Wool-gathering, she blinked, struggling to pick up the tail end of the conversation. "Oh...no. She'll be fine. Anyway, she would have killed me if I'd taken her away from those cookies. She's going to love having Maggie around."

"So is your dad," he replied. "For a little guy, he sure put the food away. I've never seen anyone eat so many biscuits at one sitting."

She chuckled. "Yeah, Maggie knocked him for a loop, thank God. I don't know what I would have done if she turned out to be a terrible cook."

Flynn didn't doubt for a minute that she'd have thought of something. She had a way about her that made a man want to give in to her—even her daddy—though she didn't seem to realize it, thank God. Heaven help him and the rest of mankind when she did.

Turning his eyes back to the road, he tried not to think about a sensuously confident Tate knowing what she wanted from a man and going after it, but the images were too strong, too hot. The road stretched out before him, long and straight, but it was Tate he saw before him, Tate he saw reaching for him, her smile slow and knowing, her hands sure and gentle, her kiss guaranteed to drive him out of his mind with need. He only had to close his eyes and he could taste her.

Suddenly realizing what he was doing, he stiffened, swallowing a curse. She hadn't even touched him and he was already out of his mind. Damn! What the hell had he been thinking of when he invited her to come with him today? He was losing his objectivity where the lady was concerned. The game didn't feel like a game anymore, and that had him worried. When had the ache she stirred in him become something that wouldn't go away?

Unsettled more than he cared to admit, he steered the conversation to shop talk and kept it on the upcoming rodeo all the way to Cedar City. Even if Tate noticed, she didn't say anything but seemed to be perfectly content to follow his lead.

An hour later, they pulled into the parking area behind the open-air arena at the fairgrounds and parted company to prepare for their prospective competitions—just like two distant acquaintances disembarking a bus.

Flynn shouldn't have given her a second thought after that. The bareback riding was usually the first event after the opening ceremonies, so he usually didn't have much time to think about anything else but his ride once he stepped behind the chutes. But this time, much to his disgust, it was Tate's ride, not his own, that nagged at him.

She needed a win here, not only because she was short on funds, but because another loss would be a real blow to her confidence.

And what about your own confidence? a voice in his head goaded him. *You haven't exactly been setting the world on fire, either. Take care of your own business and let the lady handle hers.*

Scowling, he tried. Pacing restlessly behind the chutes, he focused his thoughts on what he knew about Spinner, the horse he'd drawn for his ride. Quick out of the chute, the black mare had a habit of jumping into a spin, then whirling back the other way just when a cowboy thought he had caught her rhythm. If he wasn't damn careful, he'd end up flat on his face in the dirt. The last thing he needed to be thinking of was Tate.

Still, it was her face that flashed before his eyes just before he carefully lowered himself to Spinner's back. The chute help crawling all over the sides of the chute to help him with his rigging wished him good luck and warned him to watch out for Spinner's first hard turn to the left, and then there wasn't time to think of anything. He nodded his head at the cowboy operating the gate; it swung open, and the horse under him jumped out into the arena with a high whinny of fury.

Flynn was braced for that first hard turn to the left—he'd seen her do it a dozen times himself, each time dumping her rider with infuriating ease. But this time, instead of whirling in a tight circle, she arched her back and lunged straight up into the air. Caught off guard, Flynn almost went flying before he managed to catch himself. When the buzzer sounded a few seconds later, he was still clinging to the infuriated horse like a burr to a saddle blanket.

It wasn't the most graceful ride he'd ever had, but his score was respectable and put him in second place. There were three more riders yet to come, however, and anyone of them could knock him out of the money.

Pacing restlessly behind the stalls, he listened to the crowd as they each took their turn, knowing that wild applause would pretty much mean he could forget about celebrating, at least for that day. But it never came, and then the announcer was announcing the first- and second-place finishers. Hearing his own name, he let out a whoop and suddenly found himself being congratulated.

Elated, he wanted to find Tate immediately, but she still had her own ride to get through and he didn't want to distract her. Wandering up into the crowded stands, he waited impatiently for the barrel racing.

She was the first contestant to compete, which wasn't an easy position to be in. She was racing against the clock, not against the other riders, but having a time to aim for always helped. More nervous than if he was competing himself, Flynn leaned forward as her name was announced, and a split second later she came flying into the arena at a full gallop, urging Sugar on for all she was worth.

Flynn's breath caught in his lungs at the sight of her. He'd seen a lot of barrel racers, but never one who moved like her. Fluid and graceful, she rounded each barrel like an ice skater skimming over ice as smooth as glass, without a single wasted motion. Totally focused, her face was etched with concentration, her eyes narrowed on the next barrel. God, she was beautiful.

Only seconds after she came racing into the arena, she was gone, disappearing from view behind the chutes to the thunder of wild applause that only grew louder when her time was announced. It wasn't a record, but it was close…damn close. Grinning broadly, Flynn had seen all he needed to see. Hurrying down the stands, he went looking for her.

She was out back, cooling Sugar down, so excited she could hardly stand still. Her cheeks bright with exhilaration, her blue eyes sparkling, she looked like a kid at Christmas. Flynn took one look at her and reached for her.

It was an unthinking reaction, an instinctive one that took hold of him before he could think to fight it. He meant to give her a fierce hug, nothing more, to congratulate her on a damn fine ride. But before he could stop himself, he was dragging her close and covering her mouth with his.

As far as kisses went, it was a short one. A brief, fleeting brush of lips, a tantalizing taste of tongue, a flash of heat. It lasted only a second, no more, and was no different than any of the other casual kisses he'd bestowed on countless women over the years.

The pleasure he felt sweet and mild, he should have drawn back with a lighthearted laugh. But when he pulled back, he didn't feel like laughing, and there was nothing sweet or mild about the heat that coursed through him. He ached. And he couldn't seem to make his fingers let her go. What the hell was going on here?

Abruptly releasing her, he stepped back, struggling to find an easy grin. When he had to force it, he knew he was in trouble. "Great ride," he said huskily. "Looks like we're both going to go home winners."

Her mouth throbbing and her blood racing in her veins, Tate stared up at him blankly, hardly hearing him. Somewhere in the mush that was her brain, she knew she should move or at the very least shrug off the kiss as though it had never happened. That was the only way to handle a flirt like Flynn Rawlings, who handed out kisses as easily as a politician looking to get elected. But her head was in a fog and her knees had this crazy tendency to melt and if he would just hold her...

There was no telling what would happen.

The truth, refusing to be denied, sent her stomach plummeting to her toes, and with a startled exclamation, she quickly stepped back, heat firing her cheeks. "I haven't won yet," she said, wincing at the revealing thickness of her voice. "I'm only the first rider."

"First, last, it doesn't matter," he predicted gruffly. "You're still going to win."

He was right, but ten minutes later when the last time was announced and it was clear that Tate had held on to the lead, there were no celebratory hugs or kisses. In fact, there was no touching whatsoever. Flynn congratulated her on the win, she collected the prize money and they headed home. End of story.

On the way back to the farm, they were as reserved as two strangers who suddenly found themselves sitting side by side at the dinner table. They spoke, but each was teeth-grindingly polite, and neither spoke of anything that could be construed as the least bit personal. It was all perfectly respectable and exceedingly civil. Not to mention damn frustrating.

For the life of him, Flynn couldn't figure out what had gone wrong. He'd never been uncomfortable with a woman before, never felt like he couldn't be casually affectionate. But there was nothing casual about the heat that streaked through him every time his hand so much as brushed Tate's. With a will of their own, his heart thudded, his gut clenched and need twisted in his groin, hard as a fist. And he didn't like it one little bit. Time, he told himself, clenching his jaw on an oath. He just needed some time alone to clear his head.

That night, he lay wide-awake in the darkened guest room while the rest of the house settled down to sleep, determined to put his feelings into perspective. But there was an ache deep inside him that defied logic, an emptiness that burned, a restlessness that had him shifting on the sheets, seeking a relief that just wasn't there. Irritated, cursing Tate and himself, he stewed about it for hours and got nowhere. When he finally fell asleep, the answer was just as elusive as ever.

The next day was a repeat of the latter part of the previous one. They both did well in their respective events at the Mesquite rodeo, finishing in the money, but there was no spontaneous celebrating. And on the way home, the too-friendly politeness between them grated on Flynn's nerves until it was all he could do not to reach for Tate and kiss her until he got some honest-to-God real emotions out of her.

Caution held him back though, the need for it irritating the hell out of him. He'd never lost his head over a woman yet, and he didn't intend to start now. And just to prove it to himself, he brought up a subject he had decided last night it would be safer to avoid.

"Now that you've got Maggie to watch over your father, I imagine you're going to get right back on the circuit," he said casually as they headed home. "Where are you going next?"

"Flagstaff," she replied. "Then Durango, Raton and Golden, Colorado. Why?"

"Oh, no reason," he said with a shrug. "I was just planning on hitting most of those myself, and since we're both going the same direction, it seems kind of stupid to go in two trucks. Splitting expenses yesterday and today worked out pretty well, so I thought we might try it again and save ourselves some money."

It was a logical suggestion—and the last one Tate expected him to make. He'd been so distant since he'd kissed her, she'd assumed he regretted it and couldn't wait to take off on his own. Stunned, she stared at him, her thoughts reeling, her senses already jumping with anticipation at the mere idea of stretching out their time together.

Suddenly realizing that she was actually considering his proposal, she stiffened, panic backing up in her throat. Was she out of her mind? Of course traveling together would save them money, but how much was it going to cost her in heartache in the long run?

He'd already slipped past a guard she considered charmproof, and she couldn't sleep nights without having him tramp through her dreams as though he owned them, flashing that wicked smile of his and making sleep impossible. And all he'd done was kiss her a couple of times. What kind of shape would she be in after traveling cross-country with him all summer long, sharing every waking moment? Just thinking about it made her hot.

No, she couldn't do it, even if it saved her a small fortune. And what did he need to save money for, anyway? she wondered, sudden irritation sparking in her eyes. Who did he think he was kidding? It wasn't like they were both struggling to keep their heads above water. His family was rich as Midas and he was just running up and down the highway from one rodeo to the next for the fun of it. He didn't *have* to do this.

"I don't think so," she said flatly. "I appreciate the charity, but I don't need it. Haily and I can get by by ourselves."

"Charity!" he exploded, jerking his eyes from the road to scowl at her in confusion. "What charity? What the hell are you talking about?"

"Money," she retorted, matching him frown for frown. "There aren't any secrets on the circuit. I know all about your family and the ranch you own in New Mexico."

"So?"

"So you can quit pretending you don't have two nickels to rub together. All this talk about splitting gas money to keep expenses down is just bull. You only made the offer because you know how low my funds are right now."

"Is that so?"

His tone was stiff, his expression shuttered. Caught up in her own indignation, Tate never noticed. Afraid that if she looked at him now, she'd swallow her pride and jump at the chance to be with him every day, she kept her eyes stubbornly locked on the highway in front of them.

Her hands clutched tightly in her lap, she continued huskily, "I know it may not sound like it, but I really do appreciate the offer. I just can't accept it. Haily and I make our own way in our own truck, or we don't go."

Her words were laced with regret...and steely with determination. His hands clenching on the steering wheel, Flynn stared straight ahead, his teeth clamped tight on an oath. He could have told her that he, too, had standards. That except for his original stake money, which his family had insisted on giving him and was by now long gone, the only funds he used for rodeoing was what he earned by climbing on the back of a bareback bronc week after week after week. But he, too, had his pride.

"Don't sweat it," he said with a shrug, his tone not quite as cool as he would have liked. "It was just a suggestion, and probably a dumb one at that. I wasn't really that interested in going to Flagstaff anyway, so this way I can stick to my own schedule and you can stick to yours."

"I think that's for the best."

Her cool words grated, and it was only through sheer strength of will that he kept his eyes narrowed on the road. "Then I'll make plans to leave for Price tomorrow. I guess we'll see each other somewhere down the road."

She nodded, refusing to let fall the tears burning her eyes. What was the use of crying when there was nothing left to say?

Leaving the next morning wasn't as easy as Flynn had thought it would be. He'd figured that after a stiff thank-you for the hospitality, he'd just climb in his truck and be on his way. Only Allen asked his advice on repairs on a truck first, and Maggie promised to make him a peach cobbler if he'd just stay till lunch. But it was Tate and her daughter who got to him and found a way to squeeze his heart with regret.

Haily, confused by his sudden leaving when she'd thought he was staying at least another day, was hurt and mad. He tried explaining to her that they'd run into each other at the next rodeo, but she knew her mother's schedule as well as his, and she wasn't buying it. When her big blue eyes filled with tears, he almost changed his mind and damned the consequences. But one look at Tate's face, and he knew he couldn't.

God, had any woman ever looked at him the way she did? There was something in her eyes that tugged at his heartstrings and scared him to death. He found himself wanting to make excuses, to justify his leaving, and abruptly swallowed the words before he started to sound like a tongue-tied idiot. *She* was the one who had made it clear she didn't want to travel with him, not the other way around. There was no need for excuses.

But as she stood on the porch and watched him leave, walking away from her was just about the hardest thing he'd ever done. And that was reason enough to get the hell out of there while he still could. Climbing into his truck, his eyes met hers for a long, tense moment. If she'd have given the slightest sign that she didn't want him to go, he'd have been out of his truck and at her side in a split second. But she didn't. With a muttered curse, he started the motor and drove away. It took him hours to convince himself it was for the best.

Chapter 6

Fate, Flynn decided a week and a half later, was a tricky little bitch. Now that he'd decided he wanted nothing to do with Tate, he seemed to be running into her every time he turned around. He went to Price, just as he'd planned, but it was a washout and he didn't make a dime. Disgusted, he headed for Durango...and ran into Tate and Haily at the concession stand buying hot dogs and sodas.

He shouldn't have been surprised. He had known Tate was going to be at three of the next five rodeos he was entered in and had told himself that it was a free country and he didn't give a damn what she did. She could follow him around for the next year, compete in every rodeo he did, and it wouldn't affect him in the least. But then, just when he thought he had her out of his system, their eyes would meet, and it was all he could do not to cross to her and grab her.

He didn't, of course. He didn't go anywhere near her. But it was the nights that drove him crazy. His guard down while he slept, he had no defenses against the woman who slipped into his dreams as easily as if they'd been lovers for years, her mouth sweet and hot as she came to him, her hands soft and seducing. Reaching for her, his body hard with need, he'd wake up cursing her.

Disgusted with her and himself, it was the rodeos themselves he found the hardest to get through. The days were long, with endless hours to fill before he competed each evening, and invariably his thoughts wandered to Tate. He remembered every conversation they'd ever had, but it was the one in which she accused him of not taking his rodeoing seriously that really rankled. The criticism stung. During practice rides, he found himself watching the more successful bareback riders like Shorty Hawkins and Winn Nelson, men who had been on the circuit for a couple of years, worked hard at sharpening their skills and were consistently in the money. Every one of them made a deliberate effort to have a definitive drag when they spurred their horses, one of the critical scoring points that all judges looked for.

Nine times out of ten, he didn't do that. He was a "flopping and popping" kind of rider, and the loose and free style was obviously hurting him. Which meant he had a lot of work to do to change his technique.

He borrowed a bucking machine from a friend to practice his spurring action, but it wasn't something he could keep for any length of time, so he returned it and got himself a bale of hay instead. After strapping on his spurs, he straddled the bale like he would the back of a horse and repeated the correct spurring motion over and over again, familiarizing himself with it until it was as instinctive as chewing gum.

And for a while, he was actually able to push Tate to the back of his thoughts. Then it was his turn to ride at the

Raton rodeo. The chute boss had given the order for the first three riders to "Pull 'em up," so he scrambled to tighten the cinches and his rigging. The gate in the first chute clanged open, and Jake Reader exploded out into the arena. By the time he finished and the second rider took his turn, Flynn had already climbed up over the railing and was waiting for the signal to slowly lower himself down onto the back of the gray he'd drawn to ride.

He had only seconds, but it seemed like hours. Murmuring softly to his tense mount, he was totally focused on the ride to come. Visualizing the correct spurring action, he hardly heard the jarring buzzer or the roar of the crowd as the announcer congratulated the second rider for an excellent score. It was his turn to ride.

When the gate clanged open, his heart seemed to be pounding a thousand beats a second. His hand wrapped tight in his rigging, he raked his spurs down the gray's neck, then dragged them back up again, just as he had done during his countless practice rides on the hay bale. The gray, furious that she couldn't dislodge him from her back, whirled and spun until the surrounding arena full of spectators became a blur of color.

Time seemed to grind to a halt; eight seconds stretched into an eternity that would not end. Then the buzzer sounded, signaling the end of his ride, and the concentration that had helped keep him stuck to the horse's back like a flea to a dog broke. Elated, a wide grin splitting his face, he glanced up when the pickup man came charging toward him and forgot all about staying on the gray. Suddenly he went flying. He hit the dirt hard, but not even his less than graceful dismount could wipe the grin from his face. He'd done it! He'd just had the ride of his life, and he didn't have to hear the score to know that the long hours of practice had paid off.

"Let's have a big hand for Flynn Rawlings, ladies and gentleman," the announcer said over the P.A. system. "That's the first time Old Gray's been ridden in six weeks and Flynn gets a score of seventy-nine."

Ecstatic, Flynn let out a whoop and punched the air with his fist as the crowd cheered. Now that was more like it! Acknowledging the applause, he dusted himself off and hurried out of the arena so the next rider could have his turn, accepting the congratulations of other cowboys as he made his way behind the chutes. He'd never scored higher than a sixty-one, and if his luck held, he'd have a damn good shot at winning the first day go-around.

All because of Tate.

The thought sobered him, but he couldn't deny the truth. The infuriating woman had forced herself into his thoughts, her remembered scolding about his poor rodeo skills nagging him until he'd had no choice but to do something just to get her out of his head. Like it or not, he was going to have to hunt her down and thank her for opening his eyes.

He hurried behind the chutes, anxious to get the task over with, but before he could start to look for her, a familiar voice drawled behind him, "I think he paid off the judges. He had to. How else could he have gotten a seventy-nine?"

"Beats me," another familiar voice retorted. "Maybe the judges are women. That would explain it. I've never met a woman yet that could resist those damn dimples of his. I guess there's just no accounting for taste."

A broad grin split Flynn's face. Turning, he surveyed his brothers with twinkling eyes. "Jealousy rears its ugly head. Who let you outlaws out of jail? Do Josey and Susannah know where you are?''

Lean and weathered, Gable stepped forward to give Flynn an unabashedly affectionate hug. ''Who do you think sent us over here?'' he retorted. ''We hadn't heard from you in a while, and they were worried about you.''

''Yeah, they told us not to come back until we were sure you hadn't gotten trampled by a horse or something,'' Cooper added, his tanned, angular face alight with amusement. ''We've seen what we came for, so I guess we can go home now.''

''The hell you will.'' Chuckling, Flynn grabbed him for a hug, too. ''Damn, I've missed you guys! Why didn't you tell me you were coming? I would have gotten you tickets for out front.''

''We didn't want to make you nervous,'' Gable said. ''Though you probably wouldn't even have noticed us, you were concentrating so hard. You did good, kid.''

''Just like you knew what you were doing,'' Cooper teased. ''You never rode like that at home when we were breaking wild mustangs. You've been practicing.''

Flynn nodded. Then, as the last bareback rider completed his ride and his score was announced, it hit him. He'd won the competition for the day. If his score the following day was halfway decent, he'd have a good shot at winning the whole thing.

''All right, bro! Way to go!''

''I knew you could do it! This calls for a drink. Come on, let's go get a beer.''

Laughing, the three of them headed toward the beer concession stand on the backside of the arena, where other cowboys were gathered like horses around a watering trough. Walking on air, Flynn said, ''So what's been going on at home? Everybody okay? How's Mandy?" he asked, glancing at Gable. "Growing like a weed, I'll bet."

His older brother nodded, his chiseled features softening at the mention of his nine-month-old daughter. "She's a real handful, just like her mother. Josey says when she starts walking, she's going to be hell on wheels."

Flynn grinned, imagining his curly-haired niece running around the big old Victorian home that was the heart of the Double R, wrapping every adult in sight around her little finger. "You think she's going to be trouble now, just wait until she's old enough to date. You're going to be pacing the floor every night."

Chuckling at the thought of his always-in-control brother at the mercy of a daughter who already showed signs of being every bit as beautiful as her mother, Flynn started to order three beers from the potbellied man behind the counter when he suddenly spied Tate across the concourse. Caught off guard, he stopped short at the sight of her, not even noticing that his brothers had stopped, as well.

She was talking to Haily, killing time until the barrel racing started, the affectionate smile that curved her mouth as she joked with her daughter fading abruptly when she glanced up suddenly, as if sensing his eyes on her. Without so much as looking around, her gaze met his unerringly from forty yards away.

Time ground to a halt. All around him, his brothers, the rodeo grounds, the world, faded into nothingness. There was only Tate, a becoming blush blooming high in her cheeks, standing as still as he. Feeling as if she'd reached out and grabbed his suddenly racing heart, Flynn couldn't take his eyes from her, the need to cross to her so strong, he actually started to take a step toward her.

"You know the lady?"

Cooper's question dragged him back to his surroundings with a start, and he glanced back to his brothers to find them both watching him speculatively. At the sudden mischief he saw in their eyes, he growled, "Oh, no you don't! Don't go getting any ideas about getting me hog-tied and butchered just because you two are. I'm perfectly happy just the way I am."

"So that's why we haven't heard from you in weeks," Gable said, amused, ignoring Flynn's less-than-flattering description of marriage. "What's her name? Maybe we'd better go talk to her and check her out. You never did have a lick of sense when it came to women, and a man can't be too careful these days."

Cooper snorted at that. "Careful? Anyone who plays the field like he does doesn't know the meaning of the word. Let's go talk to her, Gable, and see what she's got to say for herself. There must be something wrong with her. She doesn't look like his usual type."

"You mean big—"

"Her name's Tate Baxter," Flynn growled out in exasperation. "She's a barrel racer, that's her daughter with her and she wants nothing to do with your baby brother. There, you know the whole story. Can we have a beer now? It's hotter than hell in here and I'm thirsty!"

Cooper and Gable exchanged silent, knowing looks of amused understanding, then Gable slapped Flynn on the back and gave him an easy grin. "Sure, kid. What'll you have? I'm buying."

The arena campground was quiet by the time Flynn made it back to the small tent he'd pitched there. Over dinner and a couple of beers, he had caught up on all the gossip and latest news from home, then stood in the dark and watched his brothers drive away. A loneliness he hadn't expected assaulted him, hitting him right in the gut. And for a wild, crazy moment, he was half tempted to throw everything in his truck and head for home himself. Riding the circuit could be damn lonely, and he didn't have any trouble admitting to himself that he missed the companionship of the Double R.

But he wasn't a quitter, he reminded himself, especially after just winning his first go-around. Growing up the youngest of three brothers, his position in the pecking order hadn't always been an easy one and he'd found himself constantly competing with two brothers who were damn good at just about anything. And he was still trying to prove something, though more to himself now than to Gable and Cooper. Rodeoing was something he'd always wanted to do, and when he'd decided to compete, he'd vowed to stick with it long enough to convince himself that he was more than fair competition for the big-name cowboys. It would take more than the fluke of one win to do that.

But damn, it wasn't much fun doing it by yourself, he thought grimly as he crawled into the tent and tried to make himself comfortable in the sleeping bag he'd laid out earlier. Sleep, however, refused to come. The campground was too quiet, the night too still. The younger cowboys who hadn't learned the value of a good night's sleep during a competition were out whooping it up at local watering holes and would probably come straggling in sometime after midnight without a thought to the other campers they were disturbing. But for now, the place was as silent as a tomb.

The thunder of his own heartbeat echoing in his ears, Flynn punched his pillow into a more comfortable position, muttering curses all the while, but it didn't help. He could practically hear the seconds dragging as time slowed to a crawl.

And it was cold, dammit. Too cold for the middle of summer. And mosquitoes were buzzing around as if he were a banquet especially laid out just for them. Slapping at one that feasted on the back of his neck, he growled in disgust and reached for his jeans. The hell with it, he thought irritably. He wasn't sleeping anyway, and there was no use lying there like a fool and getting eaten alive when he could be sitting outside doing something constructive.

Seconds later, he was out of the tent and comfortably sprawled in one of the lawn chairs he carried in his truck. It was a dark night, moonless, but as his eyes adjusted, he had to smile at his shadowy surroundings. His campsite had all the comforts of home, including a crate to cook on and a large stump that served as a table. Switching on the battery-powered lantern that he'd placed on the stump when he'd set up camp, he instinctively reached for a piece of wood from the nearby woodpile and pulled his knife from the front pocket of his jeans.

"There's no place like home, Toto," he told himself ruefully, and began to whittle.

The knife was razor sharp and glistened in the lantern light as it sliced cleanly through the wood. Lulled by the repetitive motion, he whittled without rhyme or reason, the tense muscles at the back of his neck slowly unknotting with each long, sure stroke of the blade in his hand. Only when he was completely relaxed did he think to look at what he was carving.

And cursed.

Glaring down at the rough sculpture, he didn't need to hold it closer to the light to recognize the figure his traitorous hand had whittled out of the wood. Even a blind man could have seen that it was Tate, astride Sugar, her hair flying out behind her as she guided the galloping horse through a hairpin turn around a barrel.

"Well, hell!"

For what seemed like an eternity, he simply stared at it, his brows knit in a scowl. He'd seen her like that at least a dozen times, riding hell-bent for leather, pushing Sugar and herself to the edge, the delicate lines of her face intense and determined. Unable to stop himself, he ran his thumb over the rough wood and could almost feel the power of the horse, the fragility of her, under his hands. She was so small, he thought, mesmerized, and so damn stubborn—

Suddenly realizing what he was doing, he stiffened with a curse and tossed the carving back onto the woodpile with a quickness that would have been comical if he'd been in the mood to appreciate it. But he was edgy and tense and as irritable as a stuck pig. Pushing to his feet abruptly, he grabbed a towel and headed for the campground rest rooms for a cold shower.

The water felt like spring water sluicing over him, but by the time he started back to his campsite, he no longer felt as if he'd somehow outgrown his skin. Relieved, he was halfway to his tent when he heard someone on the gravel path ahead of him and looked up to see Tate walking toward him as though she'd just stepped out of one of his dreams.

Lost in her thoughts, she wore yellow shorts that showed off the tanned length of her legs, a white Windbreaker to block out the cold evening air and sandals that were nothing more than a couple of thin straps of leather. Not even realizing until then that she'd been staying at the same campground, he froze, his blood starting to heat at the sight of her. Dressed as she was, and with her hair pulled up in a short ponytail, she looked like a teenager, fresh and innocent and so damn pretty, he couldn't take his eyes off her.

Expecting to meet no one on the path to the showers at that time of night, Tate was almost upon him before she saw him. There were lights to mark the footpath, but they were few and far between, and it was a long, heart-stopping moment before she realized that the man standing before her in the shadows was Flynn.

No! she almost cried aloud. It couldn't be! He'd dogged her footsteps ever since he'd left her father's farm, turning up like a bad penny, first in Durango and now here in Raton, making it impossible for her to get him out of her head. Frustrated just at the thought of running into him again when she pulled into the arena campground yesterday, she'd vowed to find somewhere else to stay if he was anywhere near there. But she hadn't caught sight of him anywhere, and she'd relaxed with a sigh of relief, sure that he was miles away.

She should have known better, she thought in growing anger. The man thought he was irresistible and was determined to make her think so, too. And it was high time she told him it just wasn't going to happen!

Stalking up to him, her blue eyes shooting fire in the darkness, she parked her balled hands on her hips and glared at him. "What do you think you're doing here?"

Obviously, that wasn't the question he was expecting. Frowning in confusion, he said, "Walking back to my campsite. What does it look like I'm doing?"

"Don't give me that," she snapped. "You know what I mean. What are you doing *here?*"

He could have told her that he was rodeoing, but she already knew that. One corner of his mouth starting to curl in amusement, he arched a brow at her. "I thought it was pretty obvious, but I guess I was wrong. What do you think I'm doing?''

"Following me!" She fairly shouted the words at him, only to clamp her jaw tight, horrified at what she had revealed. He was getting to her, and now he knew it.

Struggling for control, she dragged in a calming breath, but she was fighting a losing battle. Like it or not, she simply could not stand before the man and remain indifferent. Especially when he wore nothing but jeans. Her heart thumping, she stared at his bare chest and felt her mouth go dry. Why, dear Lord, did he have to be so darn attractive?

Swallowing, she glared at him accusingly. "You're following me," she repeated with a coolness that didn't come easily. "And I don't like it. I'd appreciate it if you'd go somewhere else."

"Oh, you would, would you?" he replied, chuckling. "Well, that's too bad, sweetheart, because I'm not going anywhere. If you don't like the situation, why don't *you* leave?"

"But I was here first!"

At the childish remark, he had to grin. "If I'd known we were running a race, I'd have bought you a blue ribbon."

She wasn't amused. "Damn it, Flynn, this isn't funny."

"No, it's not," he agreed, surprising her. Giving her a measuring look, he said quietly, "Have you ever stopped to think that maybe there might be something going on here bigger than the two of us? Like fate? Maybe we should just quit fighting it?"

"Fighting what?" she retorted airily, her heart skipping a beat at the suggestion. "There's nothing to fight."

It was the wrong thing to say in the wrong tone of voice. Her taunting words grating on his nerves, Flynn reached for her, hauling her into his arms before she could so much as gasp. "Good. Then there's no reason why I can't kiss you," he muttered, and covered her mouth with his.

He meant to give her a quick, hard lesson about the price a woman had to pay when she continually pushed a man's buttons. But somewhere in the middle of a kiss that should have ended soon after it began, his good intentions went straight to hell in a hand basket and all he could think about was that it had been too long since he'd held her like this ... and that she was mad as hell at him. Stiff as a board in his arms, she clenched her jaw shut and silently dared him to do something about it.

He dared.

Chuckling against her mouth, he murmured, "Come on, honey, be a good girl and open your mouth."

For an answer, she stood nose to nose with him and glared at him defiantly.

She couldn't have possibly known how she delighted him. His dimples flashing, he pulled back scant inches and grinned at her. "So you're not going to make this easy for me, huh? Okay, have it your way." And with no other warning than that, he gave in to the temptation to nuzzle the sensitive skin just behind her ear.

At the touch of his tongue against her throat, Tate jumped, her heart hammering before she could think to note the danger. She wasn't going to let him do this to her, she promised herself, only to swallow a whimper as his teeth gently closed on her earlobe. "F-Flynn—"

"I know, sweetheart," he groaned against her ear. "It feels good, doesn't it?"

It felt ... wonderful. Emotions, hot and sweet and intoxicating, came out of nowhere to swamp her senses, flooding her with heat. But she couldn't tell him that, couldn't let him know. Clinging to him even when she knew she had to find the strength to push him away, she could only shake her head. "No—"

"Little liar." He laughed softly, and swooped down to drop light, teasing kisses on her chin, the bridge of her nose, the curve of her cheek.

Her eyes closing on a sigh that somehow became his name, her head dropped helplessly to his shoulder as the night pressed in on them, shrouding them in darkness. Hot. He made her feel so hot, she could hardly breathe. Gasping, she swallowed, unconsciously licking her parted lips, her heart thundering as she waited for him to once again take her mouth in a scorching kiss.

But the expected kiss never happened. Instead, he charted her face, her neck, even the inside of her wrists and elbows with slow, languid kisses, avoiding her mouth as if it didn't hold the least appeal for him. Dazed, she tried to hang on to reason and the sure knowledge that he knew just exactly what he was doing to her. But her knees were weak, her pulse throbbing, and her mouth... Her mouth actually ached!

Her hands suddenly pulling at him, she felt his lips press lightning quick to the dimple so tantalizing close to her mouth before sliding teasingly away, and she knew she couldn't stand anymore. The battle lost, she couldn't stop the sudden, inexplicable tears that spilled without warning into her eyes. How could he make her want him so easily when he was the last thing in the world she needed?

"Don't," she choked.

Flynn froze at the sound of her pain-thickened voice. Dear God, was she crying? Capturing her face in his hands, he tilted her chin up until she was forced to look at him. Even in the poor light, he could see the tears that glistened there. Stunned, guilt and an emotion he couldn't put a name to squeezing his heart, he frowned down at her in confusion. "Don't what? Tate, honey, I'm only teasing you...."

"I know," she said huskily. "But if you're going to kiss me, would you please just do it right?"

If she'd made such a request another time, another place, he might have laughed. But there was nothing funny about the hunger crawling through his blood like acid, burning him from the inside out. "You just tell me how you want to be kissed," he rasped, "and I'll sure as hell do it."

Without a word, she slid her arms up his bare chest to encircle his neck and pull his head down to hers. Tomorrow she knew she would think back on this as a big mistake. But tomorrow was a lifetime away, and there was only the here and now and Flynn. And it seemed as if she had been waiting forever for him to hold her like this. Murmuring his name, she sank against him and covered his mouth with hers.

Flynn groaned at the feel of her pressed against him as if she couldn't get close enough, her soft breasts molded against his chest, her hips cradling his hardness. With a hesitancy that was nearly his undoing, she sent her tongue gliding into his mouth, secretly telling him that it had been too long since she had let a man hold her this way, kiss her this way. Need. He could taste it, feel the hunger that had her clinging to him, and it blew him away. His blood hot and thick, he crushed her to him and forgot everything but the woman in his arms.

One kiss blurred into another, then another. Long, drugging kisses that enticed and seduced and enchanted. His hands moving over her, slipping under the hem of her Windbreaker and the T-shirt she wore under it, he found the bare skin of her midriff, but it wasn't nearly enough. He wanted her naked and soft, under him, moving with him, loving him until he felt as if he were going to die from the pleasure of it. And they couldn't do that on the path to the rest rooms. Desire clawing at him, his breath tearing through his lungs, he dragged his mouth from hers.

"Not here, honey," he groaned thickly against the side of her neck, unable to stop kissing her. "We can't do this here. Come back to my tent with me."

Aching, caught up in the moment and her mind clouded with desire, she heard the sweet coaxing in his husky voice and couldn't have resisted if her life depended on it. She took a step back, pulling him with her, lost to everything but the fire burning in her blood.

The pickup that suddenly came barreling into the campground whizzed past them without checking its speed, the driver not even noticing them in the shadows of the tree-shaded path. But the second his headlights sliced through the night, catching them in its glare for merely a flash of a second, Tate blinked as if she were coming out of a dream.

Lord, what was she doing?

Stopping in her tracks, she squeezed her eyes shut and furiously ordered herself to get a grip. Her hormones were raging. That was all it was, all it could be, all she would *allow* it to be. Because Flynn Rawlings was just playing games with her—nothing more.

Stiffening at the thought, she jerked free of his touch and glared up at him in the darkness. "I don't think so. I'm not going anywhere with you, especially to your tent."

Stunned, Flynn blinked in confusion at her sharp change of mood. "Tate, sweetheart—"

"Don't you *sweetheart* me," she said furiously, rounding on him with blazing eyes. "Did you think I wouldn't realize what you were doing?"

"Doing? Damn it, woman, I'm trying to make love to you!"

She didn't even flinch at his irritated roar. "No, you're not. You're trying to seduce me because I'm the one that got away. Why don't you just admit it and be done with it?" she challenged, standing toe-to-toe with him. "You know it's the truth. You flashed that crooked smile of yours at me, expecting me to fall at your feet, and when I didn't, you were ticked. So you set out to prove you could make me want you."

"I didn't—"

"You did," she retorted icily. "Well, go prove it with somebody else. I let one cowboy charm me. I'll never do it again. So just stay away from me. You hear me? *Stay away from me!*"

Rounding on her heel, she turned her back on him and marched off, the tilt of her chin just daring him to try and stop her. He didn't. Furious, he stood in the middle of the darkened path and told himself he didn't care. But as he watched her storm all the way back to her camper and disappear inside, he knew that he did.

And her scathing words struck awfully close to home.

He tried to deny it. Returning to his own campsite, he tried to convince himself that he had nothing to be ashamed of. She was a good-looking woman and he was attracted to her. He hadn't needed any other reasons than those to pursue her.

But as he threw himself into the lawn chair still sitting beside the lantern burning in front of his tent, he found himself searching the darkness for her camper nestled under the trees in the distance. There were no lights on to show him where she was, but he was so damn aware of her, he could have made his way to her blindfolded.

Scowling, he just barely resisted the urge to throw something. How could a woman who could make him burn faster than anyone ever had turn around and flip the switch on his temper with only a few words? He didn't have a short fuse. Hell, he couldn't remember the last time he even got hot enough to raise his voice! But for two cents, he'd go over there to that damn camper and give the lady a piece of his mind.

All right, he admitted it. When she gave him the cold shoulder when they first met, she not only bruised his ego, she threw it down in the dirt and stomped all over it. Not that he expected every woman he came across to drop at his feet, he added irritably. But he'd never had one treat him like he had fleas, either. He hadn't liked it, and he'd vowed to prove to himself that the lady wasn't quite as indifferent as she pretended.

I let one cowboy charm me. I'll never do it again. So just stay away from me.

Her parting words echoed in his ear, scraping his nerves raw. Dammit, that rankled! Just because he'd tried to charm her didn't mean he was anything like the pond scum who had fathered Haily. That jerk had taken advantage of her, then dumped her, and he didn't appreciate the comparison! He would never hurt her. She should know that.

And he wouldn't apologize for wanting her, he vowed. Not when he'd just held her in his arms and tasted her passion . . . for *him!* She could resent it, fight it, even hate what sparked between them whenever they got within touching distance of each other, but by God, she couldn't deny it. Not when it only took one touch from him to prove her wrong.

Engulfed in a silence that seemed to come from the very depths of his soul, he stared at her camper, loneliness twisting his heart. For a long, tense moment, he wished that what he felt for her was nothing more than unadulterated lust. Sex he could handle; that he could walk away from. But not Tate.

He liked her, dammit. Too much. Reaching for the unfinished sculpture he'd tossed back onto the woodpile earlier, he ran his fingers over the rough lines of what would eventually be Tate's face. Sweet, soft, full of fire. He could practically feel her in his hands.

For the first time in his life, he wanted to impress a woman, but he'd already learned that charm and smiles weren't going to cut it with Tate. So he'd have to find another way. It wouldn't be easy, of course. After tonight, she probably wouldn't let him get anywhere near her. But he was going to change her opinion of him; the only question was how.

Possibilities tumbling over themselves in his mind, he picked up his knife and began to whittle.

Chapter 7

"And the winner is Flynn Rawlings!" the announcer declared to the crowd the next day. "Let's have a hand for this cowboy, ladies and gentlemen. Flynn's a rookie on the pro rodeo circuit, and this is his first win. And let me tell you, that's quite a feat for someone who's only been riding the circuit a few months. He had some tough competition over the past few days. Let's give him a big round of applause. You can bet we'll be seeing more of this young man."

Clinging to the back of the pickup man's horse, Flynn grinned, feeling higher than a helium balloon on its way to the sun. He'd done it, by God! He'd finally gotten his act together and won instead of just placing in the money. And it felt good. Damn good! Now if he could just keep it up, he might finally be getting somewhere.

"That was a damn fine ride," Joe Caufman, the pickup man, told him with a grin as he brought his horse to a stop behind the chutes so Flynn could jump down. "I don't know if you know it or not, but you just shocked the hell out of a lot of cowboys. You've been practicing.''

Chuckling, Flynn didn't deny it. ''Yeah, and it finally paid off. I still can't believe it.''

Unable to stop grinning, he retrieved his rigging and stowed it in his equipment bag and found himself accepting congratulations from men who had always finished ahead of him in previous competitions. It felt strange, but he wouldn't have traded the experience for anything.

Only one thing would have made the win sweeter—Tate. Her congratulations would have topped off an unbelievable day, but he didn't even know if she'd watched him ride. When he'd left for the arena earlier, her camper had still been parked under the trees at the campground. He knew she had a barrel race coming up later, so he'd kept an eye out for her, but he might as well have saved himself the trouble. She was nowhere in sight.

He wasn't surprised. After last night, he'd expected her to go out of her way to avoid him, and she hadn't disappointed him. Finding her would have been easy enough—she couldn't have gone far since she hadn't taken her truck, but he was willing to give her some space...for now. She wasn't, however, going to be able to avoid him forever. He'd make sure of it.

Shifting his equipment bag to his other hand, he headed up into the stands to watch the rest of the rodeo and relax with some of the bareback riders. He was joking with Tex Sanchez when he spied Haily coming up the steps. ''Hey, kid,'' he called, grinning at her. ''Where you been? You missed my ride.''

Her freckled face broke out into a smile at the sight of him. ''I know, and you won! Who'd you draw?''

"Killer," he retorted, and watched her eyes widen. As familiar with the circuit stock as the riders themselves, she knew every horse and bull by name and reputation.

"Oh, wow," she breathed as she dropped down on the bench next to him. "You rode *Killer!* Jeez, I wish I'd seen that. But we just got here."

Not surprised by the innocent admission, he merely lifted a brow. "How come? I thought your mom liked to come in at least an hour before the barrel racing started."

"She does. But she's just been dragging around all day like she was sick or something."

His eyes sharpened. "Is she?"

"I don't think so. But she didn't sleep much last night. Maybe she's tired." Glancing back to the arena floor, she said excitedly, "Oh, good, the barrel racing's starting. Mom said if she won, we'd go out for pizza."

The first rider burst into the arena, the rodeo band broke into a fast-paced, frenetic song and there was no more time for words. Haily scooted to the edge of her seat, her eyes trained on the woman and horse who flew around the barrels with her hat and pigtails flying out behind her. Leaning forward himself, Flynn had to give the woman credit. She was good. Damn good. And she was just the first contestant. If Tate was going to win this thing, she was really going to have to haul ass.

The second rider charged into the arena, and impossibly, had an even better score. Glancing at up Flynn, Haily bit her bottom lip and asked worriedly, "Mom's in trouble, isn't she?"

He hesitated, tempted to tell her there wasn't a doubt in his mind Tate was going to win hands down. But Haily had been rodeoing with her mother since she was a baby, and she knew a good score when she heard it. "Maybe," he said reluctantly, "but don't give up on the pizza yet.

Tate's a fighter. And she's tough to beat when she's the underdog.''

Her gaze drifting back to the arena floor, Haily nodded. "Yeah, she likes being behind. It makes her try harder.''

A few seconds later, when the chute boss gave Tate the signal and she and Sugar bolted into the arena, it was obvious that she knew it would take a record-breaking time to win. She and Sugar were flying.

Elbows on his knees, his chin resting on the heels of his hands, Flynn couldn't take his eyes from her. Lord, she was something to see! The previous riders had all had the technical skills needed to score a good time, but Tate had something else, something more, a gracefulness that caught the eye and made her a joy to watch. Rounding the barrels like that ice skater gliding into a spin, she didn't make a single wasted motion. And when she crossed the finish line, she had the crowd on its feet and the time she needed to win.

"All right!"

"Way to go, Mom!"

Laughing, Haily launched herself at Flynn for a big hug, chattering a dozen words a second. "I knew she could do it. I *knew* it! Did you see her, Flynn? Wasn't she great? Let's go down and congratulate her.''

Without waiting to see if he followed, she started toward the steps, only to realize he hadn't moved. "Aren't you coming?" she asked, frowning in confusion as she glanced back over her shoulder at him. "Mom'll be waiting for us.''

Tate was waiting, all right, but not for him ... not after last night. "You go on, honey, and enjoy your pizza," he urged. "I've got to get on the road, anyway.''

"But I thought you were coming with us," she wailed. "Please? We never see you anymore. And you haven't congratulated Mom yet."

"Oh, she's probably got so many people around her right now, she won't even miss me. You can tell her I saw her ride and she was great. And give her this." Setting his equipment bag on the seat, he scrounged around in it and finally found what he was looking for—the wooden sculpture he'd stayed up half the night finishing.

"Here," he said gruffly, his fingers unconsciously caressing the slim lines of the rider before he realized what he was doing. Frowning, he thrust it into her hands. "Tell Tate I want her to have this. She can give it to your grandpa or something if she doesn't want it."

Stunned, Haily stared down at the smooth, sanded lines of the sculpture and immediately recognized the rider. "Gosh, it's Mom!"

"Yeah." Flynn chuckled. "I wasn't planning to do it, but it just came out that way. I thought she should have it."

"But don't you want to give it to her yourself? She's right downstairs."

Just stay away from me!

Her words from last night ringing in his ears, he shook his head. "You do it for me. Okay? I want to get on the road and you've got pizza to eat. So get going, kid, and I'll see you down the highway somewhere."

She wanted to argue—he could see it in her eyes—but he didn't give her the chance. In one smooth motion he grabbed his equipment bag, gave her a hug and headed for the steps, all the time telling himself he'd made the right decision. But as he got in his truck and drove away, his thoughts on the woman he'd left behind, it didn't feel like the right decision at all.

* * *

Flynn Rawlings was, Tate decided, the most infuriating man she'd ever met! He kept his distance, just as she'd ordered him to, but he still entered every rodeo she did over the course of the next two weeks. Oh, he made no attempt to approach her, but he was still following her, still turning up like the proverbial bad penny.

And even when he was nowhere in sight, the wood carving that he'd had Haily deliver to her was right there with her to remind her that he wasn't far behind. A dozen times or more a day, her eyes drifted to where it sat on the front seat between her and Haily, the sheer beauty of it drawing her gaze like a magnet. How many hours had he sat working on it? Thinking of her? Fascinated in spite of her best efforts not to be, she found herself picturing his hands on the wood, on her, stroking her, molding her....

Suddenly realizing where her thoughts had wandered, she swallowed a curse, determined to toss the damned carving into the trash, along with all her maddening memories of the man who had shaped it out of a plain piece of wood. But it was so gorgeous, she couldn't bring herself to part with it. And that only infuriated her more. Damn Flynn Rawlings, she wasn't going to let him get to her!

But he did. He didn't say a word to her, barely even nodded when their eyes happened to unexpectedly meet, but he still managed to make her more aware of him than she liked, and there wasn't a thing she could do about it. It was still a free country, and he could enter any rodeo he wanted to.

In spite of that, she might have found a way to ignore him if he'd continued to take his rodeoing less than seriously. But he didn't. According to Haily, who visited with him every chance she got, he was working hard to improve his skills. And the extra effort was paying off—he was starting to win.

Watching him from a distance, she saw him compete against some first-class cowboys, men in serious contention for the title of World Champion Bareback Rider of the Year, and *win!* And she was impressed in spite of her best efforts not to be. Wondering if he knew how unusual his success was, she wanted to go to him and tell him. He was a rookie competing against cowboys who had been riding the circuit for years, cowboys who had paid their dues to win the respect and higher scores of the judges. *They* were the ones who should have been winning, not Flynn.

But he was good, and she wasn't the only one who was beginning to notice that he was getting better every day. And when he climbed into a chute and lowered himself down onto one of the ornery stock animals, she couldn't stop herself from watching him.

She knew she was headed for trouble, but reason had nothing to do with her feelings for him. She'd thought she wanted him to stay away from her, but now that he was avoiding her like a sinner cutting a wide path around a preacher, she conversely wished he wouldn't. To her growing irritation, she found herself looking for him— and finding him—everywhere she went. And even though he hadn't spoken a word to her in weeks, she couldn't stop herself from respecting him more and more, liking him more and more, missing him more and more. The man fascinated her; she couldn't deny it. Or control it. And that had her really worried, but there didn't seem to be a thing she could do about it.

Expecting the rodeo at the outdoor arena in Golden, Colorado, to start in a little over an hour, Flynn arrived

to find the stands crowded and the parking lot packed.
Over the P.A. system, the announcer gave the score of
Shorty Parker, another bareback rider, drawing a roar of
approval from the crowd. Stunned, Flynn swore. He'd
been told the bareback riding didn't start until three and
had planned to be there well before noon, but he'd had a
flat and had to hitch a ride when he discovered his spare
tire was flatter than a pancake, too. By the time he'd gotten both of them fixed, he was running late—several hours
late. But he'd allowed himself enough leeway that he still
should have made it to Golden with time to spare. A quick
look at the dash clock assured him that it was only just
now two, so what the hell was going on?

Ignoring the No Parking sign near the back entrance to
the arena, he whipped his truck into the empty space there
and cut the engine. Grabbing his equipment bag, he hit
the ground running.

But he might as well have saved himself the trouble.
Just as he charged behind the chutes, a gate clanged open,
a riderless horse was turned out onto the arena floor and
the announcer told the crowd, "Flynn Rawlings was a no-
show, ladies and gentleman, so his score is a zero. Our
next rider is—"

Cursing a blue streak, Flynn didn't even listen as the
next contestant's name was given and the gate clanged
open. How could this have happened? he wondered furiously. When he'd called in to sign up to compete, he'd
forgotten to ask the starting time, so he'd gotten it from
Grady Calhoun, one of the most dependable riders on the
circuit. Nobody could remember the last time Grady had
missed a rodeo, which was why he'd gone to the other man
for the information in the first place. So how could he
have screwed up so royally?

" . . . score is sixty-five, which puts him in fifth place," the announcer continued, interrupting his thoughts. "That concludes this year's bareback riding, ladies and gentlemen, and it was a dilly. Let's have a great big round of applause for our winner and the holder of the Colorado state record in the bareback competition . . . Grady Calhoun!"

Outraged, Flynn could only stare blankly at the baby-faced cowboy who climbed up on the chutes to acknowledge the cheers of the crowd with a wide grin and a wave. Not only had Grady arrived in time to compete, he'd won!

"Son of a bitch!" he hissed through clenched teeth. He'd been set up.

Preparing for the upcoming barrel racing, Tate was soothing an excited Sugar when she saw Flynn striding through the crowd behind the chutes, fury etching the lines of his usually smiling face. Relief coursed through her at the sight of him, startling her so that it actually weakened her knees. He was here. When she'd seen his bronc turned out into the arena, she hadn't known what to think. He might not take his rodeoing as seriously as he should have, but she'd never known him to actually miss a competition. Troubled, she hadn't realized just how that had worried her until now. Traveling up and down the highway as they both did, anything could have happened to him.

Tomorrow the strength of her concern for him would bother her, but for now, she was just glad to see him. Forgetting that she was supposed to be keeping her distance, she left Sugar tied to a post and hurried over to him.

"Flynn? Are you all right? When you didn't show, I was afraid—"

Suddenly realizing what she was about to admit, she quickly clamped her teeth shut on the rest of her words, but Flynn was thankfully too angry to notice. "God, what an idiot I am!" he fumed. "Talk about setting yourself up! I couldn't have done it better if I'd tried."

Wincing at the raw fury of his words, she frowned. "What are you talking about?"

"Calhoun," he retorted, glaring at the man in the distance who was accepting congratulations from his friends and grinning like a damn jackass. "He told me the bareback competition started at three today. It never crossed my mind that he might be lying."

"Maybe he wasn't," she argued. From what she knew of Grady, he was straight as an arrow. She found it hard to believe that the man would do anything so underhanded. "He could have accidentally gotten today's time mixed up with another rodeo, or maybe you misunderstood—"

"Or maybe he was afraid I'd beat him so he made sure I wasn't even in the competition," he cut in, his tone harsh. "And I didn't suspect a damn thing."

Flynn knew a month ago, even a couple of weeks ago, such suspicions would have sounded ridiculous coming from a rookie who hadn't taken himself seriously, let alone the sport. But he was starting to make some ripples, win some competitions. Which meant that he could be a real threat to anyone trying to rack up points in the race for the title of World Champion Bareback Rider of the Year. And right now, Grady Calhoun was one of the hottest riders on the circuit.

Glancing back at Tate, he didn't have to ask her if such treachery was a common occurrence in rodeoing. It was a business, a damn competitive one, and just like any sport in which there was a lot of money to be made if you were good enough, there were a few unscrupulous jerks who would do anything, say anything, to come out on top. He just hadn't thought Grady Calhoun was one of them.

"I acted like a rank amateur," he told her grimly, "but it won't happen again. If Calhoun wants me out of the way, he's going to have to beat me on the back of a horse. If he even thinks of trying any more of his damn tricks on me, I'll be ready for him."

After that, Flynn would have sworn that he was ready for anything Grady Calhoun could dream up to get rid of him. He checked time schedules himself, and before every competition, he double-checked his equipment to make sure it hadn't been tampered with. But then, he cut himself short on time between rodeos in Coleman, Texas and Hinton, Oklahoma, and somehow he screwed up.

One minute he was racing down the highway toward Oklahoma, and the next, his truck was spitting and coughing like it had just developed a smoker's hack. Before he could do anything but choke out a curse, the motor gave one last wheeze and died. In the blink of an eye, the power steering and brakes vanished, and it was all he could do to guide the truck over to the shoulder of the road.

"Dammit to hell!" he growled when he finally got the vehicle stopped and threw it into park. "Now what!"

An eighteen-wheeler whizzed by only six feet away, hitting him with a blast of hot air that nearly pulled his hat off his head as he stepped from the pickup. Shooting the quickly disappearing semi a hard look, he turned back to his truck.

It took fifteen minutes to find the problem. Even then, Flynn couldn't believe it. Rubbing his fingers on grit he'd found around the gas cap, he bit out an unprintable oath.

Sugar. Someone had put sugar in his gas tank! And he knew just who to blame—Grady Calhoun.

Why hadn't he been on his guard last night when he'd discovered that the bastard was staying in the same campground he and Tate and a half-dozen other rodeo contestants were camped out at? But he'd been so sure that Calhoun wouldn't have the nerve to try anything that he hadn't kept that close an eye on him. After all, there'd been dozens of people around. And he'd never dreamed the jackass would go after his truck—especially when he'd been sleeping only a few feet away in his tent. Talk about nerve! And for that mistake in judgment, he was stuck afoot on the side of the road. *Hell.*

Glancing at his watch, he swore and reached for his equipment bag. If he was going to get anywhere near Hinton in time for the rodeo, he had to catch him a ride or for the second time in a little over a week he was going to be fined for having his horse turned out riderless into an arena full of people expecting to see him ride.

It was early yet, well before ten in the morning, but there wasn't a cloud in the sky and the temperature was starting to climb. Striding down the shoulder of the road, the asphalt hot beneath his boots, Flynn wiped at his brow with the back of his hand and prayed someone would come along soon.

Three vehicles passed in the next thirty minutes—two pickups and another semi. But they shied away from him and his outstretched thumb, easing over the center line as if they feared hitting him, before they raced away without even checking their speed. Disgusted, he swore at them, transferred his equipment bag to the other hand for a while and kept on walking.

* * *

Five miles after she passed his abandoned truck, Tate caught up with him. He was walking down the highway with his back to her and didn't once glance over his shoulder. He heard her coming up behind him—he stuck his thumb out in acknowledgment—but gave the impression he didn't care whether she stopped or not.

Haily, who had been engrossed in a comic book for miles, sat up straighter the minute Tate took her foot off the accelerator and glanced around in confusion. "Why are we stopping? Is something wrong?" Suddenly spying the cowboy hitchhiking up ahead of them, she grinned in delight. "That's Flynn!"

Tate nodded. "We passed his truck a couple of miles back." Pulling over to the shoulder in front of him, she rolled down her window and waited for him to catch up with them. "Need a ride, cowboy?"

Hot, sweating, his feet burning, Flynn pushed his cowboy hat back from his damp brow and tried to hang on to a scowl, but she made that impossible. Damn, he was glad to see her! His mouth curling into a grin, he fought the temptation to lean into the window to steal a kiss and said instead, "Maybe. Where you going, sweetheart?"

Her heart lurching at the casual endearment, Tate tried to steel herself against the charm he oozed so effortlessly, but she was fighting a losing battle and she knew it. She'd have died rather than admit it to him, but, Lord, she'd missed him. "How about a garage in Fort Worth? You look like you could use one."

"Sounds good to me. Let me stow my stuff in the back."

Fort Worth was only thirty minutes down the road and they quickly found a garage. Pulling into the parking lot, Tate expected Flynn to thank her for the ride, then wait there for his pickup to be towed in and repaired. Instead, he pushed open the passenger door and said, "This shouldn't take long. Then we can get on the road again."

Surprised, she ignored the sudden pounding of her heart and blurted out, "What do you mean, *we* can get on the road? What about your truck?

"It'll take days to fix it, so I'll have to leave it. You are going to Hinton, aren't you?"

"Well, yes, but—"

"Good. Then I'll just catch a ride with you and Haily. I'll be right back."

Tate wanted to object, but not a single word of protest formed on her tongue. Her heart thundering, her mouth dry, she watched him make arrangements with the mechanic to store his truck after it was repaired; then he was climbing into her pickup and before she knew quite how it happened, they were headed for Oklahoma.

With Haily sitting between them, Flynn settled comfortably against the passenger door, stretched his left arm across the back of the bench seat and grumbled about Grady Calhoun's daring. Her eyes on the road ahead, Tate tried to concentrate on his angry words, but even though she only allowed herself a few quick glances at him, she was aware of everything about him. The way his long legs were slightly cramped because she had to have the bench seat pushed all the way forward so her much-shorter legs could reach the gas pedal. The whisper of the wind as it slipped through the open window to ruffle his dark hair. The heat of his hand, resting on the seat just behind her right shoulder, so close she could practically feel his touch.

Her throat was dry, and her pulse was racing. She tightened her grip on the steering wheel and reminded herself that this was the same man who had spent nearly a month trying to prove something to her and himself...that he could make her want him. Well, he'd accomplished what he'd set out to do—he'd made her ache until she couldn't sleep nights. But he was still a low-down, finagling skunk, and she couldn't trust him as far as she could throw him.

If she'd had any sense, she would have kept on driving when she came across him on the side of the road. But she just hadn't been able to make herself do it. Fate, she thought, shaken. Once again fate had stepped in to throw them together. With every passing day, their lives became more and more entwined. And like puppets on the same string, they seemed to be at the mercy of a much stronger force. And that terrified her. She was headed down the same road she'd taken with Haily's father and could only see disaster ahead. But it was too late to turn around.

Conscious of the clock ticking on the dash, she pushed that worry to the back of her mind and concentrated on another, far more immediate one—getting Flynn to Hinton in time for the bareback competition. She didn't normally speed, especially with a loaded horse trailer hitched to the back bumper, but she didn't have much choice. Her foot depressing the accelerator, she glanced at her daughter and Flynn and said grimly, "Keep your eyes peeled. I've heard there's a couple of speed traps on this road, and the last thing I need is a ticket."

The highway patrolmen were thankfully absent all day, but the minute they crossed the city limits of Hinton, there was, unfortunately, a city cop waiting to clock Tate racing into town at ten miles an hour over the posted speed limit. Her only thought to get to the arena on time for Flynn's ride, Tate didn't even see the black-and-white patrol car parked under a low-hanging tree until Flynn glanced up from the map he was perusing and warned sharply, "Watch out! There's a live one on your left."

Her heart jumping into her throat, Tate swore under her breath and immediately lifted her foot from the accelerator. They had ten minutes to spare before the bareback competition started, but they still had to find the arena. If they got stopped now, they'd never make it.

Cruising past the patrol car at a more sedate speed, she braced herself for the whoop of a siren. Her eyes trained straight ahead, she said hopefully, "Maybe he missed me."

"And maybe we're both going to win world titles this year," Flynn replied, chuckling. "Sweetheart, he had you cold before I could open my mouth."

Later, when she got him alone, Tate promised herself she was going to have to talk to him about his growing habit of calling her sweetheart, but for now, she found the endearment too comforting to protest. "Okay, so I was speeding. But it wasn't like I was flying through town or something. I was only a few miles over the limit and I wouldn't have done that if we weren't running late."

"Hey, you don't have to convince me," he retorted with a grin. "Tell it to the judge."

Her gaze bouncing back and forth between them like she was watching a tennis match, Haily exclaimed, "The judge? Are you going to have to go to court, Mom?"

Glancing down to find her daughter staring up at her with widened eyes, she reached over to pat her on the knee. "Flynn's just kidding, honey. If I get a ticket, I'll just have to pay a fine. So don't worry, no one's going to haul me off to jail. In fact," she continued, watching the patrol car in her side mirror, "I don't even think I'm going to get a ticket. That cop hasn't moved. If he was going to stop me, he would have done it by now."

"He's probably looking for bigger fish to fry," Flynn predicted as the road curved and the cop was lost to view. "Like an eighteen-wheeler rolling into town at the speed of sound."

"Maybe," she agreed, easing up on the accelerator again to keep the speedometer below the speed limit. "But I'm not taking any more chances. Did you find the rodeo grounds on the map yet?"

He nodded. "Yeah. Take the next right, then turn back left at the second cross street. That should put us right at the entrance."

His eyes on the dash clock as Tate did as he directed, Flynn knew she was going as fast as she dared, but it seemed as if they were crawling. Trying to curb his impatience, he reminded himself that they were only a mile or two from the arena, but that did little good. By the time Tate pulled into the parking lot reserved for contestants and rodeo officials, he was sure she could hear him grinding his teeth. The bareback competition started in two minutes!

Braking to a quick stop at the entrance, Tate only had time to say, "We'll catch up with you inside after I find a parking space," before he was out of the truck and grabbing his equipment bag from the camper.

He hit the entrance at a dead run and headed straight for the chutes. As usual, the scene was a madhouse. Cowboys and stock personnel swarmed around the chutes to soothe and hold the animals and offer last-minute words of advice to the contestants.

"Watch him, cowboy. He likes to break hard to the right the second he clears the gate."

"You got a good hold? Just let us know when you're ready."

"We got us a wild one here, boys. Watch those hooves!"

The familiar phrases assaulted Flynn from all sides, but he hardly noticed. Dammit, what horse had he drawn? If they'd already turned him out—"

"Hey, Rawlings!" Joe Martinez suddenly called to him over the noise. "We'd just about given up on you. Move your butt, man. You've got thirty seconds before we turn Hot Shot out."

Swearing, Flynn didn't wait to hear more. Pushing through the crowd, he jerked his rigging out of his equipment bag. "Sorry I'm late. I had car trouble. Who do I have to beat?"

"Calhoun," he retorted as Flynn quickly strapped on his chaps and spurs. "He rode first and got an eighty-four. Nobody else has even come close to that."

His jaw tight, Flynn wanted to find the other cowboy and tell him exactly what he thought of him, but there wasn't time. Hell, there wasn't even time to warm up. Quickly rosining up his glove, he climbed into the chute and carefully eased down onto Hot Shot. Just his luck, he thought grimly, to draw one of the toughest bucking horses in the country. God, what else could go wrong? After looking over his shoulder for the past week and being on constant guard every single minute of the day, he wasn't sure he even wanted to know.

The gate before his jerked open with a loud clang. The horse and rider exploded into the arena. Seconds. He had only seconds. His hands slipped into the handle of his rigging as the chute help converged around the chute. The flank man adjusted the flank strap, drawing an angry protest from the horse. Tugging his hat down snug against his ears, Flynn looked up and met the chute boss's eyes. Without saying a word, the other man told him the arena was clear. All Flynn had to do was nod his head and the gate would swing free.

His heart slamming against his ribs, he focused on the spot on the horse's neck where he would start his spurring. A second later, he nodded his head.

The second the gate was jerked open, Hot Shot broke out of the chute like a bank robber busting out of jail. Arching his back, he hopped across the arena floor, coming down hard with every jump and drawing gasps from the crowd as he sprang straight up into the air again.

Pain streaking up his arm, Flynn caught the animal's rough rhythm, determined to ride him out. Every second seemed like a lifetime, but he only locked his jaw and hung on tight. Then, just when he thought he had the horse licked, she surprised him by coming down from a jump and suddenly whirling to the left.

"Well, hell!"

Even as he ground out the curse between his clenched teeth, he felt himself starting to slide, but there was nothing he could do. An instant later, his hand slipped from the handle in his rigging and he went flying.

The crowd gasped as he landed with a bone-rattling jolt in the dirt. Unhurt except for his dignity, he pushed himself to his feet and looked around for his hat. It was a flattened pancake in the dust. Snatching it up, he had no choice but to laugh along with everyone else as he made his way out of the arena.

But he wasn't laughing when he got behind the chutes and caught sight of Grady Calhoun through the crowd. Leaning against a post, the other man was looking right at him, grinning like a jackass. That was all it took for Flynn to lose it. Red-hot fury flashing in his eyes, he pushed his way though the people blocking his path, intent on telling Grady exactly what he thought of him.

Chapter 8

By the time Tate found a parking place, then unloaded Sugar into one of the holding pens, it seemed like an hour had passed instead of just a few minutes. Something inside her pressing her to hurry, she urged Haily toward the contestant entrance at a fast walk and prayed they'd arrived in time for Flynn to ride. They made their way behind the chutes just in time to see Flynn, dusty and disheveled from an obvious fall, charging toward Grady with murder in his eyes. Her heart jerking in her breast, Tate paled. "Oh, no!"

At her side, Haily saw the fury in Flynn's face and stopped in her tracks. "Uh-oh."

"Uh-oh is right, sweetheart," Tate replied. "Stay here."

Off like a shot, she rushed forward, but suddenly the cowboys who were supposed to be helping at the chutes realized that a fight was about to erupt and gathered to watch. Just like boys in a school yard, Tate thought irritably. Cursing under her breath, she pushed her way through them and finally burst free just seconds before Flynn reached Grady.

"Dammit, Flynn, don't do this!" she hissed, rushing between the two men without a thought to what she was getting into. Planting her hands against his chest, she held him at bay, ignoring Grady's taunts as she tried to reason with him. "This isn't the way—"

"Get out of my way, Tate," he growled. His narrowed eyes locked on Grady's smug face, he didn't spare her a glance. "This has been coming a long time and I'm finally going to tell this scumbag what a lowlife he is."

"Fine," she agreed. "But not like this. Give yourself some time to cool off—"

"No," he said flatly, and reached out to set her aside.

His jaw like granite, his eyes as cold as a winter sky, he advanced on Grady with a rage that was all the more impressive for its tightly reined control. Tense cowboys circled them, ready to step in if things got out of hand, but Flynn never took his eyes off the dirtbag standing before him. "I used to think you had class, Calhoun, but if I had to do what you do to win, I couldn't look myself in the mirror in the morning."

His smile as infuriatingly smug as ever, Grady merely lifted a brow at him. "The last I heard, hard work wasn't something to be ashamed of, Rawlings. You're just sore cause you spit dirt. Maybe if you got to a rodeo on time for once, you'd be able to stay on the back of a horse without getting thrown like a city slicker out for a Sunday ride."

"And maybe if you weren't so scared of me knocking you out of that number-one ranking of yours, I might get a fair shake. But you're going to make sure that doesn't happen, aren't you, Grady?" he demanded silkily. "You want that world title so bad, you can taste it, and you're not about to let me or anyone else get in your way."

Still leaning casually against the empty chute, Grady abruptly straightened, his green eyes as sharp as glass. "I don't know what the hell you're talking about—"

"Save the innocent act for someone who appreciates it," Flynn cut in contemptuously, fighting the urge to smash his face in. "I may be a rookie, but I'm not a fool. I know what you're up to. Oh, you can keep pulling you're dirty little tricks, but it's not going to stop me. I'm giving you fair warning that I'm going to keep getting better. So if you want to hang on to that precious ranking of yours, you'd better avoid me like the plague, mister, and find yourself some other rodeos to enter. Because I'm going to whip your ass every chance I get."

"The hell you are—"

Alarmed, Tate stepped back between the two men before they could come to blows. "Okay, guys, that's enough," she said firmly.

She might as well have saved her breath. Nobody moved. Her hands against Flynn's chest, she could feel the rage pulsing through him as he tried to get past her, and one look at his set face told her she wasn't going to get through to him. Frantically searching the crowd all but surrounding them, she spied David Hartfield, the chute boss, pushing his way through the milling cowboys, and she sighed in relief. A big, burly man, David could handle any kind of trouble that came his way. "David, thank God! Get him out of here, will you?" she said, jerking her head toward Grady.

"All right, Calhoun," he said coldly. "Take a walk. The party's over."

"Me? What about—"

"You heard me," he snapped. "Get out of here!"

Wanting to argue, Grady hesitated, but David, who outweighed him by forty pounds, gave him a hard look, just daring him to try. Snarling a curse, he promised Flynn, "This isn't over, Rawlings," then stormed off with his friends.

Silence, thick and tense, lingered long after Grady disappeared in the crowd. Tate felt the thunder of Flynn's heartbeat under her palm and suddenly realized that her hands were still pressed against his chest to hold him at bay. Heat climbing in her cheeks, she quickly stepped back, releasing him. "Sorry," she murmured.

"Somebody want to tell me what the hell's going on here?" David asked sharply, studying the two of them. "I know Calhoun can be a jerk sometimes, but I didn't think you were dumb enough to let him push your buttons, Rawlings. What'd he do this time?"

"Nothing I can't handle," Flynn retorted tightly.

His weathered face set in a scowl, David had been around cowboys long enough to know when he was wasting his breath. Shaking his head at his stubbornness, he retorted, "Have it your way. Just don't settle it with your fists."

It wasn't a threat, just a warning, one that Tate and Flynn both knew not to take lightly. As a chute boss, he was one of the best—any rodeo that had David Hartfield working behind the scenes went off without a hitch. Because he didn't put up with any nonsense.

"What happened?" Tate asked quietly as soon as the older man returned to his duties at the chutes. "Did you get to ride?"

"Oh, yeah," he drawled bitterly. "We got here just in time for me to jump on Hot Shot's back and take a dive into the dirt."

Tate winced. "Ouch. And where was Grady?"

"Standing by the chutes watching the whole damn thing. From the grin on his face, you'd have thought he'd just won the lottery or something."

"So you went after him."

He nodded. "I lost it," he admitted. "But I wasn't going to hit him...even if I did want to shove his teeth down his throat. I just wanted to tell the jackass what I thought of him."

She chuckled, able to appreciate the humor in the situation now that the crisis was over. "Well, you certainly did that. I've never seen Grady so mad."

Still seething, Flynn was in no mood to be amused. "I'll show him mad," he retorted grimly. "If he tries one more damn trick..."

Out in the arena, the emcee announced the start of the barrel racing. Tate, seeing the anger still clouding Flynn's blue eyes, knew Grady's parting shot had hit the nail on the head. The hostility brewing between the two men was far from over, and she wouldn't put it past either one of them to go looking for the other the first chance they got. "I've got to get back to work," she said, frowning. "Why don't you go sit up in the stands with Haily and cool off?"

Flynn wasn't fooled by the request. "I'm not going after him, Tate," he said quietly.

"I never said you were," she began, only to swallow the rest of the denial when he arched a brow at her in patent disbelief. Heat climbing in her cheeks, she laughed. "Okay, I don't quite trust either one of you. So sue me. But you could still sit in the stands with Haily." Glancing around for her daughter, she found her where she had left her, her blue eyes wide and anxious as she watched them. "I think she thought you were going to take Grady's head off," she said, motioning for Haily to join them.

"If the bastard keeps pushing me, I just might," he confided in a lowered voice as Haily rushed up. "Hey, kid," he greeted her with a grin, ruffling her hair. "I think we've both had enough excitement behind the chutes for one day. Why don't we grab some cotton candy and a couple of seats in the stands and watch your mom run circles around her competition?"

"Oh, wow, Mom, can I?" she asked hopefully, her eyes sparkling at the mention of the forbidden treat. "Please, please, please? Just this once? I'll brush my teeth twice tonight and won't eat any more sweets for a month!"

Tate laughed at the impossible promise and pulled her close for a hug. "I guess it won't hurt. Just don't go overboard, okay? Now get out of here, you scamp. I've got to get Sugar and get ready to ride."

Wishing her luck, they hurried off toward the concession stands, laughing and teasing like a father and daughter who were crazy about each other. Watching them together, Tate felt something catch at her heart, a yearning that she knew was dangerous. Somehow Flynn had made himself a part of their family without her even knowing how it had happened, fitting in so completely that it was hard to imagine him not always being there.

Her heart knocking against her ribs, she stared after him and reminded herself that that kind of thinking could only lead to disillusionment. No man, no matter how perfect he seemed at the time, stayed forever. If she let herself forget that, even for a moment, she was going to find herself in big trouble.

"Hey, Tate, you going to ride today or moon over Flynn Rawlings all afternoon?" David Hartfield called to her, his brown eyes twinkling teasingly. "Time's awastin' if you're going to warm up that mare of yours."

Glancing up from her thoughts, Tate found, to her mortification, every cowboy in sight grinning at her. Hot color swept into her cheeks. She was, she promised herself, going to have a serious conversation with the chute boss just as soon as the opportunity presented itself. But for now she had a race to run. "I'm going to ride," she retorted with a lift of her chin. "Don't worry. I'll be ready when you are."

She won . . . for the day. The Hinton rodeo was a two-head show, which meant that all contestants competed for two days. A small daily prize was rewarded to the top scorer in every event at the completion of competition each day; then at the end of the rodeo, the contestant with the highest average score won the grand prize in his or her event. Even cowboys like Flynn, who were thrown or failed to score for some other reason and were out of the running for the top money the first day, had a chance at winning the daily take the second day.

Which meant they had to find a place to stay for the night.

There was no arena campground, but an area farmer opened up one of his pastures for all rodeo contestants who just needed a place to park their recreational vehicles, and it was only two miles from town. There were no electrical hookups or showers, but it was free, and that suited Tate's pocketbook just fine, especially since her camper had all the amenities of home, including battery-operated lights, running water and a bathroom.

Flynn, however, wasn't so lucky. It wasn't until she joined him and Haily after the barrel racing that she realized that when she'd come across him hitchhiking on the highway, he hadn't had his camping gear with him.

Haily, as observant as ever, noticed the same thing. "But where are you going to stay, Flynn?" she asked in concern as soon as Tate told her about the farm outside of town. "You didn't bring your tent."

Flynn had been asking himself the same thing for the past ten minutes. The money he'd won recently was going to have to go toward the repairs on his truck, so he was more than a little strapped for cash. Not that he intended to tell Tate and her daughter that, especially after Tate had accused him of living off his family's money.

"Oh, I'll find something, sunshine," he told Haily with an easy grin. "George Klein's here, and he always gets himself a hotel room. He'll probably let me stretch out on his floor."

"But you don't even have a blanket to lay on," she pointed out. "Why don't you stay with us? We have plenty of room."

She made the suggestion with the innocence of a child and didn't have any idea how inappropriate it was. Startled, Tate glanced at Flynn, only to find his dark blue eyes waiting for her, watching her steadily. He didn't say a word, but he didn't have to. They both knew that his staying in the camper with them could be nothing but a mistake.

Fighting the heat that threatened to singe her cheeks, Tate turned back to her daughter. "Honey—" Lord, what was she supposed to say to her? "I'm sure Flynn would be more comfortable at a hotel. We're so cramped in the camper—"

"But we have two beds. And if I sleep with you, he can have my bed."

"That's true, but—"

"You always said we should help people in trouble," she reminded her. "And Flynn's in trouble, isn't he?"

"Well, yes, he's having car trouble."

"Then there's no reason why we can't help him, is there?"

As far as logic went, it was irrefutable. Helpless, Tate glanced at Flynn.

Caught in the trap of her big blue eyes, Flynn suddenly knew what his father had felt like whenever his mother had turned to him with a problem she couldn't solve herself. Come hell or high water, he'd find a way to handle it.

Turning to Haily, he tried a different tactic. "Honey, I appreciate the offer, but I don't think you know what you're inviting." Lowering his voice as if confiding a secret, he confessed, "I snore."

At her giggle, his brows pushed together in a fake frown. "Don't laugh, young lady. It's a serious problem. Sometimes I can really rattle the walls, and I'd feel terrible if I kept you and your mom awake. Especially since your mom's going for the top money tomorrow."

"But we never see you," she complained. "Don't you like us anymore?"

Touched by the hurt in her eyes and voice, Flynn tugged gently on one of her pigtails. "Where'd you get a crazy idea like that, squirt? Of course I like you."

"Then you'll stay with us? Please?"

Caught in her guileless reasoning, Flynn knew when he was trapped. Stuck, he grinned ruefully, avoiding Tate's eyes. "I guess so. Just don't blame me if my snoring keeps you up all night."

The night was hot and still, without a breath of air. Long after the lights had been turned out and they'd all settled down to sleep, Flynn lay in his narrow, too-short bed in nothing but his jeans and felt the sweat pop out on his skin. But it wasn't the heat that bothered him. No, his discomfort could be blamed solely on Tate. From his uncomfortable position at the opposite end of the camper, he could just make out the shadowy outline of her lying next to an exhausted Haily in the big bed over the cab. She appeared to be as tired as her daughter and hadn't so much as moved a finger in the past fifteen minutes. But Flynn wasn't fooled. She was awake, all right, and as aware of him as he was of her.

He was too old to be making these kind of mistakes, he fumed, clenching his teeth on an oath before it could escape. He'd known it the second Tate had stepped out of the bathroom an hour ago. She'd been dressed in a pale blue cotton robe that had about as much sex appeal as a potato sack; and with her face scrubbed clean and her blond hair tucked behind her ears, she hadn't looked a day over sixteen. He shouldn't have been moved by her in the least, but her total lack of artifice had slain him in his tracks and he'd been entranced before he knew what hit him. Then the clean, soft flowery scent of her had floated across the camper to grab him by the throat, and he'd almost swallowed his tongue.

Slamming his eyes closed, he forced the disturbing thoughts from his mind, determined to ignore the lady and get some sleep. But he could still smell her, for God's sake, and it was driving him out of his mind! His frustrated senses, only too happy to take advantage of the situation, projected a dozen fantasies on the inside of his eyelids, each one hotter, more tantalizing, than the last. Before he could take a steadying breath, he was teased with the image of Tate slipping down from her bed to join him, the utilitarian robe she wore to hide herself from him dropping to the floor, unnoticed, the second he reached for her. Just that quickly, heat pooled in his loins.

Naked, he thought with a nearly silent groan. She'd be naked underneath the damn thing and so beautiful, his hands would shake just at the thought of touching her. But that wouldn't stop him from caressing every sweet, delectable inch of her. Oh, no. He'd touch her with his hands, taste her with his tongue, drive her out of her mind with desire until she shattered in his arms. And then he'd do it all over again.

Suddenly realizing what he was doing, he stiffened, snarling a curse. But it was too late. His body was already hot and hard and aching. And there wasn't so much as a breeze to cool him off. His jaw locking on another oath, he jerked his eyes from Tate's shadowy figure and turned over to give his pillow a savage punch. It didn't help. He had a gut-wrenching feeling that nothing short of having Tate would.

Sweating in her bed over the cab, Tate heard him swear under his breath and the sheets of his bed whisper as he tried to get comfortable. She squeezed her eyes shut and ordered herself to ignore the sounds, ignore *him*. But she might as well have told the tides to ignore the pull of the moon. She was already hot, achy, restless. And it was all Flynn's fault! He had invaded her space, taken over the camper just by stepping into it. It was usually quite comfortable for her and Haily, but now it seemed too small, too closed in, the air too thin. And she would never again look at the bed where her daughter usually slept without seeing Flynn lying there, his dark hair flopping over his forehead, his granite jaw shadowed and unshaven, his chest bare and tempting in the darkness. Lord, how could he even think about sleeping in this heat?

Over the course of the night, she asked herself that question at least a dozen times. And with every passing hour, her resentment grew. This was *her* camper, *her* home away from home. He had no right to come into it and make her so aware of him that she found herself listening for the soft sound of his breathing. She would *not* let him do this to her!

But she did.

By the time Haily bounded up the next morning, full of sass and her usual energy, Tate felt as though she had been through the wars. She'd somehow managed to grab an hour, maybe two, of sleep, but even that hadn't been restful. Because of Flynn, damn him. Every time she'd let her guard down enough to slip into an exhausted slumber, he'd been there, waiting for her, just beyond her dreams. If she'd have gotten her hands on him then, she liked to think she would have killed him. But she was horribly afraid that the second she touched him, she would have been lost.

This tension between them couldn't go on, she decided, refusing to admit that there could be anything else but pure animal attraction between them. *Lust,* she corrected herself, staring in fascination at his bare chest as he pushed himself up from the twisted sheets he'd slept on and reached for his shirt. What she felt for the man was nothing but lust, and there was no use pussyfooting around the truth. Especially when she was tired and grouchy because *he* had kept her awake most of the night and all she could think of was how wonderful he looked first thing in the morning.

After last night, she had no choice but to admit that she was never going to be indifferent to him. She didn't know how or when he had been able to slip through her defenses; she just knew it couldn't continue. He was becoming too important to her—and to Haily. She could take care of herself, but she couldn't let him hurt her daughter by being part of her life now, then walking away when he had better things to do. And just as soon as she got the chance, she would tell him that.

She had to wait until after breakfast, when Haily found some friends to play with, before an opportunity presented itself. By that time, the small confines of the camper had gotten to both adults. Flynn wasn't used to spending any time in a camper, and they practically danced in each other's arms to negotiate the narrow aisle when one of them tried to move.

Frustrated, irritated, her heart pounding and her cheeks fiery, she wasn't in the best of moods when she finally got the chance to speak her mind. Turning to face him after Haily slammed out the camper door, it didn't help that he lounged at the kitchen booth with his long legs stretched out before him as if he didn't have a care in the world.

Her mouth flattening into a thin line, she said bluntly, "After today's competition, I think it would be best if we each went our separate ways in the future. I won't have Haily hurt."

The accusation coming out of the blue, Flynn jerked up out of the booth as if she'd zapped him with a cattle prod. *"Hurt!"* he echoed thunderously. "What the hell are you talking about? I'd cut off my right arm before I'd hurt that kid!"

Flynn in a temper was something to see, but Tate didn't even blink. Standing her ground in spite of the pounding of her heart, she glared right back at him. "Oh, really? And what about last night? When you tried to back out of staying with us, you saw how she was. She thought you didn't like her anymore."

"Dammit, Tate, you know it's not that—"

Oh, yes, she knew. That was why she was going to do whatever it took to stay out of his way in the future. Her cheeks hot, she said stiffly, "And the more attached she gets to you, the harder it will be for her when we go back to St. George at the end of the summer. She'll be hurt, and I won't allow that to happen. So just stay away from her."

It was a logical request from a protective mother. But seeing the emotions swirling in her eyes like the churning waters of a stormy sea, Flynn suddenly had a funny feeling that they weren't talking about Haily at all. "What about you?" he asked abruptly, his eyes narrowed on her flushed face. "Am I supposed to stay away from you, too?"

For the first time, she looked flustered. "Well, of course. Since I'm her mother and we're usually to-gether—"

"I can't see you, either," he finished for her. "Which is exactly what you wanted in the first place." At her startled gasp, he gave her a hard look that didn't cut her any slack. "I never would have taken you for a coward, lady."

"A coward!"

"You're damn right. You're hiding behind your daughter when you know this has nothing to do with her."

"Oh, really?" she retorted, stung. "Then suppose you tell me what this has to do with."

"You. Us. Haily's not the one afraid of being hurt. *You* are."

"I am not!"

"No?" he asked softly, stepping toward her until he towered over her. Staring down at her, he saw the pulse beating wildly at the base of her throat and suddenly, in the small confines of the camper, there wasn't enough air to go around. But he couldn't move away from her. Not yet.

"Admit it," he urged her thickly. "You're scared of us . . . of this. . . ." Giving her every opportunity to draw back, he slowly reached out to lay his fingers against the pulse fluttering in her throat. At his touch, it surged into a wild rhythm that seemed to leap from her skin to his. Just that quickly he felt his blood heat. Lord, had he ever met a woman who could set him on fire so fast?

His eyes holding hers captive, he slowly traced a line from her pounding pulse down her chest to the first button of her blouse. She stared back at him defiantly, not making a sound, but beneath his hand he felt her breath catch in her throat and her skin begin to heat.

"You're afraid I'm going to turn out like that bastard who fathered Haily, and it scares you spitless," he whispered hoarsely. "And I don't blame you. You haven't had an easy time of it. But, dammit, Tate, I'm not like him! You have to know I'd never hurt you or Haily."

For a moment, he thought she was finally going to stop running from the truth and admit that he was right. Beneath his hand, she quivered, and for the flash of a second, no more, he could've sworn he saw longing darken her sapphire eyes. But then she stiffened like a maiden aunt who'd just received an indecent proposal and said tightly, "What I know is that this conversation is pointless. I've made up my mind, and I'm not changing it."

Her jaw had a mulish set; her eyes held a warning that she was prepared to resist whatever argument or persuasion he could come up with. Furious, he scowled down at her, tempted to shake her until her teeth rattled. But he wasn't so desperate for a woman's company that he stayed where he wasn't wanted.

"If my presence offends you so much, why wait until this afternoon's performance to split company? I can get out of your hair right now."

"That's not necessary—"

"Oh, but it is, sweetheart," he said coldly, turning away to grab his equipment bag. "I don't stay where I'm not wanted."

His words hurt, but not nearly as much as the wounded look in his eyes. That struck her right in the heart. "Don't be this way," she began, regret knotting her stomach as she instinctively reached for him. But he only pushed past her to the door. "Where are you going?"

"Back to town."

"But it's two miles!"

"I don't care if it's fifty," he snapped. "Tell Haily I had to go in early to get in a few practice rides."

"Flynn, wait—"

Ignoring her, he stormed out, heading for town without a backward glance. It was a long walk in the heat.

By the time he reached the rodeo grounds, his temper had cooled a little, but every time he thought about Tate, he got steamed all over again. And deep in his gut, there was a gnawing ache that felt an awful lot like hurt. Muttering a curse, he told himself there was no way in hell he'd let Tate Baxter or any other woman hurt him. But the ache persisted, refusing to be ignored.

His jaw rigid, his eyes hard, he paused at a concession stand on his way to the chutes and gave serious consideration to drowning his anger in a beer or two. But only a fool looking to get seriously injured played around with alcohol, then climbed on the back of a bucking horse. Turning his back on temptation, he headed for the chutes, dropped his equipment bag with some of the other cowboys', then went looking for some of his friends.

He didn't see Tate again until the stands started to fill up and the riders involved in the Grand Entry began to line up behind the chutes. She spied him at the same time he saw her, and across the crowd of people that separated them, her eyes held a silent entreaty that Flynn couldn't have missed if he'd tried.

Don't be mad. We can part friends.

Like hell, he thought grimly. How could they be friends when she didn't trust him not to hurt her? Still too angry to go anywhere near her, he deliberately turned away from her.

By the time it was his turn to ride, he was looking forward to working some of his frustration out on the back of Lazy Bones, the bronc he'd drawn. A tough little mare that usually didn't pull any surprises, she could be depended on to give a cowboy a good, steady, high-scoring ride. If he was lucky, he'd do well enough to win the daily money, since he was already out of the running for the championship.

As he'd expected, the minute the gate clanged open, Lazy Bones jumped into the arena and started her usual, regular rhythm that was a bronc rider's dream. Settling down for a fast, smooth ride, Flynn immediately started his spurring action, his mind totally focused on the horse and what he had to do to win.

The break in his rigging happened so fast, he had no time to brace for it. One second he was spurring Lazy Bones for all he was worth, and the next his rigging suddenly snapped free from around the horse. He went flying and landed hard against the chute railing.

The pain was immediate, hot, intense. It circled his ribs like a tight band of fire, constricting his lungs until he could hardly breathe. Groaning, he crumpled to the dirt like a rag doll.

Watching from behind the chutes, Tate gasped in horror and rushed forward onto the arena floor, ignoring the chute boss's order for everyone to keep back so the medical staff could get through. Someone got the horse out of the arena, but Tate couldn't have said who. She had eyes for no one but Flynn.

As pale as the now-dusty white cowboy shirt he wore, he lay on his back in the dirt next to the chutes, pain etching deep furrows in his brow. Her heart in her throat, Tate dropped down to her knees at his side, reaching him before anyone else. Afraid to touch him for fear she would hurt him more, she said shakily, "Flynn?"

Gasping, his eyes squeezed shut against the pain, he reached blindly for her hand. "Yeah, I'm here, sweetheart," he said, choking on a laugh that wasn't the least bit humorous as his fingers tightly wrapped around hers. "Eating dirt...again. I just can't win at this rodeo."

"Where does it hurt?"

"Everywhere." He chuckled painfully. "Pick a spot, any spot."

The medical staff arrived then with a stretcher, and Tate had to move out of the way. Standing back, hugging herself, she watched the paramedics, who were always on hand for any competition, take over. Carefully examining Flynn to make sure there was no back injury, they carefully lifted him to the stretcher to carry him behind the chutes, where they would do a more thorough examination to see if he needed to be taken to the hospital. As they exited the arena, the crowd, which had stood in hushed silence the entire time, came alive to clap in appreciation as Flynn gave a halfhearted wave to signal he was all right.

Minutes later, behind the chutes, he told the paramedics the same thing. "I'm fine, guys," he insisted, struggling to push himself up into a sitting position. But with every move, his ribs burned white-hot. Wincing, sweat popping out on his brow, he gasped. "I just got the breath knocked out of me. After I walk around awhile, I'll be good as new."

"We'll check you out just the same," the older of the two men said firmly. "Hold still while we get that shirt off you."

If he'd had any breath left, he'd have told both men to stuff it. But he didn't, and they knew it. Scowling, he let them ease him out of his shirt, determined not to let them see the agony he was in. But they were too experienced to fool.

"You've got a couple of cracked ribs, buddy," the younger one announced, his probing fingers expertly exploring Flynn's rib cage. Glancing up, he shot him a sharp look. "Hurts like hell, doesn't it?"

His mouth pressed flat, Flynn merely said, "Just wrap me up so I can get out of here. In a couple of days, I'll be good as new."

Hovering close by, Tate heard the entire exchange and frowned. "Damn it, Flynn, cracked ribs aren't anything to play around with!"

"She's right," the older of the men agreed, handing Flynn his shirt. "Right now they're just cracked. If you climb back on a horse before they're healed and break them clean through, you could puncture a lung. Then you really would be hurting. So if you want to stay out of the hospital, you're going to have to give up rodeoing for a couple of weeks."

Flynn couldn't have been more stunned if he'd ordered him not to breathe. "What! You've got to be kidding!"

"Nope. Pay me now, pay me later. Either way, you're just going to have to stay still and let those ribs heal on their own. It's up to you how much time it takes."

"But I can't take a two-week break. I'm just starting to get good."

"Yeah, life's a bitch, isn't it?" the younger man said with a rough sympathy that was hardly appreciated. "Don't try to get up. We'll help you."

His teeth gritted on an oath, Flynn suffered through their help without a word of protest, but it cost him. By the time the two men finally got him on his feet, his face was washed free of color and he was weak as a baby. Every ragged breath he took was an agony.

Two weeks, he thought furiously. He was supposed to suffer through this for *two* weeks? Like hell!

"What are you going to do?" Tate asked huskily, hovering close as if she were afraid he would collapse at any moment.

"I don't know." He started to shrug, only to catch himself at the first twinge of pain. "Go home, I guess. I'm sure not much good around here like this."

Looking around for his things, he saw the chute boss making his way toward him, a scowl etching his chiseled face, Flynn's rigging in his hand. "Oh, good—you found it," he said as David reached him. "I want to take a good look at it. I can't imagine what caused the damn thing to come apart that way."

Seeing the obvious pain Flynn was still in, David hesitated, but what he had to say wouldn't keep. "You must have really ticked someone off, son," he said flatly, holding out the rigging, which was the only thing a bareback rider had to hang on to when he was on the back of a bronc. "It's been cut."

Chapter 9

"**W**hat! What the hell are you talking about?"

"Take a look," David said, motioning to the leather body of the rigging.

Just as he'd said, it had been smoothly cut at the narrowest part. But whoever had done the damage had been smart enough to slice the leather from underneath so it wouldn't show when the rigging was strapped to the horse. Still intact when Flynn had started his ride, it had taken only the rough, continuous bucking motion to make the weak spot tear completely free.

"Son of a bitch!" Flynn muttered half to himself, rubbing his thumb over the cleanly cut spot where a knife had pierced the leather. "I never thought the bastard would go this far."

"Who?"

Lost in his thoughts, Flynn glanced up at David's sharp question and clamped his teeth shut on Grady Calhoun's name. He had no proof, only his gut instinct, but his gut was seldom wrong. And right now his belly was telling him he had to look no farther than Calhoun to find the bastard who had done this.

Before the rodeo had started, he'd carelessly left his equipment bag unattended with a dozen others behind the chutes, then joined his friends. Anyone could have come by, found his bag simply by looking at the name tag attached to the handle, then sabotaged his rigging with the quick swipe of a razor-sharp blade. Considering the fact it was always a madhouse behind the chutes before the competition began, he could have done it without drawing a second glance.

It wasn't just anyone who had it in for him. It was Grady Calhoun. He knew it as sure as he knew his ribs were killing him. But he didn't have a shred of evidence, and until he did, he could hardly go around slandering the jerk without sounding like a sore loser.

"Whoever did this," he retorted, avoiding David's watchful eyes. Wishing his cracked ribs would allow him the luxury of slamming the rigging into the nearby trash can, he had to content himself with casually dropping it in instead. "Looks like I'm going to have to get myself a new rigging."

"I want a name, Rawlings," David Hartfield growled. "And don't tell me you don't suspect someone because you're a damn poor liar. So spit it out. When this kind of garbage goes on behind my chutes, I've got a right to know who's doing it."

"I don't have any proof—"

"I didn't ask for any. But something like this doesn't happen to a man without him having a damn good idea who did it. So who is it?"

Scowling, Flynn almost told him to go dig up a suspect by himself—he wasn't ratting on anyone. But he knew

David well enough to know that he wouldn't let up until he got the name he wanted. "Grady Calhoun," he said in disgust, then sat back to wait for his reaction. He didn't have long to wait.

"Grady Cal—" David broke off the shocked exclamation to spit out a harsh curse. Glancing around quickly to make sure his outburst hadn't reached anyone else's ears but Tate's, he hissed, "Have you lost your mind? If Grady keeps going the way he's been going, he's finally going to get that gold buckle that he's been trying for all these years. He wouldn't jeopardize a world-champion title pulling something stupid now."

"You wanted a name— I gave you one," Flynn snapped. "Don't blame me if you don't like the sound of it. Oh, I know Calhoun's reputation. And how many friends he's got. But believe me, I'm not one of them."

Unconvinced, David's salt-and-pepper brows knitted in a scowl. "Look, I know Calhoun can be a real pain sometimes. But come on, Flynn, even he wouldn't stoop this low. What could he hope to gain by seeing you hurt?"

"You said it yourself," Flynn said mockingly. "That gold buckle he's been trying for all these years." Seeing the shock on the other man's face, he urged, "Think about it, David. For Calhoun to get the World Champion title and the buckle that goes with it, he's got to win the most money by the end of the year. He knows that as well as I do. Two weeks ago, I knocked him out of the top money in two straight rodeos. That's when the trouble started."

Standing close by, Tate saw pain ripple across his face as he drew in a ragged breath and quickly stepped forward in alarm. "He gave Flynn the wrong starting time for the rodeo in Golden, Colorado," she said quietly, worry clouding her eyes as she watched his labored breathing.

"So he made a mistake," David replied. "It happens."

"He won, David. He made sure Flynn was out of the picture. Then he won."

If another rough-and-tumble cowboy had done such a thing, David would have had no choice but to judge the evidence as damning. But Grady wasn't a rookie looking to make a name for himself. He'd already done that and didn't need tricks to win. There had to be another explanation.

"Maybe he got mixed-up." At the hard look Flynn shot him, he defended himself. "Come on, Flynn, you know what it's like to be on the road week after week. One town starts to look like another, the rodeos all blur together and it's a wonder anyone gets anywhere on time."

Hearing her own words raised in Grady's defense, Tate had to smile. "I told him the same thing, and maybe it *was* an honest mistake. But that doesn't explain the sugar in the gas tank of his truck yesterday or this today," she said, motioning to the trash can where Flynn had dropped his rigging.

"If Tate hadn't come by when she did after my truck broke down in the middle of nowhere yesterday, I never would have made it here in time to ride," Flynn added tersely. "And then I didn't have any time to warm up. I ended up eating dirt, and Calhoun loved every minute of it. You saw his face when I dusted myself off and walked out of the arena. He was as smug as a pig in slop."

"But you think that wasn't enough for him?" the older man asked speculatively. "He wanted you out of the way permanently. Is that what you're saying?"

Flynn merely shrugged. "I don't know if he'd go that far, but he certainly accomplished what he set out to do. I'm not a threat to him or anyone else as long as I can't ride."

It was a wild plan, and an even wilder story. Flynn wouldn't have blamed David if he'd thought he was paranoid. But instead of rejecting his suspicions immediately, as he'd expected, the older man studied him for a long, tense moment, his frown fierce, before he abruptly retrieved the cut rigging from the trash. "I'm going to ask around about this," he promised grimly, "and see what I can find out. I'll get back with you."

He returned to his duties at the chutes and the rodeo that had continued as soon as Flynn had been removed from the arena floor. One glance at the usual activity around the chutes told Tate that the barrel racing would start soon. She was the third competitor and didn't have any time to waste if she was going to get Sugar warmed up beforehand.

But as she turned back to Flynn, the argument they'd had earlier was forgotten in the face of his obvious pain. He was as pale as a ghost and hurting. Struck by the need to hold him, to wrap her arms around him and just feel his heart slam against hers, she started to reach for him, horrifying images tearing at her. Flynn, flying into the railing and collapsing to the ground. Flynn, always grinning like he knew a secret no one else did, lying unmoving in the dirt. If he'd been really seriously injured . . .

She shied away from the thought, afraid to follow it to its logical conclusion. Dear God, how had he come to mean so much to her in so little time? "I've got to go," she said huskily. "What are you going to do?"

"Do?" He started to laugh cynically, only to suck in a sharp breath as pain slipped between his ribs like a finely honed sword. "I don't guess I'm going to do anything, thanks to Grady. The bastard's made sure of that."

He should have been as weak as a kitten and damned uncomfortable, but fury and resentment flashed in his eyes, and her heart jerked in alarm. "You're not going after him, are you?" she demanded, closing her fingers over his arm. "Dammit, Flynn, I want your promise right now that you're not going to do something stupid—or I'm not letting you out of my sight."

The minute she touched him, she felt the change in him, the tension that had nothing to do with Grady Calhoun and everything to do with the sparks that sizzled between them like grease in a hot skillet. His eyes, as dark as midnight, probed hers. "Since when did you become my keeper?" he asked roughly. "I didn't think you wanted anything to do with me."

Not want him? she thought, swallowing a hysterical laugh that sounded suspiciously like a sob. Was the man blind? Of course she wanted him! That was the whole problem. He made her think of things she hadn't allowed herself to think of in years, dream things that she'd sworn she wanted no part of, ache for him when she knew he was a risk she couldn't take.

For the first time since she'd given her heart to Rich Travis, only to have it thrown back in her face, she wanted everything to do with a man. Only this time, she wasn't a seventeen-year-old girl who didn't have the slightest idea how painful life could be. She'd known the taste and feel of hurt, and just the thought of enduring that kind of pain again was enough to send her running for cover.

Heat blooming in her cheeks, she met his gaze unflinchingly and prayed he couldn't hear the jackhammer beat of her heart. "I said I thought it would be for the best if we avoided each other in the future," she corrected him huskily. "That doesn't mean I'm going to stand back and watch you get turned into hamburger meat by Grady just because you haven't got enough sense not to go after him until you're in better shape. Promise me, Flynn."

"I'm not an idiot—"

"Good," she cut in, her lips twitching at his irritated scowl. "Can I take that as a promise? I'm running out of time, so you'd better make up your mind."

He didn't want to; she could see the struggle going on behind his eyes. But she just stared back at him steadily, refusing to back off, and he finally ground his teeth on a curse of defeat. "Oh, all right! I promise I won't go anywhere near the bastard... for now. But as soon as these ribs are healed..."

"You can beat him where it hurts—on the back of a bucking horse in front of an arena full of people," she said with a smile. Surprising them both, she slipped her arms around his waist for a hug that wouldn't hurt his ribs. But the second he lifted his arms to return the embrace, she was gone. "Gotta go, or I'm going to miss my ride."

"Dammit, Tate, come back here!"

Grinning, she threaded her way through the crowd, ignoring his bellow of protest, as she made her way to where she'd left Sugar in a holding pen. But as she climbed into the saddle and began to warm up, she wasn't smiling. If Flynn had hit his head instead of his ribs, he'd be on the way to the hospital now.

"Earth to Tate," one of the cowboys working the chutes called. "What planet are you on, darlin'?"

Jerking back to her surroundings, she blinked... and realized that it was her turn to compete. Heat staining her cheeks, she forced a smile. "Sorry. I was off in the ozone somewhere. Just give us a second and we'll be right with you."

With a touch of her heels to Sugar's flank and a pull on the reins, she backed the horse up until they had enough room to get a running start. Sugar, sensing what was coming, tensed, then danced nervously and pulled at the reins, anxious to get started.

The cowboy standing at the arena entrance signaled that the floor was clear. Sugar, recognizing the signal, strained at the bit, drawing a laugh from Tate. "All right, all right. Let's show 'em what you've got, girl. Let's go!" Leaning forward in the saddle, she touched her heels to the horse, and within seconds, they were galloping onto the arena floor.

Too late it struck Tate that she probably shouldn't even have competed. She put Sugar through her paces, urging her faster and faster through her turns, but her timing was off and she just couldn't seem to get into the race. She felt as if they were moving in slow motion and pressed Sugar to increase her speed. Always anxious to please, the horse responded and they circled a barrel with a swiftness that had the crowd gasping in appreciation. But just as they came out of it and sprinted toward the finish line, Sugar stumbled and started to limp.

Their momentum alone carried them out of the arena with a fairly good time, but it wasn't one that was likely to keep them in first place the rest of the day. Not that Tate cared. Worry etching her brow, she jumped to the ground the second she pulled Sugar to a quivering stop and bent to examine her right front leg.

"What happened? Is she okay?" Flynn asked, rushing toward her as fast as his injured ribs would allow. Pale and gasping, he took hold of Sugar's bridle as the horse flinched from Tate's touch. "Easy, girl," he murmured, stroking her soothingly. "Believe me, I know exactly how you feel."

Straightening, Tate announced guiltily, "She's lame and it's all my fault. I pushed her harder than I should have."

And now, because of her own stupidity, Flynn wasn't the only one who was going to be laid up for a couple of weeks. Until Sugar healed completely, Tate was virtually grounded, the rodeos she had already paid to enter a total loss. Another disaster, she thought, stricken. How many more could she take? Summer was passing far too swiftly, and at the rate she was going, she'd be lucky to have even half the money she needed for her last semester of school by the time fall arrived. What was she going to do?

"It was an accident," Flynn said quietly, watching her. "It could have happened to anyone. You can't race a horse week after week after week, honey, without expecting a few injuries. Give her a little time. She'll be fine."

But time—and money—Flynn knew, were things she didn't have a lot of. Watching the way she babied the mare, apologizing for pushing her, he found himself struggling with the urge to tell her to forget the damn money. He had enough cash in his checking account at home to give her whatever she needed to finish school, and she could pay him back when she got the chance.

The only problem was she wouldn't take money from him or any other man. Independent to a fault, she'd do it by herself or she wouldn't do it at all.

Carefully easing his thumbs into the front pockets of his jeans, he said gruffly, "So what are you going to do now? Go home to your dad's for a while?"

She nodded, her expression grim. "There's not much else I can do. I guess you'll be heading back to New Mexico. What are you going to do about your truck? Have one of your brothers drive over to Fort Worth and get it?''

It was a logical assumption, one Flynn knew he would be wise to let her go on thinking. But he'd never lied worth a damn. Bracing himself for the explosion sure to come, he said, "Actually, I was going to get it myself—if I could talk you into making a detour to Fort Worth before you go home. I'd pay you for the trouble, of course, since it's out of your way."

"But you're in no shape to drive."

"Oh, I'll be all right in a couple of days. Anyway, I'm not going home. I've got to be in Cody, Wyoming, by Friday, so I'll just go early so I'll have some time to rest before the rodeo starts."

Stunned, Tate could only stare at him, unable to believe she'd heard correctly. "You can't be serious!"

"Now, Tate—"

"Don't you 'now, Tate,' me," she tossed back. "In case you've forgotten, you've got a couple of busted ribs—"

"Cracked," he stressed, interrupting. "They're cracked, honey. There's a difference."

Tate was in no mood to appreciate the lesson in semantics. Her mouth compressed into a thin, flat line. "They might as well be broken," she snapped. "They're just as painful. And don't you dare stand there and tell me they're not. In case you haven't looked in the mirror recently, you're as pale as a ghost."

Unexpectedly enjoying himself at the chewing out, Flynn made no attempt to stop the smile that insisted on curling up the corners of his mouth. Eyes twinkling, he drawled, "Why, Tate, sweetheart, you surprise me. If I didn't know better, I might think you cared. And just this morning you were telling me to take a hike."

Hot, telltale color rose in her cheeks, but she didn't give him the satisfaction of looking away. "Any man stupid enough to climb back on a horse with a couple of *cracked* ribs obviously needs somebody to care about him so he won't wind up flat on his back in the hospital."

"That's not going to happen—"

"You're damn right it's not, because you're not going to Cody or anywhere else."

He lifted a brow at that, his dancing eyes narrowing. "Oh, really? And who's going to stop me?"

"I am." Raising her chin to a belligerent angle, she took a step toward him and poked him right in the middle of his chest with her index finger. "And don't think I can't do it." She hardly touched him, but he still winced. "And you think you can ride," she chided softly. "Face it, cowboy. You're out of commission. The only place you're going is home, so you might as well accept that right now. If you insist on acting like a child, then I guess I'll have to treat you like one."

But staring down at her, the last thing Flynn felt like was a child. His ribs were painful, but with her so close, her finger searing him through his skin and the sweet, clean scent of her teasing his senses, all he could think of was how much he wanted her. Giving into temptation, he reached for her.

He couldn't hold her like he wanted to—his ribs wouldn't allow it—but he could damn sure kiss her as if there were no tomorrow. Capturing her face in his hands, he took advantage of her startled, "Oh!" and covered her mouth with his right there in front of God and everyone.

Somebody laughed, and some jerk of a cowboy yelled, "Way to go, Flynn!" but he couldn't hear anything but the pounding of his own heart and the jagged whisper of Tate's breath as she clung to his wrists with both hands.

Then her tongue touched his, setting him on fire, and whatever arguments he had left all fizzled into smoke. Groaning her name, his hands dropped away from her face, but only to slide around her shoulders and drag her against him.

The pain was immediate and hotter than hell. Sucking in a sharp breath, he jerked back, swearing, and released her. His breath tearing through his constricted lungs, he took one look at her dazed eyes and saw she was as shaken as he. Unable to stop himself, he reached for her again, but this time just to cup her hot cheek in his palm. "Honey, you can boss me around all you like," he said gruffly, rubbing his thumb along her throbbing bottom lip. "Just remember . . . I'm no child."

Her heart thumping madly, Tate had to swallow twice before she could get her teeth and tongue to work properly. Lord, the man could kiss! "I— I don't think I'll have any trouble remembering that." Not in this lifetime or the next.

Knowing she'd never be able to think straight as long as he was touching her, she pulled back abruptly, only to have heat flare in her cheeks at his knowing look. Damn the man— He knew exactly what he did to her and he enjoyed every minute of it! "All right," she said, too flustered to care that she was being less than gracious. "I'll take you to Fort Worth. But only so you can make arrangements to have the garage store your truck until you can come back for it. Your family's place isn't too far out of my way, so I'll drop you off there on my way home. I'll just get Haily from the stands, and we can be on our way as soon as we load up Sugar."

She didn't give him a chance to argue. Turning on her heel, she headed for the stands before he could so much as say yes, no or maybe. Staring after her, Flynn couldn't

stop the grin that tugged at his mouth. He might be playing with fireworks, but Lord, there was nothing like a
bossy woman to stir up a man's blood.

Within thirty minutes, they were on the road again, the
three of them piled into the pickup just like a family
starting out on a vacation. Haily, thrilled that Flynn was
riding with them all the way to New Mexico, innocently
relayed the gossip that had erupted in the stands when
Flynn was thrown. More than a few cowboys had suggested that Grady Calhoun had had something to do with
the incident, though no one quite knew how.

Over Haily's head, Flynn's eyes met Tate's, and she sent
up a silent prayer of thanks that she had gotten him away
from the jerk before he tried to do something stupid.
"David Hartfield's still looking into it," she reminded
him. "And he's going to notify the PRCA. If anything
else happens and there's any evidence to be found,
Grady'll be dead in the water. He might was well forget
about rodeoing because he'll be kicked out of the Professional Rodeo Cowboys Association, and it'll be no more
than he deserves."

Flynn wanted to believe her, but he had to give Grady
credit. The bastard was damn clever. He'd covered his
tracks well. "He's got to make a mistake first," he said
grimly, "and so far he hasn't done that. And once David
and PRCA officials start questioning him, he'll be more
cautious than ever. He's going to be a hard rat to run
down."

Fort Worth was hot and sweltering when they reached
the garage where Flynn had left his truck, the temperature edging toward the century mark. Leaving Tate and
Haily in their rig with the air conditioner running, Flynn

promised to hurry and pushed open the passenger door. Heat, like a gust from a blast furnace, hit him in the face. Before he'd taken two steps, he was sweating.

"The gas tank needs to be put back on," Ray Johnson, the mechanic and garage owner, told him as he greeted him and handed him the bill. "Everything else is just about done. If you want to check out the Stockyards down the street and maybe get something to eat, we can have it ready for you by the time you get back."

"No problem," Flynn said easily. But when his eyes dropped to the bottom of the page, where the total amount owed was written out in large numbers, he almost swallowed his tongue. Good God!

"I know it's a lot," the other man said apologetically, noting his stunned reaction. "Believe it or not, I tried to keep the total down, but someone sure did a number on that truck for you. There was a lot of damage."

Flynn couldn't doubt his sincerity. The mechanic looked almost sick at the idea of having to present anyone a bill that resembled the national debt, but short of taking a loss on the long hours of labor involved, there was little else the man could do.

"Yeah, I know." Glancing up from the invoice, he smiled ruefully "I figured it would be a bundle, just not *that* much."

"If payment's going to be a problem, we could probably work something out—"

Already shaking his head before the words were out of Ray's mouth, Flynn said, "Thanks for the offer, but I can get it."

Because of the dangers of the road, he didn't carry a great deal of money with him, and all his credit cards were safely locked away in the desk back at the Double R. Gable and the rest of the family had assured him all he had to do was call if he ran into trouble and they'd send him whatever he needed. But he was thirty years old, dammit, too old to be calling home like a teenager who'd run out of money. When he'd gone on the circuit, he'd vowed he was going to make it on his own come hell or high water, and that was exactly what he was going to do.

"I just need to get something out of my truck," he said, making a snap decision. "Then I'll be back with your money in an hour."

Ten minutes later, he walked down the street to the historic Fort Worth Stockyards and Cattleman's Exchange. Cattle and livestock were still auctioned there, but many of the old buildings had been restored and were now home to restaurants, specialty shops that catered to the city's cowboy heritage and galleries that specialized in Western art. It was the latter he went looking for, stepping into the first one he found, the small duffel bag he carried his wood carvings in in his hand. What he knew about art could pretty much be summed up in a couple of sentences, but from what he could tell, his wood carvings would fit right in with the paintings of Native Americans and Southwest landscapes on the walls.

"May I help you?"

Expecting an artsy-fartsy snob of a clerk, he turned to find himself confronting an older woman who was dressed in a colorful broomstick skirt, white peasant blouse and flats, her only touch of elegance the real pearls at her neck. Seeing her smile and the twinkle in her eye, Flynn grinned. "I certainly hope so. In case you haven't noticed, I'm a little bit out of my league here."

"I never would have noticed," she replied graciously, extending her hand. "I'm Sydney Alexander, the owner. Is there anything in particular you're interested in looking at?"

"Actually, I'm not here to buy," Flynn confessed as he took her hand and introduced himself. Unconsciously, he tightened his grip on his duffel bag. "I probably should have made an appointment or something, or at least called, but—"

"You have something you would like to put on consignment," she guessed, smoothly cutting into his ramblings with a grin. "Let's see what you've got."

The moment of truth upon him, Flynn hesitated. He'd sold his carvings before, but never to anyone but friends and family and fans on the circuit. And they were biased. What if they'd just raved over his work to spare his feelings? What if he really wasn't any good and just thought he was? Was he about to make a fool of himself in front of a total stranger?

He almost backed out then and there, but the gallery owner was already reaching for his duffel bag and tugging it open. Bracing himself, he watched her pull out a carving of a bull rider clinging to an angry Charolais bull who seemed to be trying his damnedest to dislodge the cowboy from his back.

In the few silent moments Sydney Alexander stood as if turned to stone and stared at the smoothly sanded sculpture, Flynn learned what it meant to measure time in eternities rather than seconds. Tension curled into his gut. "You don't like it," he said flatly.

Startled, she looked up at him as if he were out of his mind. "Not like it! Are you cra—"

"Oh, how gorgeous! May I see it?"

Without waiting for an answer, a richly dressed woman who had been looking at the sculptures tastefully displayed throughout the gallery snatched the carving from Sydney Alexander's hands and fairly squealed, "Isn't it absolutely beautiful! Why, I can practically feel the power in the bull. My husband will love it. How much is it?"

She looked up, her gaze bouncing from the gallery owner to Flynn, then back again. Flynn, caught flat-footed by the sudden turn of events, opened his mouth, but before he could he come up with the usual twenty dollars he charged, Sydney Alexander named a price that he almost choked on. Horrified that she had lost him a sale, he was about to tell the potential customer that the real price was actually a fraction of what Sydney had quoted her, but he never got the chance.

Beaming, the woman held the carving to her as if she'd just stumbled across a long-lost child. "I'll take it," she said promptly, without batting an eye. "You do take American Express, don't you?"

Sydney smiled like a cat who had swallowed a bird cage full of canaries. "We certainly do. Come with me, and I'll wrap that for you. You wouldn't want anything to happen to it on the way home."

Stunned, Flynn watched the two women cross to the French provincial desk discreetly positioned at the far end of the room. He had to be dreaming, he thought dazedly. His whittling was just a hobby, something he did to pass the time and always felt guilty taking money for. He was usually satisfied with the finished product, but he never would have considered it art. And he'd never have dreamed of selling it for the small fortune Sydney Alexander just had.

"Thank you, Mrs. Winters," Sydney told the woman again as she left with *his* sculpture. "I'll let you know as soon as we get any new pieces in." Her mouth twitching with amusement, she waited only until the bell over the door signaled that the woman had left. Then she turned back to Flynn. Lifting a delicately arched brow at him, she teased, ''Do you still need to ask if I like it?''

By the time he returned to the garage a short time later to pay his bill and make arrangements to leave his truck there until one of his brothers could come for it, he was in a numbed state of shock. He had money in his pocket, and there was more where that came from. A lot more, if Sydney Alexander was to be believed.

And if anyone should know art, it was Sydney. She had galleries in Aspen, Tahoe and Santa Fe, and was considering expanding into San Antonio, New Orleans and Key West. Raving over the other pieces he'd had in the duffel bag, she'd accepted all of them on consignment, then wanted more. If her predictions came true, he would be the next big rage in Western art.

Dazed, Flynn returned to Tate's pickup feeling as if he'd just fallen down the rabbit hole in *Alice in Wonderland*.

Sitting behind the wheel, Tate had seen him head for the Stockyards with the duffel bag that he kept his carvings in. The Stockyards, where there were places to eat, shops to see…galleries. One look at his face as he climbed into her truck, with a now-empty duffel bag, and she knew what he'd done.

She shouldn't have been surprised…or bothered. The carvings were his and he could do whatever he wanted with them. But something cringed deep inside her at the idea of people who didn't know a thing about him buying something he'd put his time and heart into, buying a piece of *him*. After all, it wasn't as if he needed the money.

Oh, he'd had a run of costly bad luck lately, she silently admitted to herself, the kind that would have probably sent anyone else into a panic. But he was one of the New Mexican Rawlingses, and according to rumor, they—

and Flynn—were rolling in it. Unexpected expenses that would have knocked the legs out from under the rest of the cowboys on the circuit wouldn't even faze Flynn.

So what was going on? She was dying to ask, but it was his business, and if he didn't want to tell her about it, that was his choice. However, convincing Haily of that, who was sitting impatiently at her side, just waiting to ask him what he'd been up to, wasn't going to be nearly as easy.

Seeing the question forming on her daughter's tongue, she said quickly, "Now that that's all taken care of, why don't we go get a hamburger and find a park somewhere? Getting out of the truck for a while will do us all some good."

Distracted, Haily said, "Oh, good. I'm starving! Can we go to McDonald's, Mom? I'm sure I saw one right around the corner."

Not surprised by the request, Tate laughed. They couldn't go within a mile of a McDonald's without Haily spying the golden arches. "I guess so... if Flynn doesn't mind. He might not like McDonald's."

Horrified at the thought, Haily glanced up at Flynn as if her mother had just suggested he'd rather have spinach. "Hey, not me," he laughed. "You won't see me ever turn down a Big Mac. We'll get the works—my treat."

"All right!" Thrilled, her mind already working on what she would get to eat, Haily immediately forgot all about seeing Flynn walk out of the garage with his duffel bag in his hand.

Tate, however, wasn't so easily distracted. All during the impromptu picnic at the park they'd finally found, she kept seeing Flynn's face as he'd headed toward the galleries down the street from the garage. His jaw had been set determinedly, his usually laughing eyes dead serious. He may have sold his carvings, but he hadn't seemed all that eager to do it. And that worried her.

Chewing over all the possibilities of why he would have done such a thing, she kept coming back to the certainty that he had to. Which made no sense. Finally, unable to stand it another minute, she waited only until Haily had raced over to the playground equipment to swing before she blurted out, "Dammit, Flynn, why did you sell your carvings? And don't try to tell me you didn't. I saw you!"

Chapter 10

"Because I needed the money," he said simply. "The truck repairs were more than I'd expected."

Her eyes searching his, Tate frowned in confusion. It was a logical explanation—for someone like her, who'd never had an emergency fund in her life because there was never anything left over to put in one after the bills were paid. But Flynn Rawlings shouldn't have had that problem. "I don't understand. I thought you were—"

"Rich?" he supplied with a smile when she suddenly realized what she was about to say and hesitated. "Actually, we have more land than money, but we're doing all right...especially since we diversified last year and don't have all our money in just cattle."

"Then why didn't you call your family for the money? Surely they would have sent it."

"In a heartbeat," he agreed, grinning. "But then I would have had to explain about Grady, and there's no way in hell my brothers would have let me take care of the bastard in my own way. They'd have been fighting mad and up here so fast, Grady wouldn't have known what hit him." His eyes rueful, he admitted, "We have a tendency to be protective of each other, even when we don't want to be protected, so sometimes it's just better to keep certain information to yourself."

Tate watched the angles and planes of his face soften at the mention of his family, saw his smile light with affection and wished, not for the first time, that she'd been lucky enough to have brothers and sisters. She knew siblings fought sometimes, but they also had each other to depend on and were usually there for each other through thick or thin. And that was something she'd missed.

Her eyes drifting to where her daughter played on the swings, she felt regret squeeze her heart that Haily, too, would grow up alone, with no one to fight with, to play and laugh with. But some things were meant to be. Whatever chance she and Haily had had of having a Norman Rockwell all-American family had died the day Rich Travis walked out on them both.

Turning her attention back to Flynn, she said, "But if you all are that close, surely they'd want to know that you were low on funds and in trouble. If the situation was reversed, and you were at home and one of your brothers or sister was out on the road, wouldn't you want them to call home for help?"

"Yes, but this is different."

"Why?"

"Because I made a deal with them before I went out on the circuit," he admitted reluctantly. "The family put up my original stake money, and after that, I was on my own. I would either make it or go bust without their help."

His words hit Tate like a slap in the face. How many times had she raked him over the coals for playing at rodeoing like a spoiled little rich boy while the rest of the cowboys were busting their butts just to get by? She'd been scathing in her contempt of his use of his family's money, and all the time, he'd been scrimping and saving and supporting himself just like the rest of them. And he'd never once defended himself, never once said anything to change her opinion of him. He knew she thought he was nothing but an irresponsible, woman-chasing thrill seeker just looking for a good time, and he'd never said a word.

"Oh, God," she whispered, mortified, lifting stricken eyes to his. "I'm sorry. I didn't realize . . . I never should have said . . . God, I must have sounded like a sanctimonious fool—"

Swearing, Flynn cut her off, reaching across the picnic table for her hand. "You did not," he said gruffly. "Anyway, you didn't think anything that everyone else wasn't already thinking, so don't beat yourself up over this. You didn't know my finances— No one did."

With his hand holding hers, it would have been so easy to let him take the blame for her own poor conduct. But she couldn't. She'd misjudged him from the very beginning because that smile of his had gone straight to her heart and scared the hell out of her. And now, one by one, he was knocking down her defenses, leaving her nothing to hide behind, forcing her to face the emotions he stirred in her whether she wanted to or not.

Agitated, needing to think, she tugged free of his hold and jumped up, grabbing up the litter from their lunch. "Break time's over," she said briskly, avoiding his eyes. "We need to get back on the road. We're going to be driving all night as it is."

"Honey—"

"Haily, time to go!" she called, turning away to put the trash in the nearby garbage can. "It's getting late."

Cursing, Flynn started to haul her back down next to him and refuse to go anywhere until they talked this out. But Haily was already running toward them, and any chance of a private discussion was lost. Swearing under his breath, he headed for the truck.

The drive to the Double R in southwestern New Mexico was interminable. Because of Flynn's injured ribs, Tate drove the whole way, which was a blessing in disguise. With her eyes on the road, she didn't have to look at Flynn, and could even try to pretend when the silence stretched for miles at a time that it was just her and Haily on the road together, just like always.

But then he would shift in his seat, curse the pain that flared to life every time he moved too fast, and the awareness she couldn't deny for long was back, stronger than ever. Tightening her hands on the wheel, she forced herself to stare straight ahead and fought the panic rising in her, mile after mile after mile.

By the time they arrived at the Double R, it was close to three in the morning. Tired to the point of exhaustion, Tate followed Flynn's directions and drove through the simple, unassuming ranch entrance. This was it, she thought, blinking back the sudden hot tears that stung her eyes. The end of the road. The end of their time together. She'd been trying to shake free of him for longer than she cared to remember and now she finally had a chance to put some distance between them. She would leave him with his family to recuperate, and she would head for home, where she would stay until Sugar was rested and ready to compete again.

And when she hit the road again, she'd make sure that there were no more chance meetings with him up and down the interstate. He tended to stay in the southwest, roaming states that weren't all that far from his home, so she'd just have to go somewhere different—like up north to Wyoming or Montana, or maybe even the South— anywhere that was a long ways away from that roguish smile of his.

The decision made, she should have been relieved. She'd had a hard enough time resisting him when she'd thought he was nothing but a well-heeled rancher's son looking for a good time. But now that she knew there was so much more to him than that, he was even more dangerous. Because he was still a flirt, still a fun-loving cowboy who wasn't the least bit interested in commitment. She wanted him, ached for him, but there was no room in her life for such a man.

Pain a lead weight in her heart, it was several long moments before she realized that they'd left the ranch entrance far behind and there still wasn't a sign of a house anywhere in sight. Scanning the darkened desert surrounding them, she said huskily, "Is the house in this county or the next?"

"It's right over this rise. The barn's just beyond the house, so stop there first and we'll unload Sugar before going up to the house."

"Going up to the house?" she echoed, startled, as the Victorian homestead that had been the center of the Double R for generations came into view. "Oh, but we're not staying!" They couldn't! "We'll just drop you off and go find a campground somewhere."

"The hell you will!" he exploded, only to suddenly remember Haily's sleeping figure between them. Swearing under his breath, he struggled to lower his voice. "Dammit, Tate, it's late and I know you have to be tired. The nearest campground's at least forty miles away. Do you really want to drive all that way when you and Haily can stay here and sleep in a real bed for a change?''

He held the invitation out to her so temptingly, it was all she could do not to jump at it. He didn't know what he was asking of her, she thought, swallowing a sob as she braked to a stop in front of the barn. She couldn't stay here. She couldn't meet his family, couldn't take the chance that she might like them, couldn't take the chance that when she left here, she'd leave all of her heart behind, instead of just the chunks he'd already claimed.

"But we can't just walk in on your family in the middle of the night," she began desperately.

"Why not?" he retorted with maddening logic. "I am."

"But this is your home," she reminded him, searching her brain for excuses. "You're family— Haily and I aren't."

But it was too late. Someone in the house must have heard them drive up. A light came on upstairs, then downstairs. Flynn, seeing the back door open, grinned as his oldest brother stepped outside and frowned at the sight of the unfamiliar truck and trailer parked in front of the barn. "You might as well stay now," he said, glancing back at Tate as he pushed open the passenger door. "Everyone's awake, anyway." And without giving her a chance to object further, he went to meet his brother.

"It's just me," he called, striding out of the darkness into the light supplied by the floodlights his brother had turned on before stepping outside. "The prodigal's come home."

"And a little the worse for wear, I see," Gable retorted, frowning in concern as he watched the careful way Flynn was moving. "You all right?"

"Well, that depends on which part of my body you're asking about." Flynn chuckled, then paid the price for it. Sucking in a sharp breath, he wrapped his arms around his ribs. "A couple of my ribs are a little the worse for wear from a run-in with a metal railing, but the rest of me's fine."

His sister, Kat, stepping out onto the porch in time to hear his last few words, snorted, the corners of her mouth curling up into a quick smile that was a carbon copy of her youngest brother's. "You should have landed on your head, then you would have been fine."

Flynn, not fooled by the cutdown, only grinned up at her from the bottom step. "Nice to see you, too, brat. I see that tongue of yours is sharper than ever."

"You better believe it." Her smile dying as she saw how pale he was, she asked worriedly, "Are you sure you're okay? You look like you haven't got the energy to take another step."

Before he could assure her he just needed a couple of hours of sleep, Josey called from inside the house, "Gable? Kat? Who is it? Somebody in need of a doctor?"

"Just your crazy youngest brother-in-law, sweetheart," Gable told her as she rushed out onto the back porch. "Evidently rodeoing's not what it's cracked up to be."

Flynn groaned, trying to hold back a laugh. "Dammit, Gable, don't make me laugh. It hurts bad enough as it is."

"Oh my God, he *is* hurt," Josey said in alarm. The doctor in her never far from the surface, she hurried down the porch steps with Kat right on her heels. "What have you done to yourself this time? Come inside and let me take a look at you."

"Wait," he said as both women started to slip an arm around him and help him up the stairs. "There's someone in the truck I want you to meet. Come on."

Watching his family hover protectively around Flynn, then start off across the yard to where she waited in the truck with Haily, Tate finally had her excuses all ready. She would politely, but firmly, turn down any invitation they issued and explain that she planned to leave at dawn for home. She'd already disturbed their sleep once; she couldn't possibly do it a second time. Anyway, she was just here to drop Flynn off. She'd never planned to stay.

Tate forced a smile as Flynn opened the driver's door to introduce her to his brother Gable and Gable's wife, Josey, and his sister, Kat. The words were lined up on Tate's tongue like ducks in a row but she never got to say her piece. The minute she alighted from the truck, Josey gave her a warm smile and took over with a graciousness that wouldn't be denied.

"You must be exhausted, driving all this way," she said sympathetically. "Come on inside while the men take care of your horse, and I'll show you to the guest room. The bed's already got clean sheets on it. All I have to do is turn them back for you. And in the morning, you can sleep as late as you like—"

"Oh, but I couldn't," Tate began. But Gable and Flynn, ignoring her objections, were already moving to the horse trailer to unload Sugar.

"I don't know why not," Kat retorted easily. "We've got plenty of room."

Josey nodded. "That's right. The house is huge, though it feels pretty empty at times now that Cooper's married and living next door at Susannah's and Flynn's off rodeoing. When Kat goes back to school in the fall, it'll just be me and Gable and the baby rambling around in this big old place. And Alice, of course," she added, smiling. "She's the housekeeper, and I don't know what we'd do without her sometimes, especially when the flu is going around and I'm swamped with work."

Seeing the look of confusion on Tate's face, Kat explained, "Josey's a doctor—the only one for forty miles...so sometimes things are pretty hectic around here. Do you need to get anything from your camper for the night?"

Exhausted by the long, emotionally draining day and dazed by the two women's friendliness to a total stranger, Tate blinked at the sudden change in subject. "No. I mean, yes! My daughter!" Lord, how could she have forgotten Haily? And when had she agreed to stay?

Josey's face softened with surprise. "You have a daughter? So do I. Poor thing, I bet she's out on her feet, isn't she? She probably crashed hours ago. Let's get her inside." Moving back to the pickup as if there wasn't a doubt in her mind that they were staying, she said, "Since she's asleep, we better put her in your room. We wouldn't want her to wake up during the middle of the night and get scared in a strange house."

"No...please..." Rubbing at her throbbing temples, Tate tried one last time to regain control of the situation. "I appreciate the invitation. Really, I do. But Haily and I couldn't possibly impose. You weren't expecting guests tonight."

"Sure we were," Gable said as he and Flynn came out of the barn after stabling Sugar. "We always keep a couple of rooms ready in case a patient shows up in the middle of the night too sick to drive home."

"And since you went out of your way to bring Flynn home when he was hurt, the least we can do is offer you a bed for the night," Josey added. "Please don't say no."

Tate hesitated, but she knew she'd just lost. How could she deny them the chance to repay her even though she didn't want to be repaid? "Okay, we'll stay," she said, sighing in defeat. "But we have to leave first thing in the morning."

Tate figured that spending what was left of the night at the Double R would be as easy as carrying Haily to bed, then crawling between the sheets next to her and crashing till dawn. She was so tired, she'd zonk out the minute her head hit the pillow.

But fifteen minutes later, she lay flat on her back on the bed and stared up at the ceiling in the dark, wide-awake. She never should have agreed to stay. She was already dangerously tempted by Flynn Rawlings, the rookie bareback rider who liked to flirt. The Flynn Rawlings who owned and worked the Double R with his family was something else altogether.

The youngest boy of four children all named after their mother's favorite movie stars of the forties, he was as rich as she'd feared, though one would never have known it from the way he and his family acted. No one put on any uppity airs, least of all Flynn. At home and relaxed in a way she had never seen before, he laughed and joked with his family, the teasing that jumped back and forth between them warm with affection.

Watching them, envying them, Tate had found herself picturing Flynn as a little boy, pulling practical jokes and no doubt drawing laughter from his brothers and sister even when they wanted to kill him. Now, alone in her room, she was forced to admit to herself that she liked the scamp he must have been...and the man he had become.

Out in the hall, she heard Flynn and the rest of the family come upstairs and whisper good-nights to each other, then the sound of booted feet passing by her door. Her heart stumbled. She didn't have to see the face that went along with those feet to know that it was Flynn. His room was two doors down from hers.

It took her hours to forget that long enough to go to sleep.

Dawn came early in the desert in the summer, but well before the first rays of the sun peaked over the horizon, Tate groaned and forced herself to get up. The need to flee urging her on, she hoped to get Sugar loaded in the horse trailer before Flynn and the rest of the family knew what she was up to. Feeling around in the dark, she hurriedly pulled on her jeans and a scooped-neck red T-shirt. Seconds later, she left Haily sleeping in the bed and quietly made her way down the stairs to slip outside to the barn.

At the first sound of her footsteps, Sugar lifted her head over the stall door and whinnied a greeting. "Well, good morning, sweetie." She laughed softly, hurrying over to the stall. "How're you feeling? I bet you're ready to go home, aren't you?"

"I already am home, honey," Flynn said from inside the stall. Grinning at her gasp of surprise, he nudged Sugar over and joined the horse at the stall door. Propping his arms on it, he laughed down into her eyes. "And good morning to you, too. Since you asked, I'm feeling better. Just don't ask me to move too fast. How about you?"

Caught in the trap of his amused gaze, Tate couldn't manage to squeeze a single word through her tight throat.

In the early-morning light that was just pushing aside the darkness of the night, he looked as if he had just crawled out of one of her fantasies. His blue eyes sparkling with mischief and his jaw rough with a night's growth of beard, he was the sexiest thing she had ever seen.

She swallowed and tried to force a frown, but the flash of Flynn's dimples made that impossible. "I was speaking to Sugar," she retorted.

"You can call me sugar anytime you want to, honey. I don't mind at all."

"The horse," she huffed, her lips twitching traitorously. "I was speaking to the horse."

He only clicked his tongue at her, his eyes dancing. "Obviously you didn't get enough sleep last night if you're going around talking to horses. What's the matter? Did you spend the night dreaming of me?"

The teasing taunt struck a little too close to home, and it was all Tate could do to hang on to her smile. Heat climbing in her cheeks, she reached out suddenly to pat him lightly, teasingly on his granite jaw. "In your dreams, sweetheart. In your dreams. Now move, please, so I can get Sugar out of there and into her trailer. Haily and I have a long way to go today."

He didn't budge. His eyes suddenly turning serious, he said quietly, "I know you want to get home, but I think you're going to have to change your plans. The drive yesterday in the trailer didn't help Sugar's injury. If anything, it made it worse. The last thing she needs is another long ride today."

"Oh, no!"

"It's a twelve-hour drive to your dad's place," he continued as she pulled open the stall door and dropped to her knees in front of the mare. Even in the poor light, it was obvious that Sugar's right front leg was hot and swollen. "Do you really want to put Sugar through that? Considering the shape she's already in, it could prolong the time it takes her to heal."

Tate knew he spoke nothing less than the truth, but what choice did she have? She couldn't stay here!

As if he could read her mind, Flynn took her arm and pulled her to her feet. "Stay here," he suggested. "We've got plenty of room for you and Haily *and* Sugar. She can heal here just as well as she can at your dad's place, and it won't take her nearly as long to recover because she won't have to suffer through another long drive."

Standing only inches away from him, the closeness setting her pulse skipping, Tate tried not to listen. Every instinct she possessed screamed for her to get out of there, away from the Double R, away from him, before it was too late and she completely lost her heart to him. But he was right—the drive yesterday had aggravated Sugar's injury; another one could keep the mare off the road for much longer than a couple of weeks. And when Sugar didn't race and earn money, neither did she.

Stay, her heart whispered in her ear, tempting her. *This is the only time you will have with him. What harm can it do?*

What, indeed, she thought cynically, but it was too late. Her heart had made the decision for her, damn the consequences. "We'll stay," she agreed. "But only until the swelling has gone down and it's safe for Sugar to travel again."

The two or three days that Tate had planned to spend at the Double R stretched into four, then five, slipping away before she could get a handle on them. Surrounded by Flynn's welcoming family and secluded from the rest of the world, it was easy to forget about rodeoing and a college fund that was alarmingly low. Tomorrow seemed like it would never come, let alone fall and her last semester of college before medical school.

Whenever her conscience reminded her that she really was taking advantage of the Rawlingses' hospitality, she resolved to leave the next day. Sugar was much better, and if they took the trip home in stages instead of trying to make it all in one day, the horse would be fine. But every time she brought up the subject of leaving, Kat, Josey and Susannah, Cooper's wife, would press her to stay a little longer, and she had a hard time coming up with a reason not to. Her father was taking his blood-pressure medicine on a regular basis now that Maggie Donovan was at the farm to watch over him, so there was no reason to rush home on his account. And Haily was having the time of her life. The ranch hands, more than willing to spoil her rotten, took her all over the ranch, just as they had Kat years ago when she was the same age, and taught her how to be a cowgirl. As far as Haily was concerned, they could stay forever.

And Tate, no longer able to run from the truth, was forced to admit to herself that she, too, wanted to stay... days, weeks, years. Because of Flynn.

Shaken, panic backing up in her throat, she tried to tell herself that nothing had changed. He was the same Flynn Rawlings who had flirted outrageously with her at rodeos all over the Southwest. The same Flynn Rawlings whom she had thought was just like Rich Travis—charming, boyishly mischievous, with a quick smile and equally quick line when it came to women. The same Flynn Rawlings who was totally committed to being *un*committed.

But he wasn't. With his admission that he lived on what he earned rodeoing, she'd known she'd misjudged him.

But even then, she'd thought that as one of the Rawl-ingses of New Mexico, he—and his family—would enjoy the life-style that owning a cattle operation the size of the Double R could give them. She'd expected them to leave the actual work, the day-to-day-down-in-the-dirt grind, to the ranch hands.

Nothing could have been farther from the truth.

Flynn and his brothers asked nothing of the Double R cowboys that they weren't willing to do themselves. Every morning, they were up at dawn for a quick breakfast, then outside, getting an early start on the day's work before the real heat set in. And there was plenty to do. The cattle operation alone was huge, with the herd spread out over much of the Double R and the connecting Patterson Ranch next door, which Cooper's wife, Susannah, had leased to the family before she and Cooper married. And then there were the acres of peppers to be tended, a farm-ing experiment the family had undertaken last year as a means of diversification that was, according to Kat, go-ing to pay off better than any of them had dared to hope.

The days were long, hot, the burning sun fierce and unrelenting. In spite of the fact that Flynn had been gone for months on the circuit, he picked up right where he'd left off, throwing himself into the work without having to ask, let alone be told, what to do. His ribs were still hurt-ing and the whole family insisted he take it easy, but when he came in at the end of the day, he was as hot and sweaty and dirty as his brothers and ranch hands.

Watching him day after day, seeing him laugh and work with his family, Tate tried to hold on to the protective barriers she'd built around her heart. Then late one af-ternoon, a week and a half after they'd arrived at the ranch, Flynn walked into the kitchen, a grin tugging at his mouth as he and Cooper laughed over their encounter with a mama cow who didn't want them anywhere near her newest calf. Tate, who was helping Alice with supper by setting the table, glanced up, her eyes snagging on his crooked smile, and the truth she had been avoiding for weeks reached out and grabbed her by the heart.

She loved him.

Her fingers tightened on the plates she'd been distributing around the big round table, and she froze, stricken. Dear God, how? she wanted to cry. How could this have happened? How had she *let* it happen? It wasn't as if she were seventeen again, too eager to experience life to know what she was inviting. She'd learned the hard way that a woman who made the mistake of falling for a flirt could expect nothing but heartache.

And Flynn was and always would be a flirt. It came as naturally to him as breathing, and he'd even admitted that he was amusing himself with her because she hadn't fallen at his feet the way the other girls on the rodeo circuit had. She was a challenge to him, nothing more.

So what had she done? She'd turned around and fallen in love with him.

Panic seizing her, she started to bolt, but the rest of the family came in then, and the moment was lost. The men, still in their chaps and boots, headed to the various bathrooms to wash up, while the women helped Alice dish up the food and set it on the table. Cooper and Susannah usually ate at their own home every night, but tonight the family needed to discuss the Fourth of July bash they threw for all their neighbors every year, so Susannah had driven over to join them. Within minutes of sitting down at the table and saying grace, they were all talking at once about the work still left to be done, then laughing over unexpected surprises that had made some Fourths more memorable than others.

They were, Tate realized, planning a real old-fashioned, rip-roaring Fourth of July, complete with barbecue, homemade ice cream, a barn dance and fireworks. Under other circumstances, she would have been thrilled at the thought of being involved in such a big party. But all she could think of was that she wasn't going to enjoy it. As soon as it was over and Haily had seen the fireworks Tate knew she was dying to see, they were leaving.

Seated next to her, Flynn studied her shuttered face and asked quietly, "What's the matter? Don't you like fireworks?"

Startled, she glanced up and found him frowning down at her in concern. For a wild, heart-stopping moment, she thought he had read her mind; then his words registered. "Yes, of course... when they're not handled carelessly."

"Don't worry. We don't mess with them ourselves." His lips twitched into a grin. "Knowing our luck, we'd probably burn the place down. That's why we get a pyrotechnic expert from El Paso to shoot them off for us every year. So you don't have to worry about Haily getting hurt or anything."

"I wasn't."

"Then what's wrong? And don't tell me you're fine," he retorted quickly before she could shrug off his concern. His voice pitched low so it wouldn't carry to the rest of the family, he said, "You haven't said two words since we sat down to eat, and I want to know why. It's not like you to be so quiet."

Not surprised that he had noticed—she'd felt him watching her for what seemed like hours—Tate prayed he couldn't see the pain she knew was clouding her eyes. "I guess I'm just tired," she said with a shrug. "Alice has already started making some of the ice cream for the party and I've been helping her."

It was a logical explanation, but Flynn wasn't buying it. She'd been avoiding his gaze ever since he'd come in earlier with Cooper, and a clenching in his gut told him something was wrong. But he hadn't had two seconds alone with her in days, and that wasn't likely to change now that the preparations for the holiday were shifting into full swing. Frowning, half tempted to drag her outside with him so they could talk in private, he promised himself he'd find a way to get her alone later in the evening.

But he didn't. Not that night or anytime over the course of the next three days. If Flynn hadn't known better, he would have sworn she was avoiding him. Every time he thought he finally had her all to himself for a moment or two, someone or something interrupted them and it was hours before he so much as laid eyes on her again.

By the time the Fourth rolled around, he was ready to spit nails. He'd caught glimpses of Tate all day long, but she was always just out of his reach, helping the other women, watching Haily to make sure she didn't get caught up in the mischief generated by some of the neighbors' rowdy kids, talking with some of the guests. She never seemed to stay anywhere for long, and then, before he knew it, it was dark. The fireworks were about to begin and would be followed by the dance, and Tate was nowhere in sight. Concerned, he went looking for her.

He found Haily first, sitting with the rest of the kids who were impatiently waiting for the first Roman candle to streak into the night sky and burst into color. Pulling her aside for a moment, he asked, "Do you know where your mom is, sunshine? I've been looking for her everywhere."

Her eyes on where the fireworks were set up, she said absently, "Oh, she's cleaning up the camper so we can leave in the morning."

Flynn couldn't have been more surprised if she'd hauled off and kicked him in the shin. "You're leaving?"

"Mmm-hmm. Mom says Sugar's all better, so we need to get back to rodeoing before we lose any more time. When are the fireworks going to start? We've been waiting *forever!*"

Fury flashing in his eyes, he gave her a hug and sent her back to the kids she'd been sitting with. "Any second now, sweetheart," he said through his teeth. "Any second now."

He was, he promised himself as he made his way to where the camper was parked next to the barn, going to kill her. All this time she'd been planning on leaving, and she hadn't said a word. Of all the sneaky, underhanded, yellow-bellied . . .

It wasn't until he saw the lighted windows of the camper that he realized how much he'd been hoping Haily was mistaken. But since Tate was the only one who had a key to the rig and the lights were on, she was obviously in there, just as her daughter had said. Hurt battling outrage for dominance, he jerked open the camper door without bothering to knock and slammed it shut behind him as he stepped inside.

"Flynn!" Caught in the act of making Haily's bed, Tate straightened at the sight of him, guilt rising in a hot tide up her neck to her cheeks. "What are you doing here? I—"

"Don't bother to come up with a quick excuse," he said flatly. "I know exactly what you're up to. I spoke to Haily."

"Then you know we're leaving in the morning."

If she'd said it with some degree of regret in her voice, he might have managed to hang on to his temper, but she was so cool, so in control, that something in him just snapped. Muttering a curse, he reached for her. "Then we have tonight."

Too angry to think straight, he'd meant to just kiss her. But the second he tugged her into his arms, he knew he wasn't going to be able to let her go. Not this time. Groaning her name, he crushed his mouth to hers.

Somewhere in the rapidly sinking depths of her reason, Tate figured that he would let her up for air when his anger ran out and he was thinking more clearly. Wrapped close by the steel bands of his arms, she could feel the rage, the heat, seething in him. And though she knew he would never physically hurt her, she wasn't foolish enough to antagonize a man who had already been pushed to the limits of his control. All she had to do was wait him out and he would let her go.

It was a logical deduction, but somewhere in the thinking of it and the execution, his last words slipped into her consciousness to tease and tempt her. *We have tonight.* It was all they would ever have. And if she didn't take it, she knew she would regret it for the rest of her life.

Lost in the fury and need that burned in his gut like a red-hot coal, it was several long, hazy minutes before Flynn realized that she wasn't standing stiff as a board in his arms, but melting against him, her arms clinging to him, her mouth hot and sweet and hungry under his.

For just an instant, sanity returned and his head cleared. The lady had already proven she wanted nothing to do with him—she'd been planning to leave without a word, for God's sake! Where was his pride? He should let her go and get the hell out of there. Now!

But as his hands were reaching for hers to pull her arms from around his neck, she was standing on tiptoe to press her mouth to his. Groaning, Flynn tried—he really tried—to make her see reason. "Honey, this isn't what you want—"

"Yes, it is," she murmured huskily. "I want you."

"But you're leaving."

"You said we have tonight," she reminded him, gently nipping his lower lip. When he stiffened as though she'd just shot a bolt of electricity through him, she laughed softly. But when she pulled back far enough to look him in the eye, her own were dark with need. "Everyone else is watching the fireworks. No one will bother us—"

Outside, a sudden boom, then a gasp of appreciation from the crowd, supported her claim. Without a word, Flynn reached behind him and locked the door.

Chapter 11

Before the next Roman candle exploded in the sky, he had the lights off and was reaching for her again, his mouth finding hers in the sudden darkness as his hands fumbled with the buttons of her blouse. Her fingers climbing his shoulders, she turned boneless and pliant in his arms.

"The bed," she murmured, breathless, when he finally lifted his head a fraction.

But he only laughed softly and changed the angle of the kiss. "We'll get there, sweetheart. I promise."

Her heart thumping, she tried to explain that the bed over the cab was much larger than the one he was nudging her toward, but then he had her blouse off and his fingers found the front snap of her bra. In the blink of an eye, she was naked from the waist up and her breasts were spilling into his waiting palms.

Whimpering, she leaned into him and buried her face against his shoulder. Sweetness. She hadn't expected sweetness from him. But he held her as if he'd never touched a woman before, as if her softness fascinated him, as if she were fragile, delicate, infinitely precious. Touched in a way she'd never been before, she wanted to cling to him, to rush the moment before it was somehow inexplicably snatched from her, but his hands were slow, his kisses lazy and thorough. Aching for more, she strained against him.

"Easy, sweetheart," he murmured, trailing his lips over her face to press teasing kisses to the curve of her cheeks, her eyes, the shell of her ear. "There's no hurry. We have hours."

"But someone might come—"

"No one would dare," he growled, nipping at the lobe of her ear. "Everyone's watching the fireworks."

But there were fireworks, and then there were *fireworks*. As he stripped away the last of her clothes, then shed his own, the explosives were suddenly in the camper. He pressed her down into the cool sheets of the small bed that Haily normally slept in, every hard inch of him sliding against her softness. As quickly as if someone had flipped a switch, the air turned hot and starry and magical. Watching her, his eyes midnight blue and wanting in the darkness, he stroked his hands over her, slow and easy and seducing, and she could only moan, shuddering.

Too long, she thought, dazed. It had been too long since a man had held her, loved her. Years, a lifetime ago. And even then it hadn't been like this. No one, not even Rich Travis, had ever been able to move her so easily. Wherever Flynn touched her, she melted, pleasure dribbling through her like hot candle wax, burning her all the way to her soul.

Need clawing at him, Flynn struggled for control, the effort to go slow almost more than he could bear. It seemed as though he had wanted her forever, and all he could think about was taking her fiercely, hotly, until they were both weak with pleasure and so sated they could hardly move. But this was Tate, his conscious reminded him sternly, a woman who had been so hurt by Haily's father that she hadn't let another man come anywhere near her since. Until now.

Emotion clutching his heart, he promised himself that he would do whatever it took to make this good for her. But she was so sweet, so damned responsive, he felt like a teenager about to explode in the back seat of a car with his first woman. She made him ache!

Ignoring the small confines of the bed, he shifted over her, taking painstaking care with her, his every thought focused just on her while the blood pooled and heated in his loins. Soft. Her skin was as soft as silk under his hands, his mouth, the thundering of her pulse hot and wild under his tongue. Then he captured a breast in his palm and rubbed his thumb with agonizing slowness across her sensitive nipple, and she gasped, his name a fractured cry on her lips.

It was enough to almost drive him over the edge. But not yet, he told himself, dragging a calming breath into his straining lungs. They'd only just begun and there was so much more pleasure he wanted to give her. Ignoring the throbbing in his loins that screamed at him to hurry, he moved lower.

Shuddering, she groaned, wanting him to rush, praying he wouldn't. Torture. She'd never dreamed that this kind of torture existed. Hot, wet kisses that burned; lazy, indolent caresses that teased; time that ceased to exist. Like a mind reader who knew all her secret yearnings, he touched her just where she needed to be touched, every stroke of those long, sure fingers of his driving her out of her mind.

And then, just when she thought she couldn't stand any more, he dipped his tongue into her belly button, followed the curve of her hip and trailed openmouthed kisses up the soft, tender skin of her inner thigh. When he continued the kiss up to the hot, wet heart of her, she cried out, startled, and bucked against him, blindly reaching for him. "Flynn!"

"I know, sweetheart," he said, murmuring praise as he slowly made his way back up her body. "I know. I'm right here."

He'd spent more nights than he cared to remember dreaming about just this moment, but not even his wildest imaginings were close to reality. From the first time he'd kissed her, he'd known she would be like a flame in his arms when they finally made love. Yet he'd never guessed that she would make him tremble.

Sweat beading his brow, he fought to steady himself, but her hands were moving over him, her mouth tasting him as she gently pushed him to his back, and the shakes he already had just got a hundred times worse. She was a toucher, a stroker, a sybarite who loved the feel of her soft, curvy body rubbing again his hard, lean one. How could he have known?

His breath tearing through his lungs, he felt the kiss she teasingly dropped at the top of his thigh and almost came undone right then and there. Her breath hot against his loins, it was all he could do not to roll her to her back and bury himself in her to the hilt.

Grinding his teeth on an oath, he dragged her back up to him for a scorching kiss. His blood roaring in his ears, he swept her under him, his breath as fast and harsh as hers as he made a place for himself between her legs.

Outside, the fireworks finale exploded like a barrage of artillery fire. With each thunderous boom, red, white and blue stardust sparkled like glitter in the night sky. The visual display was nothing compared to the fiery heat that burst into flames when Flynn filled her. Clinging to him, her hips picking up the rhythm of his, tears flooded Tate's eyes. Then Flynn was moving faster, harder, and neither of them could think at all as they suddenly tumbled over the edge and starlight shattered around them.

Up at dawn the next morning as usual, Flynn silently made his way past Tate's bedroom door, wishing he could go in and awaken her with a slow, possessive kiss. Letting her go back to the party last night had been the hardest thing he'd ever done. But they'd both been gone a long time, and if someone had come looking for them, they'd have had a hard time explaining how they watched the fireworks from inside the camper. Anyone with eyes could have seen they were lighting their own sparklers.

So they'd each gone their separate ways, though Flynn had hoped to catch up with her later on and grab a dance with her in the barn. But he'd never gotten the chance. Haily, almost asleep on her feet, had had to be taken upstairs and put to bed soon after the dancing had started, and Tate had never come back down.

Quietly making his way down the stairs, he reasoned that she'd avoided him the rest of the evening because she was tired, and probably not yet ready to face him after the intimacies they'd shared. Lord, he couldn't wait to see her, to hold her. It seemed like forever since he'd given her that long, lingering kiss right before they'd stepped out of the camper into the real world.

Picturing the moment when he got her alone again, he stepped outside, intending to get started on repairs on the windmill in the south pasture before it got too hot. But he'd hardly started down the steps of the back porch when he stopped in his tracks. Tate, already up, was hooking Sugar's horse trailer up to the camper.

She was leaving.

The thought hit him like a flaming arrow, right in the heart. Sucking in a sharp breath, he could only stare at her, telling himself that the emotion raging through him wasn't hurt, but fury. For a moment there last night, he'd have sworn they set the world spinning on its axis. She'd felt it, too— He knew she had. But it obviously hadn't meant a damn thing to her.

Fighting the urge to grab her and shake her the minute he got close enough to touch her, he shoved his thumbs into the front pockets of his jeans before he could give in to temptation. "So you're still leaving," he said coldly. "Were you even going to bother to tell me or were you just going to grab Haily and cut out without saying goodbye?"

Her back to him, Tate stiffened, her hands trembling as she finished hooking up the trailer before turning to face him. For most of the night, she'd lain awake, preparing herself for the confrontation she knew was sure to come once Flynn realized she was still leaving. She'd thought she was ready for it, but nothing could have prepared her for the hurt blazing in his eyes.

Wincing, her throat tight, she said, "You know I wouldn't leave without a word—"

"Do I?" he taunted. "I'm beginning to think I don't know you at all."

"Don't say that."

Her stricken tone sliced at him, but then his eyes fell on the trailer again, all hooked up and ready to go, and his jaw hardened to granite. How dare she act the injured party here! "You're running," he accused harshly. "Because of last night."

She didn't deny it. How could she? The facts spoke for themselves. Her eyes hot with tears, she lifted her chin and met his gaze unflinchingly. "Last night shouldn't have happened. I have a child, responsibilities, a future all mapped out. I can't let you or any other cowboy make me forget that."

Something in her eyes, a flash of old, remembered pain, told him it wasn't him she was running from, but a past that still had the power to reach out and claw at her heart.

"Dammit, Tate, I'm not Rich Travis!" he growled. "And don't you dare stand there and try to tell me that's not what this is about. Do you think I can't see what's going on here? He hurt you, so now you expect every cowboy who comes along to do the same thing."

"No one's ever going to hurt me like that again," she said fiercely. "*No* one."

He wanted to reach for her then, to wrap her close and just hold her until he could make her see that she had nothing to fear from him. But instinct warned him all the talking in the world wouldn't get him anywhere with her. She already had her mind made up and the only way he was going to get through to her was to stick around long enough to prove himself to her.

"I know that, sweetheart, and if anyone tries, I'll be right there to bash their head in for you. What time are we leaving this morning?"

Startled, she stiffened. "What do you mean, *we?* Haily and I are leaving. That doesn't include you."

"Oh, yes it does." A grin curled his mouth, but his blue eyes were hard with determination. "Do you really think I'd let you go after last night? If you're ready to hit the circuit again, then so am I."

"But your ribs—"

"Are fine," he stated firmly. "They're still a little sore, but the pain's nothing I can't stand. So where are we going first?"

Her heart thumping, she struggled for a nonchalance that didn't come easily. "Haily and I are going to the Stampede. I haven't the foggiest where you're going."

He lifted a brow at her, his dimples flashing. "Calgary, huh? I'm impressed. That's where the big boys play. So how are we doing this? We can either go together in your rig and share expenses or I'll follow behind you in mine. Since Cooper went and got it for me last weekend, it's been running like a top. Take your pick. The choice is yours."

"You call that a choice? Dammit, Flynn, I don't take orders from you!"

"No, you don't," he agreed huskily, surprising her. "But last night gave me a whole lot of rights where you're concerned, honey." Eliminating the distance between them before she realized his intentions, he cupped her cheek in his palm and lightly rubbed his thumb slowly across her lower lip. Feeling her breath catch in her throat, his eyes burned down into hers. "I'm not letting you run up and down the highway in this old battered truck by yourself," he said thickly. "Especially all the way to Canada and back. So get used to seeing my face, sweetheart. I'm not letting you out of my sight."

Caught in the trap of his eyes, the feel of his thumb at her mouth melting her bones, Tate was shocked by her sudden need to give in. When had she come to need him so much? "What about Grady?" she asked hoarsely, desperately. "He's the one you need to be worrying about, not me. Last time you were lucky to escape with just a couple of broken ribs. Next time, he could really hurt you."

"Next time, he won't get the chance," he promised her. "So what's it going to be, sweetheart? Am I riding with you and Haily or following behind you?"

He was, she decided, studying him through narrowed eyes, the most persistent man she'd ever met in her life. It would serve him right if she made him eat her and Haily's dust all the way to Canada. But the layoff caused by Sugar's sprain had already cost her more than she could afford, and splitting expenses with Flynn would help her tremendously.

"We're leaving right after breakfast," she said stiffly. "So if you expect to ride with us, you'd better be ready."

Unperturbed by her less-than-gracious answer, Flynn only gave her mouth one last, slow rub with his thumb and grinned. "My bags are packed. I'm ready when you are."

But leaving turned out to be harder than Tate expected. She'd never met a famiuly quite like the Rawlingses. They'd taken her and Haily into their home like they'd known them for years and honestly seemed to hate to let them go. Once they realized they couldn't talk her out of leaving, Cooper and Gable teased Flynn unmercifully for insisting on going with her, claiming he couldn't let her out of his sight. But when it came time to actually say goodbye, all three of them were hugged and kissed by every family member, then gruffly ordered to take care of themselves before they were allowed to pile into the cab of Tate's truck and head north.

Warmed by the leave-taking, Tate let Flynn drive and tried to put things back on a friendly basis between them now that they were back on the road. Acting as if last night had never happened, she chattered about his family and the ranch, but then Haily brought up the fireworks and Tate's eyes, with a will of their own, flew to Flynn's. He didn't say a word, but he didn't have to. The air between them was suddenly charged with memories, the look he gave her hot and hungry. Her mouth as dry as dust and her heart pounding like a jackhammer, she jerked her gaze from his to stare unseeingly out the passenger window.

Four long days of driving stretched out before them. And four equally long nights. Seated between them, Haily rattled on about how much fun she'd had at the Double R, but all Tate could think about was making love with Flynn last night like she could never get enough of him. It should have ended with that— She'd sworn that it would. So how, then, had she ended up on the highway with him again, racing toward the next rodeo as if there were no tomorrow?

Tomorrow always came, she reminded herself, forcing back the hot tears that threatened to flood her eyes. And usually at a cost that was painful. She knew that and had, in fact, learned that particular lesson years ago. But none of that seemed to matter when it came to Flynn, and that was what terrified her. Grabbing this time with him could be nothing but a mistake. Weeks. They had a matter of weeks that they could take for themselves, no more. Then she would go back to her life and he would stay in his, and their paths would probably never cross again.

Her throat closed up at the thought, but it was too late to avoid the hurt. Like it or not, it was coming right at her, full speed ahead.

The Fort Worth of Canada, Calgary sat in the middle of the plains of Alberta, its Western heritage as deep as any city of the Old West. Since hosting the Winter Olympics in '88, it had acquired an international flavor, but the cowboys who gathered there in the middle of the summer didn't come for the ambience. The best in the business came from all over North America for one thing only—the Calgary Stampede. With over a hundred thousand dollars up for grabs, the competition was fierce.

Excitement sparking in the air like heat lightning, Tate, Haily and Flynn arrived at the arena less than an hour before the bareback competition was to begin. The crowd was already filing in, and behind the chutes, champions that Flynn had only read about were lining up for the Grand Entry. With the arena director throwing out orders like a drill sergeant, it was a madhouse.

And Grady Calhoun was there.

Not surprised, Flynn spied him the minute he walked through the contestants' entrance, and judging from the hard look the other man shot him, Grady wasn't any happier to see him than he was him. Which meant he would have to watch his back...and his rigging. The jerk had stabbed him in the back more than once, and only a fool would underestimate him again. Flynn was no fool.

At his side Tate stiffened, her gaze locked on Grady and his girlfriend, Valerie Jones, who were standing at the other end of the chutes. There was no question that the other man had seen them— He was staring at Flynn with such venom that Tate actually felt the stinglike touch of his narrowed eyes from over two hundred feet away. Suddenly chilled, Tate shivered, wrapping her arms around herself.

"Mom, why is Grady Calhoun looking at Flynn like that?" Haily asked, frowning, as she noted the direction of her gaze. "He looks real mad."

"Oh, that's just Grady for you, sunshine," Flynn answered for her. "He's always got a bee in his bonnet about something. Don't pay any attention to him."

Another child might have accepted that without question, but Tate knew her daughter well enough to know she'd keep asking questions until she got a more acceptable answer. "Are you hungry, honey?" she asked, digging in her jeans pocket for some money. "Why don't you go get a hot dog and find a seat in the stands? The Grand Entry's about to begin, and the bareback riding's going to start right after that. If you want to watch Flynn ride, you'd better hurry."

Since arena food was a treat on their limited budget, Haily wasn't about to turn it down. "Can I have a Coke, too?"

Chuckling, Flynn added a couple of dollars to the one Tate had already given her. "Get yourself an ice cream, too," he said, with a wink. "But don't tell your mother."

Laughing, Haily gave him a big hug. "I won't say a word," she whispered, cutting her eyes toward her mother. "See you later!"

All smiles, she was gone in a flash, while across the way, Grady still watched them with hostile eyes. The smile fading from her mouth, Tate glanced up at Flynn, unable to hide the worry tugging at her. "Maybe you should give your ribs another week of rest and skip this one," she said with a lightness that anyone could see was forced. "It's going to be a tough week, and you haven't really given yourself time to heal yet—"

"I'm not afraid of him," he told her flatly, following her gaze to Grady. "And I'm sure as hell not going to let him scare me off."

Making a strangled sound of exasperation, she glared at him. "You aren't little boys throwing rocks at each other," she began, but before she could say anything else, she looked up to see David Hartfield, bossing the chutes again, making his way through the crowd toward them.

"Well, Rawlings, I see you're back," he said with a smile as he reached them. "How're the ribs?"

"Much better," Flynn replied, shaking his hand. "In fact, I've got new rigging and I'm ready to ride."

Since he held his equipment bag in his hand, David had already figured as much. Frowning, he said, "I investigated your accident in Oklahoma like I said I would, but there's just not that much to report. No one saw anyone near your equipment bag before the competition started. And every cowboy I talked to had ironclad alibis for the time period when your rigging was left unattended. Even Calhoun. His girlfriend swears he was with her the whole time, and I don't have any witnesses to prove that he wasn't."

So there was nothing anyone could do. "Somehow I'm not surprised," Flynn said. "Grady wouldn't have pulled a stunt like that unless he'd covered all his bases. His alibi doesn't mean a damn thing."

Unable to comment one way or the other on Calhoun's guilt or innocence, David wisely held his tongue. "Just be careful, okay? Whoever cut your rigging wasn't playing around. Until he's caught, you could be in real danger."

The warning hung heavy in the air as he returned to his duties at the chutes, leaving behind a silence that seemed to echo. Suddenly afraid, Tate glanced up at Flynn, uncaring that her heart was in her eyes. "Don't do this, Flynn. It's not worth it. You heard David. Even he's afraid you're in danger."

"Then he should do something about Calhoun," he replied. "Don't worry, honey, I'll be careful—"

"How can you when you don't know where he's going to hit you next?" Her hand clamped around his forearm, she pleaded, "Don't ride. Not this time."

"And what about next time?" he countered, fighting the snare of her beseeching eyes. Lord, the lady could bring him to his knees with just a look, and she didn't even know it. "If I back off here, then I have to every time we enter the same rodeos. Don't you see, sweetheart? This isn't going to end until I show him that I'm not going to let him scare me off, no matter what. I *have* to ride, and if I can, beat the bastard."

She knew he was right, but that didn't make it any easier to accept. They should have gone to Santa Fe, she thought, agitated. Or Texas. There was always a rodeo of some kind in Texas. The competition wouldn't have been as fierce and they would have been a long way from Grady. "If you're going to insist on going through with this, then I'm going to watch Grady Calhoun like a hawk," she promised him. "He won't be able to scratch an itch without me knowing about it."

And just to prove it, she glanced back to where the other man had been standing only seconds before, intending to glare a hole right through him. But instead of studying her and Flynn from the other end of the chutes, Grady and Valerie were headed right for them. Her heart in her throat, Tate swore under her breath. "Oh, God, here they come."

"Stay out of it," Flynn warned just seconds before the other couple reached them. "I'll handle it."

The words were hardly out of his mouth when Grady advanced on him, his green eyes blazing with fury. "I don't know who the hell you think you are, Rawlings, but if you think I'm going to stand by and let you cause trouble for me with the rodeo officials, you hit something besides your ribs in Oklahoma. Get off my case! You got that?"

His jaw set in granite, Flynn didn't so much a flinch. "What I've got is a couple of sore ribs. Because of you, Calhoun. Oh, I know you had an alibi," he continued, shooting the leggy redhead at Grady's side a mocking look, "but we both know you cut my rigging and why. You know I'm going to knock you out of the running for world champion, and you're running scared."

"Of what?" he choked, almost strangling on his own jeering laughter. "You? I don't think so." A flush of rage singeing his cheeks, he looked Flynn up and down and snorted contemptuously. "You're just a loser looking for somebody to blame for your own poor equipment. Try looking in a mirror. It'll give you all the answers you need."

"The only answer I need is standing right in front of me blowing hot air," Flynn retorted coldly. "Get out of my face, Calhoun. *Now.*"

Her heart in her throat, Tate braced herself, her eyes flying back and forth between the two men in alarm. She knew Flynn wouldn't throw the first punch, no matter how provoked he was, but she wasn't so sure of Grady— if he had any scruples, she hadn't seen any evidence of them so far. And he was furious! She could practically see the anger throbbing in his clenched jaw.

Half expecting him to explode any second, she turned to Valerie, hoping the two of them together could defuse the situation, but one look at the other woman's face killed that hope. She was as outraged as Grady by Flynn's accusations. Great, Tate thought, fighting back panic. She could expect no help there. The tension mounting, she was giving serious consideration to stepping between the two men—in spite of Flynn's warning to let him handle the situation—when the beginning of the bareback competition was announced out in the arena. She almost wilted in relief.

"We'll settle this later," Grady promised Flynn coldly. "Just you and me."

"That's fine with me," Flynn retorted. "You just let me know where and when."

With a last angry look, Grady stalked off, dragging Valerie behind him. Staring after them, Tate frowned worriedly. "You don't think he was serious, do you? Surely he wouldn't try to settle this with his fists."

Just the thought of Grady Calhoun doing anything as straightforward as meeting him for an honest-to-God fistfight drew a cynical laugh from Flynn. "Grady? Hell, no! He hasn't got the guts for that. He'd rather sneak around behind you and stab you in the back. He's just blowing off steam."

Tate wanted to believe him, but something she'd seen in Grady's eyes as he'd stalked off left a chill lingering in her blood. Try as she might, she couldn't shake the feeling that they were headed for disaster.

Nothing, however, happened that afternoon. When it came time for Flynn's turn in the chutes, his ride went off without a hitch. Standing at the entrance to the arena floor, her eyes glued to him as he clung to the back of the wildly bucking horse, Tate didn't realize how afraid she was that something would go wrong until the buzzer sounded and the pickup man galloped out to snatch Flynn off the furious bronc. Expelling her breath in a rush, she felt her knees go weak and chided herself for being paranoid. Flynn was right. Grady was all talk. He wouldn't have the guts to do anything now that he knew Flynn was on to him.

Relieved, she felt the worry that had been sitting heavily on her shoulders lift like a cloud. Grinning, she congratulated Flynn on his second-place finish the minute he stepped off the arena floor. From the smug grin on his face, it was obvious he didn't have to be told that he'd just bumped Grady down to third place.

"Not bad, cowboy," she teased. "Especially for a rookie. How are the ribs?"

His eyes wicked with mischief, he caught her hands and dragged them to his ribs before she could do anything but gasp. "I don't know," he drawled huskily, grinning. "You tell me. How do they feel?"

Startled, her breath hitched in her throat, while in her breast, her heart knocked out a jerky rhythm that exactly matched the one being played out against her palm where it rested on his chest. She didn't have to look around to know that amused eyes were watching their every move, but for once, she didn't care. She loved him. Later, when they went their separate ways, that love would bring her a pain that would shake her to the depths of her being. But now, when he was looking at her as though he wanted to carry her off to some dark, quiet place where they couldn't be disturbed, all she could do was marvel at the wonder of the emotions he pulled from her so effortlessly.

Her eyes locked with his, she slid her searching fingers slowly along his ribs and grinned as the pounding of his heart quickened revealingly. "Pretty good," she agreed, her eyes smiling up into his. "But for a really thorough examination, you need to take that shirt off."

Without a word, he guided her fingers to the snaps of his cowboy shirt. "I'm ready when you are, honey."

Just to tease him, and because she knew he didn't believe she dared, she took hold of both sides of his shirt just below his collar, and with a sudden jerk of her hands, ripped the snaps open all the way down to where his shirt was tucked into his jeans. At his gasp, she chuckled. "Gotcha!"

"I don't know about that," he retorted, his eyes warm with laughter. Quick as a wink, he snared her wrists and slowly pulled her toward him. "It looks to me like I've got *you.*"

Too late, Tate realized he wasn't going to stop until he had her right where he wanted her—in his arms. Her pulse pounding, she tugged halfheartedly against his hold, the stern look she tried to adopt totally ruined by the smile that refused to leave her mouth. "I've got to go warm Sugar up," she reminded him. "I don't want to take any chances on her hurting that leg again."

"In a minute," he promised, drawing her with him around the corner to a relatively secluded spot behind a storage area. "First come here and warm *me* up."

Since it was ninety degrees in the shade outside and they were already playing with fire, Tate didn't think that would be too difficult to do. Her eyes smiling into his, she stepped into his arms and stood on tiptoe to bring her mouth to his.

For the span of a heartbeat, the kiss she gave him was light, teasing, playful. Then his arms closed around her, his lips sank into hers, and all she could think of was stolen moments in the dark in her camper while fireworks exploded outside. With a murmur of need, she crowded closer.

His answering groan vibrated through her, his arms crushing her to the hard length of him. For one sweet, timeless moment, there was only the two of them and the fire that threatened to rage out of control between them, sparked to life by nothing more than the slow sweep of tongue against tongue.

But it couldn't last and they both knew it. The rest of the world was just around the corner and she had a race to prepare for. "Flynn—"

His name was all she could manage, but it was enough. Reluctantly drawing back, he sighed, "I know, I know. You have to go. Just one more for good luck." And with a grin, he gave her a swift, hard kiss that made her tingle all the way to her toes. Then he sent her off to Sugar.

By the time they returned to the arena campground later that evening, Flynn's parting kiss, her own first-place finish in the barrel racing, plus the fact that Haily had begged and received permission to spend the night with a friend she hadn't seen since last year, had pushed Grady Calhoun and his threats from Tate's mind. All she could think of was the long night they would have alone together.

Her heart racing with expectation, she stepped up to the back door of her camper, only to stop when she saw a folded piece of paper wedged into the space between the door and door frame. Even before she reached for it, she knew it was bad news.

"What is it?" Flynn asked sharply as the blood drained from her face in the gathering twilight.

"Grady," she said faintly, handing him the note. "He wants you to meet him at the practice arena at eleven o'clock."

Flynn swore, scanning the note in the poor light. "Son of a bitch!" he growled, crushing the paper in his fist. "He wants a fight—well, by God, he's going to get one!"

Chapter 12

"**I** don't feel good about this," Tate told him, worry carving deep lines in her brow. Seated at the small dinette in the camper, where they'd been drinking coffee for the past thirty minutes and watching the clock, she tried one last time to reason with him. "Fighting never solves anything. You know that. Just because Grady's acting like a spoiled little bully doesn't mean you have to go along with him."

His jaw set in granite, Flynn refused to argue with her. "There are some things you can't walk away from," he said flatly, and left it at that. There wasn't time for any more talking, anyway. It was already five minutes to eleven. Setting his coffee cup down with a clunk, he pushed to his feet. "I've got to go."

"No! Dammit, your ribs have just healed! There has to be another way."

She was so fierce, Flynn had to smile. Easing out of the booth, he stood and pulled her up beside him and into his arms. "Believe me, honey—" he chuckled "—this is not the way I wanted to spend the evening, either."

"Then stay with me."

He wanted to. God, if she only knew how close he was to changing his mind, she'd be all over him like sugar on a doughnut. "I can't. The bastard has to be stopped, and if knocking some sense into him is what it takes, then that's what I'll have to do. I'll be back as soon as I can."

Letting her go while he still could, he gave her a smile and a wink and stepped outside, shutting the door behind him. But when he started across the street to the rodeo grounds, his face was set in grim lines. No one was more aware than he that his ribs were still tender, and Grady was just the kind of bastard to take advantage of that.

The arena was deserted at that time of night except for several security guards who patrolled the huge complex in golf carts to make sure none of the animals were disturbed in the stock barns. Explaining that he was checking on Sugar, Flynn waited until the guard he ran into continued on his rounds before he headed for the small outdoor practice area located halfway between the main arena and the barns.

As expected, the fenced paddock was shrouded in shadows and quiet as a tomb. Seldom used in the daytime, and never at night, it was only equipped with a security light at one end, and that provided precious little illumination. But it was enough for Flynn to see that Grady was nowhere in sight. Scowling, he bit out a curse. So the jerk wasn't going to show. He should have figured as much. Cowards had a problem with confrontations, and if the cutting of his rigging had proved anything to Flynn, it was that Grady Calhoun was a coward of the lowest kind, a real dirt crawler.

And if the jackass thought he was going to let him jerk him around on a string, he'd landed on his head once too many times, Flynn thought grimly. Tate was back at the camper probably worrying herself sick over him, and he had better things to do than to stand around an empty arena waiting on a loser when he could be with her.

Giving the shadows one last piercing look, he started to turn back the way he had come when he suddenly caught sight of what looked like a piece of paper lying in the dirt near the center of the arena floor. Stopping in his tracks, he told himself to ignore it. It was probably just a piece of trash.

But the arena grounds were well maintained, and there wasn't so much as a stray candy wrapper anywhere. Frowning, he stared speculatively at the paper, unable to shake the feeling that it had something to do with Grady. It would be just like the bastard to leave him another note suggesting a different meeting place.

It was a trick. He knew it as surely as he knew he was good enough to knock Grady out of the competition for the world-champion title. But that didn't stop him from climbing through the metal railings of the fence and trotting over to where the note lay in the dirt. Reaching down for it, he could just make out his name scrawled across the folded piece of paper in bold letters.

Inside, it was blank.

"What the hell—"

Still swearing, a sudden movement behind him warned him he was no longer alone. His blood pumping, he froze, recognizing the sound of a gate quietly swinging open and the heavy thud of pounding hooves. Too late, the fine hairs at the back of his neck warned him that he'd walked into a trap. Then he whirled and literally felt his heart stop.

There, in the shadows at the other end of the arena, stood Lucifer, the meanest son of a bucking bull on the circuit. As unpredictable as the devil he was named after, he delighted in pounding cowboys into the dirt every chance he got. And right now, there was only one cowboy in sight—Flynn. Snorting and pawing the ground, his gray hide looking ghostly pale in the shadows, the angry bull lowered his head to charge, his narrowed black eyes trained unwaveringly on his prey.

Run!

In the split second he had to think, Flynn's first instinct was to light out like the hounds of hell were after him. But there was no way he could outrun the charging animal, and they both knew it. His only hope was to jump out of his way and scramble for the fence before the bull could double back for another swipe at him. His heart clamoring like an out-of-control freight train in his chest, he forced himself to stand perfectly still while a thousand-plus pounds of rage ran right at him.

Something was wrong. Tate could feel it in her bones. Unable to stand the claustrophobic confines of the camper another second, she stepped outside, her gaze flying across the street to the arena. From what she could see, the place was as quiet as a church at midnight. Nothing moved but the security guards. She'd timed them and, in spite of her worry, had to be impressed with their punctuality. They passed just like clockwork every fifteen minutes, the putter of their golf carts a steady hum in the quiet of the night.

Staring at the spot where she knew the practice area was hidden on the other side of the barns, she tried to convince herself that she was getting bent out of shape over nothing. If Flynn was in trouble, surely one of the security guards would have noticed. Flynn was probably just trying to talk some sense into Grady and would be along any minute now. There was no reason to panic.

But logic had nothing to do with the worry tying her stomach in knots. Images kept taunting her—Flynn, taking the fall that had cracked his ribs two weeks ago, the pain that caught him by surprise every time he moved wrong, and Grady, thirty pounds heavier, strong as a bull and twice as mean, aiming right at Flynn's tender ribs, bringing him down, hurting him.

No! Denial screaming in her head, she knew she couldn't do it. Flynn would be furious with her for interfering, but she didn't care. She couldn't stand by and let Grady beat him to a bloody pulp just because his own stubborn pride wouldn't allow him to walk away from the jackass. She had to get help.

Frantic, she glanced around the campground, needing someone, *anyone,* when her eyes landed on Grady's truck and travel trailer parked two sections over. Valerie! she thought, swallowing a sob. She lived with Grady; she had to care something about him. She hadn't been much help earlier in the day, but surely she wouldn't countenance something like this. Dammit, one of them could get hurt!

Sprinting to the trailer, she pounded on the door, not caring that she might disturb the whole campground. "Valerie! Open up! I need your help!"

At the sound of someone moving about inside and the click of the latch being unlocked, her knees almost buckled in relief. Then the door was pushed open from the inside and she could only stare in stupefaction at the man who stood there scowling at her.

"What do you want, Tate?" he demanded harshly, his green eyes dark with dislike. "If Flynn sent you to apologize, you can tell him to stuff it. If he hasn't got the guts to deliver it in person, then I don't want it."

Confused, she frowned. "Apologize? He hasn't got anything to apologize for! And what are you doing here, anyway? Your note said you were meeting him at eleven."

Braced for a scathing retort, she watched in surprise as he stiffened as if she'd struck him. "Note?" he repeated sharply. "What note?"

"The one you left at my camper." Digging in the front pocket of her jeans, she pulled out the crumbled note that Flynn had tossed down on her dinette table before stalking across the street to the arena. One look at Grady's rugged face told her that something was terribly, horribly wrong. Swallowing, she forced words past the lump of inexplicable fear that suddenly lodged in her throat. "You did write this, didn't you?"

"No."

With all her heart, Tate wanted to believe he was lying, but there was no doubting his sincerity. And just that quickly, she knew who had sent the note. "Where's Valerie?" she demanded in growing alarm.

"I don't know. She said she was going for a walk." His gaze shifted to the arena, something that looked an awful lot like fear clouding his eyes. "Flynn could be in trouble," he said abruptly. "C'mon."

He took off like a shot. Hurrying to keep up with his much-longer legs, Tate raced across the street after him, nameless terror gripping her by the throat, choking her. Her heart slamming against her ribs, she wanted to ask Grady what Valerie was up to, how he knew Flynn was in trouble, but the pain hitching in her side was robbing her of breath and she was so scared, she was trembling.

Then they were running around the side of the main arena, and the small corral used for practice was right ahead, bathed in treacherous shadows. Something moved, but it wasn't until she was almost to the iron fence that ran all way around the practice paddock that she saw it was Flynn. Hot and sweating, his shirt covered with dirt from where he had obviously rolled on the ground, he was at the other end of the arena, his eyes locked unwaveringly on the angry bull that stood less than twenty feet away from him.

"Oh, God!"

She didn't remember crying out, but Flynn's eyes snapped toward her, just for an instant, and that break in his concentration was all the bull needed. His hooked horns as sharp as any lance, he bolted without warning at Flynn and caught him in the ribs, drawing blood and a grunt of pain.

"No!" Tate screamed, already scrambling up on the railing. But just as she threw her leg over the top, a male arm grabbed her around the waist and dragged her down. "Dammit, Grady, that's Lucifer in there with him! We've got to distract him—"

"I'll do it," he snapped. "The minute I get his attention, you help Flynn get the hell out of there."

He turned back toward the iron fence, but before he could take another step, Valerie Jones came flying out of the darkness like a witch from hell, her red hair streaking out behind her. "No!" she screamed, throwing herself at him. "Stop! You can't go in there!"

"The hell I can't," he growled. "If you think I'm going to stand by and watch him get pounded into the dirt, you're crazy. Get out of my way!"

But instead of releasing him, she clawed at him, refusing to let him put her from him, her fingers biting into his arm like talons. "No, you can't! You'll ruin everything.

Don't you see? We have to get rid of him. It's the only way you can win the title.''

Tate's hand flew to her mouth in horror. "All this time we blamed Grady, but it was really you. You cut Flynn's rigging—''

"It would have worked," Valerie bragged proudly. "It would have been so perfect if he'd just have fallen under the horse's hooves instead of against the railing. Then he would have been out for months, and there would have been nobody else to stop Grady from taking the title. I would have made sure of it.''

Something close to revulsion washed over Grady's face at her boastful tone. "If you think I would want a title under those circumstances, you obviously don't know me at all. And I sure as hell don't know you.''

Behind them in the arena, Flynn gasped humorously over the snorting of the bull, "I could use a little help here—hell!''

The bull, tiring of the game, charged again, then turned right back again, missing him by a hairbreadth. Swearing, Flynn jumped out of the way, wondering wildly how he even managed to move. His legs felt as if they were weighted with lead, and every breath he drew seared his lungs. He hadn't had time to check the wound at his side, but he could feel the blood slowly wetting his torn shirt.

Unable to take his eyes from Lucifer, he heard Grady swear at Valerie and shake off her hold, but all his attention was focused on the bull. It had taken only two minutes in the arena with the monster to discover why he was named after the devil. Quick as lightning and meaner than a striking rattler, he was the spawn of Satan himself.

"Just hold on, Flynn," Grady told him, ignoring Valerie's screams and declaration that he not climb up onto the railing. "While I distract him, Tate's going to help get you out of there—"

"No!" From the corner of his eye, Flynn caught sight of Tate moving into position near the gate by the chutes off to his right. Watching the bull like a hawk, he swore, "Dammit, Tate, I don't want you anywhere near this bastard! Just stay where you are and open the gate when Grady and I lure him over there."

Fear tightening her throat, Tate wanted to protest. He was hurt! Blood had already darkened his shirt where Lucifer had nicked him on the right side, and she wanted him out of there, safely out of reach of the bull's sharp horns. Damn the heroics. But Grady, obviously agreeing with Flynn's plan, was up and over the railing before she could stop him. With a soft thud, he landed on his feet in the dirt halfway down the arena from Flynn.

"Oh, God, be careful," she pleaded, her fingers biting into the metal bars of the gate. When Valerie cried out as the bull swung toward Grady, she snapped, "Oh, for heaven's sake, Valerie, stuff it!"

"Atta, girl," Flynn said, chuckling, tired of the woman's hysterics when *she* was the reason they were all in this mess. "You ready, Grady?"

For an answer, the other man moved closer to him, making sure he kept the bull between them so the animal didn't know which one of them to charge. Together, they backed slowly toward the chutes, luring Lucifer toward the gate that blocked the long loading chute leading back to the holding pen where the other bulls were.

Each step made with nail-biting deliberation, they were careful not to make any sudden moves, but they might as well have saved themselves the effort. Lucifer was already enraged. Snorting and pawing the dirt, his black eyes swung back and forth between them, as if he were just looking for an excuse to skewer either one of them with his horns.

"Easy," Flynn said soothingly. "Easy, boy. Nobody wants to hurt you. Just a little bit farther and you're home free. And so are the rest of us," he muttered. Sensing Tate less than six feet behind him at the railing, he said, "Get ready, Tate. At the same time you open the gate, Grady and I are going to run for the railing. Hopefully, he'll charge the gate instead of us."

Tate paled, horrified. If the trick didn't work, both Flynn and Grady would have their backs turned to the bull and would just be asking to be gored. "Surely there must be another way—"

"If there is, sweetheart, I haven't been able to come up with one. Grady, we'll move on three, okay?"

"Whatever you say," he replied.

"All right, here we go. One. Two. *Three!*"

At the same time Tate jerked open the gate with a loud clang, the two men pivoted and sprinted for the railing on each side of the gate. Distracted, Lucifer glanced around wildly, not knowing which way to run. And that only seemed to infuriate him. Suddenly, without warning, he charged.

His head down, he headed right for the gate, just as they'd hoped. Seconds before he ran through it, though, he abruptly changed his mind and swerved, hooking Grady with his horns.

"Oh, God, no! You've killed him!" Valerie screeched as the animal disappeared into the chute. "You've killed him! This is all your fault, Flynn Rawlings!"

Tate, already at Grady's side, turned on her so fast, the other woman didn't even have time to blink. "You say one more word, Valerie Jones, and I swear to God it'll be your last. If you want to blame anyone for this disaster, then you'd better take a good hard look at yourself! Now make yourself useful and go call an ambulance.''

Not waiting to see if the woman did as instructed, Tate turned back to Grady as Flynn dropped to his knees beside her. "How is he?" he asked roughly.

"Not good," Grady answered for himself, lying flat on his back in the dirt, his face as gray as dust. "It hurts like hell."

Praying the wound wasn't nearly as bad as it looked, Tate teasingly chided, "Quit your crying. In case you didn't notice, that was a bull you were playing tag with. Be thankful you got off with just a scratch."

Seeing the blood gushing from the ugly gash in the other man's thigh, Flynn quickly jerked off his shirt, wincing as his scraped ribs burned in protest. "Yeah," he added as he used the shirt as a tourniquet, "just think what could have happened if that son of a buck had decided he *really* didn't like you. He could have flattened you into a pancake."

Sweat beading on his colorless brow, Grady groaned as the makeshift bandage was tightened. "Yeah, I'm one lucky dude." The forced grin sliding from his mouth, his pain-clouded eyes met Flynn's. "I'm sorry, man. I knew Valerie was obsessed with me winning the title, but I never thought she'd go this far."

"Don't worry about it now," Flynn said gruffly. "Save your strength."

"I should have known," he insisted, his breathing becoming labored as he struggled to get out the words. "When I found out she'd given me the incorrect starting time for the Golden rodeo, I just thought she'd made a mistake."

"One you didn't bother to tell Flynn about," Tate retorted, her blue eyes flashing.

"By the time I'd figured out what she'd done, it was too late. I couldn't find him anywhere."

"And when my rigging was cut?" Flynn reminded him, his eyes growing hard at the memory. "Are you saying you knew nothing about that, too?"

"Not until later, when David Hartfield showed up asking questions after you'd left for New Mexico." Pain that had nothing to do with his injury deepened the weathered lines of his face. "I didn't want to believe she'd do something like that, so I convinced myself it had to be someone else. I knew it was a stupid thing to do, but I couldn't turn her in. I love her."

At the hoarse admission, a strangled sob escaped the redhead, who suddenly appeared with two security guards hot on her heels. "Oh, Grady, I'm so s-sorry!" Her face ashen, she ran to his side and collapsed in the dirt to throw herself on his chest. "I never m-meant to hurt anyone. I just w-wanted y-you to win."

With that, she burst into tears, clinging to him as if she'd never let him go. His arms tight around her heaving shoulders, Grady looked up at Flynn just as the wail of a siren could be heard in the distance. "I wouldn't blame you if you called in the police," he said stiffly. "You're certainly entitled. You could have been killed."

The fire burning in Flynn's side from his scraped ribs reminded him that was all too true. But for the grace of God, *he* could have been the one lying in the dirt, his blood spilling out of him, and no one would blame him if he didn't show Valerie any mercy. After all, how much had she shown him?

At his side, Tate shifted, and he could feel her eyes on his face. Whatever he decided to do, he knew she would back him up. Just that quickly the decision was made. All he wanted was to be finally free of the ugliness...and alone with Tate.

"I don't think that's necessary," he said gruffly as the ambulance raced up and braked to a bone-jarring stop right outside the paddock. "Now let's get you to a hospital before you bleed all over the damn arena."

Fifteen minutes later, Tate switched on the lights in her camper and made Flynn sit at the dinette while she collected her first-aid kit from the bathroom. "I still think you should have let the paramedics look at you before they took Grady to the hospital," she scolded as she bent over him. Armed with disinfectant and a whole bag of cotton balls, she warned, "This could hurt," then set to work.

At her first touch, Flynn flinched, but he was enjoying her closeness too much to move away. Staring at the blond fall of her hair as she tended his wounds, he fought the need to crush her close, every second of the time that he'd been trapped in the arena burned into his mind. He'd come damn close to biting the dust for good, and it was amazing how clearheaded a man got when he found himself looking his own mortality in the eye. Just that quickly, he'd known what he wanted out of life.

Tate. She was all he needed, all he cared about. Bent over him, tenderly nursing him while she scolded him for all she was worth, she was the beginning and end of all of his dreams. Shaken, he couldn't take his eyes from her. Why had it taken so long to see what was right in front of his nose? He loved her.

How had it happened? He'd sworn that he wanted no part of that particular four-letter word, and he'd made sure every woman he came into contact with knew it. Yet Tate Baxter had had to do nothing more than look down that pert nose of hers and dismiss him as if he were of less importance than the dirt under her feet, and he'd been good and hooked. Lord, he'd never hear the end of it from his brothers.

His mouth twitching at the thought, he reached out and gently tucked back a blond curl that kept insisting on falling in her eyes. At his first touch, she went utterly still, her eyes flying to his. In the sudden tense hush, he could have sworn he heard her heart pounding in time with his.

"You know, I had some time to think when it was just me and Lucifer in that arena together," he said in a low, husky voice that wasn't nearly as casual as he'd hoped it would be. How the hell did a man lay his heart on the line without just blurting it out? "It was a very enlightening experience."

His finger lingered to tease the curve of her ear, and between one heartbeat and the next, Tate's throat was dry as dust. "If it had been me," she replied thickly, "I wouldn't have been able to think of anything but getting out of there." Visions of Lucifer turning on him, ripping him open with those lethal horns of his, flashed before her eyes, cracking her control. And suddenly she was trembling. "You could have been killed."

"Hey, what's this?" he chided, pulling her down onto his lap, his thumb brushing at the tear that spilled over her lashes and trickled down her cheek. Murmuring reassurances, he kissed her softly, sweetly. "Shh. It's all right. God, I love you. Don't cry, honey. Everything's going to be just fine now."

It wasn't until she slowly pulled back, her tear-drenched eyes wide as they met his, that he realized what he'd said. His mouth quirked into a rueful grin. "Yeah, you heard me right. I love you. And you're never going to believe when it hit me. Right when I found myself eyeball-to-eyeball with that devil, Lucifer.''

She laughed, she couldn't help herself. "Oh, Flynn!"

"I know." He chuckled, cupping her cheek. "Talk about your timing. All I could think about was getting out of there and getting back to you so I could tell you." His eyes suddenly serious and dark with need, he slid his spread fingers up into her hair, around to her nape, unable to stop touching her. "I love you," he growled fiercely. "Believe me, sweetheart, because I've never even come close to saying that to another woman. I'm nuts about you and nothing's ever going to change that."

Before she could say a word, he kissed her, telling her without saying a word that there was no way on God's green earth that he was ever letting her go. "I love you," she said with a fierce tenderness against his mouth. "More than I could ever tell you."

"So show me," he rasped, his grin daring her.

It was a challenge she couldn't resist. Her mouth still pressed tight to his, she muttered, "In my bed. I want you in my bed."

His eyes dark with delight, he growled, "I love an aggressive woman," making her laugh as he scooted her off his lap and stood to tower over her in the narrow aisle.

"I'll remember that," she promised, her smile hot and seductive as she caught his hands and brought them to the buttons of her blouse. He was still toying with the top one when she reached for the snap to his jeans. In the next instant, the buttons to her blouse went flying.

At her gasp, he grinned. "Did I happen to mention that I seem to have a problem with control when I'm within touching distance of you? Unzip my jeans, sweetheart."

She meant to tease him, to drag his zipper down with a slow tug that would really push the limits of that control he so freely admitted was shaky. But he was having none of that. Pushing her hands away, he took care of the job himself, then shucked his jeans and briefs before helping her with hers. A split second later, the lights were switched off, his hands closed around her bare waist to lift her into the queen-size bunk over the cab, and then he was climbing in beside her.

Before he had time to do anything but stretch out beside her, she was reaching for him, determined to drive him out of his mind. It took all of two seconds and nothing more than the touch of her hand sliding down his hard, naked stomach to turn him into a wild man. Groaning, he had her flat on her back between one heartbeat and the next, his mouth hot and hard on hers, his fingers between her thighs.

The fire was instantaneous and scorching in its intensity, burning her from the inside out. Laughter went up in flames, her breath catching on a moan as she arched off the bed. "Flynn!"

"I'm here, sweetheart," he assured her, his voice as rough as sandpaper as he pressed her back into the pillows. "I'll always be here."

Taking her mouth, he kissed her long and slow, as if he could spend the rest of his life just doing that. As if he couldn't get enough of her. As if a hundred years of kissing her, loving her, every night, would never be enough. And when he finally lifted his head, it was only to tell her how she pleased him with just her smile, how she'd walked into his dreams and taken them over with the sassy sway of her hips, how the feel and taste and softness of her haunted his every waking thought and how going through this lifetime with her was only going to make him hungry for more.

With nothing but words and the touch of his hands, he made love to her until she was breathless, aching and crying out with need. And still he didn't take her. With mouth and tongue and teeth, he took her to the edge, wooing her breast, laving the silken skin of her inner thigh, tasting the fire in her, then driving her impossibly higher.

Dazed, whimpering, she knew what he was doing. Instead of giving her the chance to show him how much he meant to her, he was showing her. In the shadows that engulfed them, his eyes burning into hers, he told her how precious she was, how he'd waited a lifetime for her without ever knowing what he was missing. But now he knew. He'd found her when he wasn't looking, and she was his. Forever.

Tears were streaming down her cheeks when he slowly slid into her, not stopping until he was buried deep and they were heart to heart. The muscle ticking in his jaw the only sign of the effort the slow loving was costing him, he linked his fingers with hers and captured her in the heat of his gaze. The glow in her eyes told him that nothing had ever been so right. A slow smile spread across his face. Setting a rhythm that was uniquely theirs, he drove them higher and higher until they were racing with the wind and shooting toward the stars. When they both tumbled over the edge into ecstasy, they were still smiling.

"Marry me."

Her heart thundering, her body limp and sated, Tate was sure she'd misunderstood the words Flynn mumbled against her neck, but then he lifted his head and she knew her ears weren't deceiving her. She'd never seen him more serious.

Unable to hide her surprise, she lifted a shaky hand to the dark hair that tumbled over his brow, a joy unlike anything she had ever known before flooding her. But before she could come up with a halfway intelligent answer, he mistook her silence for something else and blurted out, "I know you've got your future all mapped out, and there's no way I would interfere with that. I think it's great that you're going to medical school, and I'm behind you one hundred percent. But that doesn't mean we can't get married. And if you're still worried that I'd turn out to be like Haily's father—"

She stopped him there with nothing more than the pressure of her fingers against his lips. "Never," she said fiercely. "I was wrong to ever accuse you of that, but I was just so afraid of getting hurt."

"I know, honey, and I understand." His fingers latched on to hers, holding tight. "But you've got to know now that I would never hurt you. I love you, for God's sake! We belong together. And where I come from, people get married when they love each other—"

"Yes."

"You have to think of Haily, of course. But anybody can see I'm crazy about her—" Suddenly realizing what she'd said, his brows snapped together. "Did you say yes?"

"Yes."

"Yes, you'll marry me?"

He was so nervous, so unsure of himself, that Tate couldn't hold back a grin. Was this the same flirty, cocksure cowboy who had approached her on the dance floor only weeks ago, expecting her to fall into his arms? "Would you like it in writing?"

"You're damn right I want it in writing," he growled, giving her a swift hard kiss, his grin broad. "I want an unbreakable contract filed at the courthouse."

"Me, too." She chuckled, pulling him back down for a long, lingering kiss. "Just in case any of those women chasing you think that you're still footloose and fancy-free, I want it on public record that you're no longer in circulation. You're mine, Flynn Rawlings, and don't you ever forget it!"

Epilogue

The candles were lit, the champagne chilling on ice in celebration of their three-month wedding anniversary, when the phone rang. Tate, locked tight in Flynn's arms, groaned. "Don't answer it," she murmured against his mouth. "It's probably a wrong number. Nobody we know would dare call tonight."

She sounded so disgusted, Flynn had to laugh. "Honey, it won't take a minute to answer it, and anyway, it could be important. What if it's about Haily? She could be in trouble—"

"Haily's perfectly fine," she assured him. "Dad and Maggie spoil her rotten every time she spends the night, but they wouldn't let anything happen to her."

"Then she's probably calling to tell us good-night," he said, and reached for the phone with one hand while the other kept her cradled close against his chest. "Hello?"

The thump of his heart a steady cadence in her ears, Tate trailed a lazy finger down his bare chest, her grin flashing as his hand suddenly flattened over hers, stilling the teasing caress. Undaunted, she merely chuckled and leaned up to nibble on his ear, knowing just how to drive him crazy.

But her teeth had hardly nipped the lobe when he suddenly bolted up in bed exclaiming, "What! Is this for real? No joking?"

Alarmed, Tate scrambled up on her knees, only to see a wide grin spread across his face. "What?" she whispered. "What is it? What's going on?"

Winking at her, he hauled her close and said into the phone, "I still can't believe it. Thanks for calling, man. You don't know what this means to me."

For a good thirty seconds after he hung up, he just lay in the bed, still holding her, a huge grin splitting his face. Watching him, Tate couldn't help but grin herself. "Well? Are you going to tell me what that was all about, or do I have to guess?"

For an answer, he swept her under him, his blue eyes sparkling with devilment. "Kiss me, woman. In case you don't know it, you happen to be in bed with the Pro Rodeo Association's newest Rookie of the Year."

For the span of two heartbeats, she could only stare at him in stunned disbelief. "Rookie of the Year!" she cried in delight as the words finally registered. "Oh my God! Honey, that's wonderful!"

Locking her arms around his neck, she pulled him down to her, laughing as she pressed a quick hard kiss to his mouth. "I knew you could do it. I knew it! This year, Rookie of the Year, next year World Champion Bareback Rider. Just you wait. You're going to win it all. I just know it."

Chuckling, he drawled, "Actually, Mrs. Rawlings, I already consider myself a winner."

"Well, of course you are," she retorted, instantly jumping to his defense. "But I thought you wanted the world title."

Staring down into her well-loved face, he swept her hair back to plant a kiss on the curve of her cheek, her brow, the tip of her nose. There had been a time when he'd wanted the title more than anything, but that was before she'd come into his life and knocked him out of his boots. God, he loved her!

"I did," he assured her huskily. "But it doesn't seem too important now. And my whittling has brought me more satisfaction—and money—than rodeoing ever did."

She had to smile at that. "Sydney does keep you hopping. She's selling everything you give her and the only thing that would make her happier was if you could whittle twice as fast." Her smile fading, she searched his eyes in the candlelight. "You're not talking this way because I'm back in school and can't go with you, are you? I know how much you love competing."

"What I love," he said thickly, "is you." Giving in to the longing that was impossibly stronger now than the day they'd married, he lowered his mouth to hers.

"Why would I want to go chasing off down the highway after a fancy belt buckle when I have the real prize in my arms every day and in my bed every night?" he rasped a long time later, his blue eyes filled with love as they locked with hers. "I have everything I need right here." His grin suddenly flashing, he arched a brow at her. "Any more questions, Mrs. Rawlings?"

Her heart thudding, tears welling in her throat, she linked her arms around his neck and hung on for all she was worth. "Not a one, cowboy. Not a one."

* * * * * *

Don't miss the showdown when the youngest Rawlings—Kat—meets her match in sexy Lucas Valentine as the Wild West series comes to a thrilling conclusion. Only from Intimate Moments!